THE GRAFTON CONSPIRACY

K. L. Kitten

1

The Hijacking

The smell of acrylic paints, old sketchpads, and pencil shavings hung thick in the air. Even though he'd been trying not to inhale too deeply, the anxiety got the best of him and Eli took another deep breath as he glanced at the clock mounted on the wall above him. According to the two paintbrush hands it was 8:58 in the morning.

Eli nervously gripped the straps of his backpack. He'd planned on hiding in the art room closet until nine o'clock, but, considering how quiet everything had been in the last few minutes, he was starting to wonder if there was much of a point. Like the rest of the student body at Meade Middle School he'd been let out of his first period class a little early for the assembly, so he guessed most everyone was probably in the gym by now. In theory, that meant the hallways were probably clear, too.

Pulling the hood of his jacket over his greasy brown hair, Eli stepped into the empty classroom and walked to the door. Once he glanced through the window and confirmed the hallway outside really was empty, he stepped out and took a left, heading for the office.

A wry grin started to creep across his lips. They weren't just making a big deal about the superintendent's speech today; they'd turned it into the event of the century. If it wasn't for the distorted sound of the band playing something from the gym, Eli would have sworn the place was deserted.

All the same, Eli pressed himself against the wall and carefully poked his head around the corner once he made it to the first intersection. The sunlight streaming in through the main doors on the right made it hard to see much against the glare, but, as best as he could tell, there wasn't a soul in sight between him and the office.

Glancing to the left, Eli could see one of the entrances to the gym about a hundred feet down the hall. The doors were open, and it was much easier to hear all the noise coming out of it now, but, thankfully, the few teachers he could see just inside the doorway weren't looking his way.

Taking a deep breath to swallow his anxiety, Eli stepped around the corner and quickly strode to the other side of the hallway towards the office. Once he'd made it to the wall next to the office's glass door, he carefully glanced inside to make sure the coast was clear.

A triumphant grin slithered across his face. The office was dark and just as vacant as the hallways outside were.

"Phase 1 complete," Eli hummed happily as he opened the door and stepped inside. "Now for Phase 2."

After quietly shutting the door behind him, Eli rounded the reception counter and found his way to the secretary's desk. He quickly slid the top drawer open and found the key to the school's network cabinet under a pad of sticky notes, just where he expected it to be. A second later, he stepped around the desk and used the key to open the door at the edge of the administrators' hallway. A series of flickering lights and a soft electric hum greeted him.

"Okay, now where's the PA terminal?" Eli thought aloud as he studied over the server rack. Even though the office was completely dark, there was just enough light filtering in from the main doors for him to see the different devices. Eventually, he spotted the PA terminal on the second shelf from the top, right below the router.

Grabbing a stepstool from inside the closet, Eli stood up on it and slid his backpack off his shoulder to cradle it against his chest. He unzipped the rear compartment and pulled out the old MP3 player his aunt had given him a few years ago before looking for a place to plug it in. Surprisingly, the terminal already had a USB drive plugged into it and it was blocking his access to the auxiliary port.

He needed to remove it before he could plug in the MP3 player.

Pulling his lips in tight, Eli reached out and unplugged the USB drive from the terminal. He froze when an audible blip played over the PA system. Feeling a twinge of panic, Eli hooked the MP3 player into the terminal and clicked on the power button.

The thought that he should have left the art room sooner shot through his mind as the device took its sweet time loading. Nearly thirty seconds passed before Eli was able to make sure the volume was turned all the way up on both the PA terminal and the MP3 player and hit Play on its only playlist.

Silence permeated the office.

Even though Eli knew the first track was nothing but five minutes of dead air to give him enough time to sneak into the assembly, he couldn't stop himself from looking at the MP3 player's cracked screen to be sure the track was actually progressing. He felt a sense of relief when he confirmed that it was.

Now all he had to worry about was making it into the gym before the next track started and hope to high heaven no one saw him before he got there. As good as he was at pulling pranks, he'd never been very good at talking his way out of them when he got caught.

Leaving the key for the network cabinet on the shelf next to the PA terminal, Eli zipped up his backpack, slipped it over his right shoulder, and closed the door. A few seconds later, he was striding out of the office, heading straight for the school's main entrance while the dull voice of Principal Espinoza echoed out of the gym behind him.

The assembly was already underway.

Letting out another sigh in an attempt to calm his racing nerves, Eli shoved the first set of doors open and then the second, stepping out into the sunlight and the crisp morning air. Turning right, he started to jog around to the opposite side of the school.

Hopefully, the bit of information he'd heard Nolan mention about the football team a few weeks ago was true. Otherwise, getting into the gym unnoticed might be harder than sneaking into the office had been.

"Thirty-two-and-a-half years. I know it's hard for me to believe sometimes, but that's how long I've been an educator here in the Grafton School District," Principal Espinoza continued in the same lethargic tone he'd been using for the last few minutes. The energy he was sapping out of the audience made Nolan feel like he'd been listening to Principal Espinoza for thirty-two-and-a-half years already.

"Thirty-two-and-a-half years," Principal Espinoza echoed in reflection. "But I can honestly say I've never been more excited about the direction this school and this district is going than I am right now."

"Boy, I can really tell," another eighth-grader behind Nolan muttered under their breath. A few muted chuckles broke out and Nolan did his best to suppress his own laughter. As usual, listening to a speech from Principal Espinoza made Mrs. Fulton's algebra class feel like a rock concert.

"In the last few years alone," Espinoza continued, "we've seen a dramatic increase in our test scores and student/teacher morale is the highest it's ever been."

"Just not in this gym," the voice behind Nolan cut in again, getting a few more snickers this time.

"And even though the hard work each and every one of you has put into studying harder, investing in your futures, and dedicating yourself to your studies is a real testament to us getting to this point, I'm certain we wouldn't have made it here if it wasn't for the strategies put in place by the person I'm about to introduce. He accepted a job with Grafton ISD when not many other people would have and put us back on the fast track to success. It is my honor to introduce him here today.

"So, let's give a big Meade Mountaineers welcome to our superintendent, Dr. Lars Richter."

With that, applause spread through the gym as Principal Espinoza stepped away from the podium that had been set up at center court and ushered a man in a black suit to take his place. Nolan watched as Superintendent Richter practically leapt out of his chair and strode over to the podium.

From what Nolan could tell, the superintendent was probably in his early fifties and well-trimmed for his age. Based on the way he moved and carried himself, Superintendent

Richter seemed to be in pretty good shape too, even though the man's gaunt, wrinkle-free face made Nolan wonder if he had gone through a round or two of plastic surgery.

Nolan quickly found out the superintendent's demeanor matched his youthful looks, too.

"Good morning, Meade Mountaineers!" Superintendent Richter shouted through the microphone once he'd unclipped it from the stand on the podium. Then, pointing out into the sea of brown and gold shirts in front of him, he added, "How y'all doing this morning?"

A few mumbles and surprised chuckles echoed across the gym. Most, like Nolan, were taken back by the superintendent's exuberance. He even started to wonder if someone had spiked the guy's coffee that morning.

Superintendent Richter rolled his eyes, bowed his head, and waved his hands in the air. "Oh, come on! I know it's Monday morning and everyone's bummed out because they asked you to wear your school shirts today, but surely your principal didn't suck that much life out of you.

"Now, one more time. With feeling. How y'all doing this morning, Meade Mountaineers?"

This time, a thunderous hodgepodge of students shouting various forms of the word, "Great!" bellowed out across the gym.

"Alright! Now that's more like it!" Superintendent Richter exclaimed with a beaming smile. "And I've got to say, every one of you–teachers and students alike–should be that excited right now. Because I don't know if you've heard or not, but Meade Middle School is in one of the best school districts in the country."

The superintendent was forced to pause for a few seconds while applause graced the gym, even if most of it was coming from the teachers and the staff. He quickly lifted a hand to silence it.

"Now, I'm not just saying that because I'm the superintendent and that's what superintendents are supposed to go around saying. No! I'm saying that because Grafton ISD truly is one of the best school districts in the country. And I'll give you three reasons why."

Counting it out on his fingers, Superintendent Richter stated, "Test scores are up across the board, student attendance is at the highest level it's been in twelve years, and the consolidated testing syllabus we implemented two years ago has vastly improved classroom efficiency and unified the district.

"So," Superintendent Richter said with a smirk, "this is the point where I say: you know, things are *so* good at Grafton ISD right now..." before gesturing at the audience with the microphone.

Nolan cocked his eyebrows when some people in the stands shouted back almost in unison, "How good is it?" mixed in with some laughter.

"Things are so good right now that Grafton ISD was just named one of the top twenty school districts in the country by Teachers' Apple magazine!" Superintendent Richter announced.

A few astonished gasps rose across the gym.

"Seriously, I don't think I have to tell you what an achievement this is for us. So, Meade Mountaineers, why don't y'all give yourselves a round of applause for that?"

More out of obedience than anything, Nolan started to lightly clap along with everyone else. But as much as he was warming up to Superintendent Richter's charisma, he got the feeling he'd been forced into yet another mandatory pep rally, just a lot lamer than the ones the school usually put on.

After raising his palms to silence the crowd again, Superintendent Richter continued with his speech.

"All that being said, as much as I like to brag about it–and, I'm not going to lie, I do like to brag about it," he added with a smile and some laughter from the audience, "it's not just about bragging rights.

"No. As I'm sure most of you are fully aware, when the school district isn't doing good, the community isn't doing too good either. And like Principal Espinoza mentioned a few minutes ago, when I first took this job a lot of people were trying to avoid moving into the Grafton School District, let alone work for it. I mean, let's face it, there were a lot of people moving or transferring out of this community back then."

A few agreements murmured over the audience.

"But now... things-are-turning-around," Superintendent

Richter said, pressing his index finger down on the podium in time with the last four words out of his mouth.

"And even though Principal Espinoza wants to give me the credit for the rising test scores, I firmly believe that honor belongs to the awesome young people and educators in the stands right in front of me. It's your hard work and your determination that helped Grafton ISD get an exemplary rating on the BEAKS test last year."

An enthusiastic, "Yeah!" erupted from a teacher somewhere in the gym. Superintendent Richter continued.

"And, sure, the academic advantages that come with that are important, but the ways it's helping this community pull itself out of the dirt is just as important. For the first time in years, I can tell everyone is starting to believe in themselves again.

"Meade Mountaineers, thanks to all of you, we are on our way to a brighter, more successful future!"

Within seconds, the audience was swept up in a standing ovation with a few teachers even whistling out their praise. Nolan stood and clapped along with everyone else, taking care not to clap too hard because of the bright yellow cast over his left hand and forearm. However, his eyes were quickly drawn to the way Superintendent Richter's high-octane gaze had shifted from the audience to the news cameras positioned at the edge of the basketball court.

Eli was nearly out of breath by the time he made it to the west side of the school. Without wasting a second, he opened the door leading into the boys' locker room and walked in.

Just as he hoped, a few members of the eighth-grade football team were still there, in the final stages of getting dressed back into their school clothes. The ones that were done were on their way out, heading through the practice gym that led back to the school. It was just the opportunity Eli needed.

"Thank you, Nolan!" Eli exclaimed under his breath as he passed through the musky locker room and started filtering in with some of the other guys. For once, he was glad Nolan had griped about being late to second period so much this fall–before the broken wrist landed him in athletic study hall for the rest of the season, anyway.

Unable to contain his smile, knowing he might just pull this off, Eli made his way to the main basketball gym in line with a few of the straggling football players. It wasn't long before he was stepping through the side entrance with the rest of them. A person he guessed was Superintendent Richter was already in the middle of an animated speech at center court.

"Yeah!" Coach Robbins yelled out as Eli passed by, making him jump a little. He quickly realized it was in response to something Superintendent Richter had said, though, so he kept moving. By the time he found an empty seat near the back corner of the gym, the audience rose and gave the superintendent a standing ovation.

Eli had no idea what Superintendent Richter had just said, but he started clapping too after he slipped off his backpack and slid it under the metal bleacher seat. As he clapped along with everyone else, he started looking around the gym for a clock to see how much time had gone by since he left the office. Unfortunately, the only one he could see was bolted to a cinderblock wall directly across from him and Eli wasn't at the right angle to read it.

Frowning, he glanced back down at the superintendent as he soaked in the praise. After about fifteen or twenty seconds, the applause finally died down and the audience was allowed to take their seats again.

"Okay. So, to get off my soapbox," Superintendent Richter began with a smile, "I didn't come here today just to make a big speech."

Yeah. Sure you didn't, Eli thought, noticing the TV cameras that had come out to cover the event.

"The fact is, I'm sure a lot of you out there are thinking, 'Hey! What's the deal with Superintendent Richter coming to our school just for some crazy assembly?'" he exclaimed, making a point to shrug his shoulders in an exaggerated fashion. "Am I right?"

A few mumbled affirmations escaped the audience, but, for the most part, they remained silent.

"Well, I'll give you one big reason why I'm here today," Superintendent Richter said as he presented his index finger to everyone. "A few weeks ago I received a letter from the Bureau of Education. They're the agency that writes the BEAKS test y'all take each spring."

A few isolated boos wafted over the gym. Eli was surprised when it only brought a wry grin from Superintendent Richter.

"It was all about Meade Middle School," he continued, his smile broadening. "Do y'all want to know what the letter said?"

"Yes!" was the single answer that erupted in pockets across the gym.

Eli watched as Richter's smile seemed to get even bigger. "Okay, then," the superintendent chuckled. "Well —"

"I like BIG BUTTS and I cannot lie! You other brothers can't deny."

The boisterous voice of Sir Mix-a-Lot shouting out the opening line to *Baby Got Back* cut Superintendent Richter's sentence short. In an instant, the audience burst into laughter as the song continued to blare over the PA system.

It didn't take long for the beaming smile on Richter's gaunt face to get replaced by a look of confusion that quickly turned to unbridled anger. Eli watched on excitedly as Superintendent Richter's cheeks and forehead turned bright red and he slammed the microphone down onto the basketball court, making it squeal.

He quickly grabbed Principal Espinoza by the shoulder and pulled him out of his seat. Even though the principal looked just as bewildered as the rest of the faculty did, Superintendent Richter started yelling something right in his face while waving a hand back at the stands. An instant later other members of the faculty sitting nearby bolted out of their seats and started running for the exits, desperate to put an end to the lewd song playing over the PA system.

While everyone else around him was either laughing hysterically or singing and dancing to the music, Eli could only smile and shake his head. He'd pulled some pretty awesome pranks before, but never anything like this. Never anything this epic.

And he'd pulled it off without a hitch, too!

Eli was still smiling about it when he dipped his hands into his jacket pockets and felt something plastic brush against his right hand. Suddenly, all the commotion around him faded into a distant clamor.

Biting his lip, Eli slowly wrapped his fingers around the object and pulled it out of his pocket. An intense sinking feeling lurched through his stomach and a chilled, "Oh, crap!" slipped out of his mouth as soon as he saw the USB drive from the office in his hand.

Without giving it a second thought, Eli shoved the USB drive back into his pocket and glanced at the crowd around him. Even though he figured most everyone was either too caught up in the music or watching Superintendent Richter's arm-waving rant to notice, he still knew he had to get rid of this thing before anyone saw him with it.

Thanks to where he was, though, he knew there wasn't a shortage of options.

2

Lost and Found

Conrad did his best to ignore the lingering hunger pangs in his stomach as he slipped his backpack off and sat down in front of one of the computers in the library. As bad as the school's lukewarm steak fingers were, trying to eat them with freshly adjusted braces certainly didn't make them any better. Then again, the topic of conversation in the cafeteria was getting pretty stale, too.

Just about everyone kept talking about how mad Superintendent Richter looked when the big butts song came on or how Cory Schultz nearly had an asthma attack from laughing so hard. As funny as Conrad thought it was at first, he was starting to get tired of all the overdone impersonations and weak re-enactments the other kids were doing.

Plus, he couldn't get that stupid song out of his head now.

Doing his best to put it all behind him, Conrad turned his attention back to the computer and plugged in the USB drive he'd found in the gym earlier. He knew he should probably take it to the office and hand it over to the lost and found, but he figured he might as well see if it belonged to anyone he knew first. However, the drive contained something much different than he was expecting.

"Audio files?" Conrad thought aloud as soon as the contents of the drive flashed across the screen.

There were about thirty in all, mixed in with a few executables. Stranger still, every one of them had a weird file name that looked like it was part of a programming code.

Biting his lip, which sent a jolt of pain searing through his teeth, Conrad glanced at the headphones sitting on top of the computer tower. He wondered if the audio files meant the drive belonged to someone in band or orchestra.

After grabbing the headphones and slipping them over his spikey red hair, Conrad double-clicked on a random file in the list. He heard a blip from a prompt appearing, asking him which program to open the file with. After choosing the media player option, it opened up a short time later and started playing.

Conrad leaned forward in his chair and rested his elbows on the computer desk. Unfortunately, all he heard was silence.

A quick glance at the media player's control panel confirmed the sound wasn't muted, and the volume was set about halfway up the bar. All the same, Conrad went ahead and used the mouse to turn the volume all the way up. The dissonance inside the headphones got louder, but he still couldn't hear anything.

Conrad slouched back in the chair and waited a few seconds, watching the dot on the audio track creep to the right. According to what he was seeing, the track contained exactly fifty minutes of audio, but, after a full minute, Conrad still couldn't hear anything.

Clicking on the progress bar, he moved it to 35:53 on the track. Once again, nothing.

With a perplexed grunt, Conrad closed the file and tried opening another. Unfortunately, opening a second or even a third file didn't change anything. Every file he clicked on was completely silent.

Biting his lip, Conrad took the headphones off and closed the media player. If anything, at least he had tried to figure out who this thing belonged to.

After pulling the drive out of the computer, Conrad glanced over it one more time to make sure he hadn't missed seeing someone's name or their initials on the device. As before, though, all he found was a red logo engraved into the back.

The only thing left to do was turn it over to the lost and found.

After sliding his backpack over his left shoulder and putting the USB drive in his pocket, Conrad started to make his way to the office, which was just across the hall from the library. He felt his cheeks getting warm when he saw a bright yellow laminated sign taped on one of the computer towers warning students not to plug unknown USB drives into the computers.

A sense of dread started to build up in the back of his mind. If they found out what he'd done, he'd probably get detention for a few days and then his parents would ground him on top of that–especially if he'd just uploaded a virus to the school's network.

All the anxiety Conrad was feeling intensified the second he walked into the office and found Principal Espinoza, Superintendent Richter, and some younger guy with long black hair huddled around a small closet behind the reception counter. They were in the middle of a heated argument.

"I don't care if you think it was just some childish prank," Superintendent Richter sneered while glaring at Principal Espinoza. Jerking his thumb back at the younger guy, he added, "Troy just said that stupid MP3 player's so old that it's untraceable, so I want you to look through that security footage and figure out who the little punk was that came in here during *my* speech and jacked with the network cabinet."

Principal Espinoza was about to respond when the younger guy tapped the superintendent on the shoulder with his knuckles and nodded his head at Conrad. He was staring at them wide-eyed from behind the front counter.

Without saying a word, the superintendent motioned towards the administrators' hallway and the three quietly resigned to Principal Espinoza's office, leaving Conrad alone with the secretary. She didn't speak to him until the door to the principal's office clicked shut.

"So, um, can I help you, Conrad?" she asked gently, though she still looked a tad rattled. "You're not here for your headache medicine already, are you?"

"No, not this time," Conrad said after letting out a deep breath. He reached into his pocket and put the USB drive on top of the counter. "I was just going to drop this off to put in the lost and found. I found it in the gym earlier."

"Okay, then," the secretary said as she grabbed the drive off the counter. Her eyes went wide a second later when she took a closer look at it and she reflexively glanced over her shoulder at the principal's office.

"You said you found this in the gym?" she asked quickly.

"Um, yeah. Why?"

The secretary stumbled over her next word for a second before she shakily lifted her index finger. "Okay. Um, yeah. Conrad, sweetie? Would you mind staying right here for just a second?"

"I guess so," he said slowly, feeling his stomach tighten up.

An instant later, the secretary stepped away and gingerly knocked on the principal's door. Conrad's eyes barely cleared the front counter, but he watched on as best as he could as the door opened and the secretary poked her head inside. She handed the drive to someone in the room before she looked back at Conrad and motioned for him to come over.

"Conrad? Could you please come here? The principal needs to speak to you."

Conrad took in a deep, trembling breath before nodding his head and making his way over to the principal's office. Once the secretary ushered him in and closed the door behind him, a renewed sense of dread washed over him when he found Superintendent Richter, Principal Espinoza, and the third guy with long black hair he guessed was named Troy staring back at him from behind the principal's desk. Every one of them looked like they were about to melt him with their minds.

Principal Espinoza eventually gestured toward an empty chair in front of his desk. "Why don't you go ahead and take a seat, um…?"

"Oh. Uh, Conrad Slater," he spat, sounding just as nervous as he looked.

"Right. Mr. Slater. Could you please take a seat over here?" the principal asked. "And what grade are you in?"

"Sixth," Conrad answered bluntly. His legs felt like lead weights had been tied to them, but he still managed to walk over to the chair. "Am I in trouble or something?" he asked as soon as he sat down, nervously gripping the ends of the armrests.

"Well, we're about to find out," Principal Espinoza said while looking up at Superintendent Richter. He picked the USB drive up off his desk and exhibited it to Conrad. "First off, how did you get ahold of this?"

Conrad's heart skipped a beat and he froze momentarily under the gazes of the three. "I found it in the gym after the assembly this morning," he said uneasily, which only seemed to heighten the others' suspicions.

"Where in the gym?" Superintendent Richter demanded.

"On-on the floor," Conrad stammered. He could tell they wanted more, so he added, "It was near the exit. I figured someone must have dropped it on accident."

"Did you see who dropped it?" Troy asked. Conrad quickly shook his head.

"No. I couldn't find anyone's name on it either."

A panicked jolt shot down Conrad's back when he saw Principal Espinoza's lips dip into a scowl. Obviously, that wasn't the answer they were looking for.

"So, tell me, Mr. Slater: if you knew this wasn't yours, why didn't you bring this into the office right after the assembly?"

"Because I had an orthodontist appointment then," Conrad explained, hoping that made enough sense. "It was during third period. I didn't even get back until fourth period had already started."

"Wait. You mean you took the USB drive with you to the orthodontist?" Troy asked with genuine concern seeping out of his voice. Conrad swore Superintendent Richter looked just as bothered by it.

"Well, no," Conrad said shakily. "I left it in my locker. In my backpack. That's what I usually do when I go to the orthodontist. I put my backpack in my locker before I go."

"And I guess you've got the second lunch period, then?" Principal Espinoza asked flatly, knowing what lunch period was going on right then. Across from him, Conrad nodded.

"Yeah. B-Lunch."

He was disappointed when the response still drew a disapproving glare from Principal Espinoza.

"So, basically, you waited until you were through with your orthodontist appointment and your lunch before you decided to bring it in?" the principal asked. Conrad nodded.

"Yeah. I mean, yes. Yes, sir."

Principal Espinoza bit his lip and slowly nodded as he mulled over the sixth-grader's story. "Do you have a doctor's note?"

"Yeah, but I already gave it to the secretary before I went

to Ms. Matty's Latin class," Conrad said, still looking extremely anxious. Even though he was focused on Principal Espinoza, he could feel the superintendent and his associate staring him down.

Principal Espinoza pursed his lips and nodded again before he grabbed the phone off his desk and put the receiver to his ear. He tapped in an extension a second later.

"Yes, Mr. Espinoza?" Conrad heard the secretary say after one ring. He could just barely hear her voice over the phone line and through the closed door behind him.

"Um, yeah, Sally. Can you please tell me if Conrad Slater brought in a doctor's note? Might have been about an hour ago."

Even though his face didn't entirely show it, Conrad felt a sense of relief wash over him as soon as he overheard the secretary's response.

"Yes, Mr. Espinoza, he did. Did you need to see it?"

Principal Espinoza shook his head. "No, that won't be necessary. Thanks."

A heavy sigh whisked out of the principal's lips as soon as he hung up the phone.

"Okay. I guess your story checks out," he said sullenly as he slouched back in his chair. "But if you ever come across something like this again, please try to bring it in sooner. Okay, Mr. Slater?"

Conrad nodded and was about to respond when Troy nudged his head down at the USB drive. "You didn't tell anyone about this while you were at lunch, did you?"

A confused look swept over Conrad's face. He wasn't sure if it was the man's shoulder-length jet-black hair, his narrow face, or a combination of the two, but something about Troy made him look much more intimidating than the others.

"Um, no, sir. I didn't."

Principal Espinoza gave Superintendent Richter and his associate a bewildered look. "Why does that matter? I thought you said this was just something to cut down on cellular interference over the PA system."

Superintendent Richter and Troy exchanged brief glances before the associate spoke up. "It is, but we'd still like to keep this quiet for the time being. So far, we're the only ones that know the perpetrator took the drive this morning. So, if anyone else mentions it…"

"Then they're the prankster or know what the prankster did. Got it," Principal Espinoza grumbled with a nod.

"Plus, all we know for sure right now is that they tampered with the PA system," Troy added. "Like we were talking about earlier, the fact that they had access to the network cabinet means they could have done a lot more. And even if they didn't, why did they take the USB drive with them?"

"That's the part I want to know," Superintendent Richter cut in. "That and how this kid knew exactly what to do. Seriously, they knew where to find the key to the network cabinet, knew exactly how to bypass the PA system, and, on top of all that, they used something so old and outdated we can't even trace it back to them."

Superintendent Richter paused and shot a frigid look at Principal Espinoza. "It almost makes you wonder if someone here helped them do it."

Conrad looked back at Principal Espinoza in time to see the man shriveling up in his leather chair. "I still think this was just some kid's prank, Dr. Richter," he choked out. "Whoever did it probably just knows a lot about computers."

"Well, I think that goes without saying," Troy said.

"I don't care," the superintendent shot back. "I don't think I have to remind you we're one of the top twenty school districts in the country. This sort of crap shouldn't be happening here. Y'all need to find this kid and find out why they did it."

Principal Espinoza nodded before he turned his distant gaze back to Conrad.

"You didn't hear anything during your lunch about who might have done this, did you?"

Conrad shook his head. "No. I don't think so."

"Well, if you do, let your principal know right away, alright?" Troy answered ahead of Principal Espinoza.

"Or Assistant Principal Horne, when she gets back from her conference trip," Superintendent Richter added somewhat grudgingly.

Principal Espinoza stared at Conrad for a second or two before continuing. "So, is that understood, Mr. Slater?"

"Um, yes. Yes, sir, it is," Conrad said shakily.

Principal Espinoza slowly nodded back. The tired look in his eyes made Conrad wonder if the principal actually felt worse than he did right then.

"Alright," he said, gently nudging his head back towards the door. "I guess that's all we need from you. Thank you for your cooperation."

"And make sure you keep your eyes and your ears peeled, alright, kid?" Superintendent Richter suggested sternly as Conrad rose out of his seat.

"Sure, I will," he choked out, intentionally looking down at his backpack as he picked it up off the floor. He was more than happy to get out of the principal's office.

3

Showdown at Fryer Tuck's

An uneasy feeling rumbled through Nolan's stomach. He wanted to blame it on his growing hunger and the inescapable scent of freshly grilled hamburgers, but deep down he knew it was thanks to the smug glint coming from Sabrina's eyes across the table.

Evasively, he glanced down at the sealed envelopes on the dark green tabletop between them and tried to settle his mind down. Their report cards had come in today, and, just like they'd been doing since the sixth grade, he and Sabrina had met up at Fryer Tuck's after school to see who had the best grades and who would be buying the drinks.

It rarely went Nolan's way.

"Well, it's the moment of truth," Sabrina announced. "A new year and a new set of six weeks. You ready?"

"Ready for you to buy the drinks this time? Yeah, I'd say I'm ready for that, Sabrina. And I'll have a Cherry Coke, by the way."

Sabrina's eyebrows cocked above the rim of her narrow glasses. "Really? You actually think you're going to win this time?" she said with a haughty smile. She knew just as well as Nolan did that she'd only bought the drinks three times in the last two years.

Nolan answered Sabrina's smirk with his own. "Well, since Superintendent Richter himself came to our school this morning and said that we made a perfect score on the math part of our BEAKS test last year, let's just say I think my chances are pretty good."

"You do realize that stupid standardized test has

nothing to do with our report cards, don't you?" Sabrina said, remembering all the eagle posters she'd seen around her school proclaiming, 'This school has sharp BEAKS!' just because they got at least a satisfactory rating on the test.

"Yeah, I know," Nolan conceded. "But it doesn't change the fact that I'm feeling lucky today."

Sabrina rolled her eyes and shook her head, making a few loose strands of her dark black hair sag over her forehead. She quickly whisked them back into place.

"Whatever," she snorted as she started tearing off the perforated edges of her report card. "Let's just get this over with. I still have to finish my Spanish homework and then do some more studying for my history test tomorrow."

Nolan looked up as he started opening his report card. "Same here. About the history test, anyway. Is yours also over the time between the French and Indian War and the start of the Revolutionary War?" he asked. Unlike him, Sabrina went to a magnet school across town called River View Middle School.

"Yeah. I'm sure our tests will be identical again thanks to Superintendent Richter's awesome consolidated system," she snipped.

"Not a fan?" Nolan asked. He'd finished opening his report card but hadn't looked at his grades yet.

"Well, my mom certainly isn't. I can tell you that much," Sabrina said matter-of-factly. "Anyway, it looks like I got a ninety-eight in algebra, a ninety-five in English, a perfect one hundred in history, and a ninety-four in science."

Sabrina used the calculator on her phone to average out her core subject grades. "That gives me a score of 96.75. How'd you do, hotshot?"

Nolan nervously looked down at his report card. "Ninety-two in algebra, ninety-nine in English, ninety-eight in history, and a ninety-seven in science. And that, ladies and gents, comes out to— Oh, for crying out loud!"

"How much?" Sabrina pried, grinning maliciously.

Nolan tossed his phone down on the table and slouched back in his seat. "96.5," he grunted. "Seriously, you only beat me by, like, twenty-five hundredths!"

Sabrina leaned in close and the grin on her face got

bigger. "Yeah, but I still beat you. I believe I'll have the usual, Mr. Leere."

"Yeah, yeah. Coming right up," Nolan said as he got up out of the booth seat, folded his report card in half, and slid it into his pocket. Grudgingly, he made his way over to the front counter to buy a pair of drinks for both of them.

About a minute later he came back with Sabrina's bottle of cream soda and his Cherry Coke out of the fountain machine. Sabrina took a moment to slip her report card into her pocket before twisting the cap off of the cream soda bottle.

"So, Superintendent Richter came to your school today?" she said after taking a sip of her drink. "Was that just because of the BEAKS test?"

Nolan shrugged and slouched back in his seat, slurping his Cherry Coke out of a straw. "Sort of. Mostly, I think he just wanted to brag about how much things have gotten better since he took over. There were news cameras there and everything."

"Yeah, that sounds like him," Sabrina grunted. In the back of her mind, she knew her mom wouldn't have been surprised either. She was a high school chemistry teacher and had vented about Superintendent Richter's inflated ego, among other vices, many times before.

"Of course, he wasn't able to tell us about our test scores exactly when he wanted to," Nolan said eagerly, catching Sabrina off guard.

"What do you mean?"

"You know that song, 'Baby Got Back?'"

A hint of disgust crossed Sabrina's eyes. "The big butts song? Yeah, I'm familiar with it. Why?"

"Alright, so Superintendent Richter is up there giving his speech and is about to tell us about this letter he got from the Bureau of Education or something, right? Then, just when he's about to start telling us what the letter said, someone started playing that song over the PA system!"

Nolan looked on expectantly, as if he'd just delivered the punchline of the century. However, Sabrina was only half-smiling back at him.

"The timing was flat out perfect!" Nolan explained. "He started to tell us what the letter said, and was right at the word,

'Well', when all of sudden all you hear is, 'I like big butts and I cannot lie!' It almost made it sound like he was into that sort of thing."

"Yeah, that's a riot, alright," Sabrina said as she rolled her eyes and took another sip out of her cream soda.

"Okay. So, maybe you had to be there," Nolan said. "Still, it was freakin' hilarious. Everyone was talking about it the rest of the day."

"And how'd Superintendent Richter take it?"

"Not too good, even for a teacher," Nolan scoffed. "I swear, the guy just about lost his mind. He spiked the microphone like it was freakin' football and his face got so red I thought it was going to pop."

Laughter burst out of Sabrina's mouth before she could hold it back. She even clasped her hand over her lips and glanced off to the side like she was embarrassed about it.

"Okay," she choked out as her face started to turn pink, "I actually wish I could have seen that!"

Nolan smiled back at her. "Yeah. Like I said, it was hilarious. Probably one of the best pranks I've ever seen, too."

"I'll bet. And it probably couldn't have happened to a better person either."

Sabrina felt another stab of embarrassment when she noticed the curious look in Nolan's eyes.

"Who? You mean Superintendent Richter?"

The tingling sensation in Sabrina's cheeks intensified, and she glanced down at the dark green tabletop again. "Yeah," she said reluctantly. "From what my mom tells me, he's not exactly the greatest guy out there."

Nolan gave Sabrina a puzzled look and took another sip of his drink. "Really? He seemed pretty cool to me. Well, at least until that song interrupted him, but that's different. What's your mom got against him?"

Sabrina bit her lip and looked around the half-empty dining area for a second as if Superintendent Richter might have undercover agents listening in.

"Okay. Maybe he seemed *pretty cool* to you today, but my mom's not a fan of his attitude. It's like what you said about his speech. He takes every chance he gets to brag about his own amazing accomplishments and how much better we are with him."

Nolan shrugged and glanced off to the side to escape Sabrina's imposing glare. "Okay, so maybe he is kind of full of himself. But maybe he's also getting stuff done. I mean, he did say some teachers' magazine said our district was one of the best in the country."

"Yeah, like no one's ever said that about us before," Sabrina snorted.

"They haven't?"

Sabrina looked at Nolan like he should know better. "Well, yeah, of course they have. It's the sort of thing people used to say about us before Superintendent Evans got busted for the cash-for-grades stuff a few years ago."

"And you think Superintendent Richter's doing the same thing?"

Sabrina closed her eyes, took off her glasses, and pinched the bridge of her nose. Just bringing up Superintendent Evans' name had regurgitated some painful memories.

"No, probably not. I'm just saying that having a superintendent get up in front of a lot of people and say things are going great doesn't actually mean that they are."

Nolan still didn't get where Sabrina was going with this. "So, what, my school getting a perfect score on the math part of the BEAKS test last year doesn't mean anything?"

"Look, all I know is that my mom doesn't like the guy or his system, so that's good enough for me," Sabrina said bluntly as she slid her glasses back on and took a sip of her cream soda.

"Okay, okay. Fair enough," Nolan conceded before he diverted his eyes away from Sabrina again. He reached down to get another sip of his Cherry Coke when Sabrina nudged her head at the bright yellow cast on his left hand.

"So, when did that happen?"

"During football practice about two weeks ago," Nolan said. "I landed on it wrong when one of the guys tackled me. Hurt like hell, too. I'm not going to lie about that."

Sabrina took a deep breath, still trying to shake off the discussion they'd just had about Superintendent Richter. "You think you'll be able to play again before the season's over?"

"Probably not," Nolan grumbled. "And basketball's looking pretty iffy, too. I think the doctor said the bone won't be fully healed until about a month or so from now. Hopefully, I'll have it off by the middle of November, though."

"Well, that sucks," Sabrina said somewhat halfheartedly. "That must be driving you nuts."

Nolan shrugged and lowered his left hand down below the table again, getting his cast out of sight. "It did at first, but it's got its perks. Like, I'm going to study hall during athletics now, so at least I'm not getting to second period late anymore because Coach Adams lost track of time and caused football practice to run long. Plus, I think the extra time in study hall has really helped me get a better handle on all my Pre-AP classes."

"And yet you still lost today," Sabrina chided with a playful smile.

"Hey! I didn't get hurt until a few weeks ago and most of the first six weeks was already over by then," Nolan protested.

"Yeah, yeah. Excuses, excuses," Sabrina cooed. Nolan just glared back at her, knowing better than to encourage her with more arguing.

"Anyway, it definitely helped me do some more studying for the history test both of us have tomorrow," he said. "I just hope I can remember the different things affected by the Townshend Acts and some of the important dates."

"Yeah, that's something I've been struggling to get a handle on, too," Sabrina admitted. "Honestly, I kind of wish I had a study hall period like you. It would make my life immensely easier for stuff like this."

Nolan cracked a knowing smile and took another sip out of his Cherry Coke. "No kidding. Then again, if I was more like Eli, I probably wouldn't have to worry about studying at all."

"Yeah," Sabrina said absently. Suddenly, a confused look swept over her eyes. "Wait. You're not talking about Eli Reznik from Batts, are you?"

"Yep, that's the guy," Nolan said as if Sabrina should know better. "I swear, he hardly ever studies for his tests."

The confusion didn't fade from Sabrina's eyes. Granted, she hadn't seen or heard much of the guy since fifth grade when they were all going to Batts Elementary School, but, from what she remembered, Eli was one of the worst students in their grade. He was also one of the most obnoxious.

"Yeah and I'm sure he hardly ever passes those tests, too," Sabrina snipped back, still not sure why Nolan was so jealous of Eli. Across from her, Nolan just shook his head.

"Not anymore. Sure, he's just in the regular classes and not in any of the Pre-AP ones, but from what he's told me he's actually been getting A's on his tests this year. And I think he was getting B's on some of his tests last year, too."

"Seriously? A's and B's?" Sabrina echoed skeptically. "And he doesn't even study for his tests?"

"Nope," Nolan said frankly. "As far as I know, he just sort of shows up and takes it, then gets, like, an A or a B. I think he even likes to brag about how he barely even does his homework, too. I don't know, maybe the regular classes are just easier like that."

"I seriously doubt they're that easy," Sabrina snorted. She glanced down at the table to think for a second. As bad of a student as Eli was at Batts, she doubted he could be something close to an honor roll student now.

"And you're sure he's not cheating or something?" she asked while staring at the tabletop. Even though she didn't mean for it to come out so bitterly, she could still hear the accusatory tone in her voice just as easily as Nolan could. He didn't seem to take too much offense to it, though.

"Actually, it's sort of crossed my mind a few times, especially when Eli first told me about it. But if he's been cheating, he's been getting away with it for a couple of years now, and, like I said, his grades have actually been getting better."

Nolan paused and seemed to stare at some distant point behind Sabrina for a few seconds. "Still," he began, "it kind of makes me wonder..."

"What?"

Nolan slowly met eyes with Sabrina again. "Well, Eli didn't start doing better on his tests until *after* Superintendent Richter got here. What if the superintendent's system really is working? I mean, both of us know what Eli was like back at Batts. The guy could barely pass a test if the answers were right there in front of him."

"Probably because he was too busy making fart jokes,"

Sabrina huffed, drawing a dirty look from Nolan. He took another sip of his Cherry Coke before continuing.

"Either way, Eli's still the same crazy guy he's always been, but he's getting good grades now. If it's not because of whatever Superintendent Richter's doing, then how else do you explain it? I mean, maybe we're just not seeing it as much since we usually make good grades anyway."

"Or maybe it's because he started going to a different school," Sabrina shot back. "Seriously, Superintendent Richter's first year here was the same year we all started going to middle school. It's probably just a coincidence."

Nolan slouched into his seat and took another sip of his soda. "You really don't want to give Superintendent Richter any credit, do you?"

Sabrina let out a deep breath and glanced through the panel window next to their booth. The sun wasn't down yet, but it was certainly getting darker outside. Most of the cars on Crescent Avenue were already using their headlights, too.

"If you'd heard half of the things my mom has said about him, you'd be in the same boat," she insisted quietly. "Either way, I'd better head back home before it gets too dark. I need to get started on my Spanish homework anyway. Same time next six weeks?" she asked with a competitive smile.

"You know it!" Nolan shot back, opting to drop the debate like Sabrina had. "Except next time you'll be buying the drinks."

A thin smile crept over Sabrina's lips. "Yeah, like I haven't heard that one before."

"Hey, I'm serious this time," Nolan insisted. Sabrina still didn't look convinced, though, so he tried to take it up a notch. "I'll bet I even get a better grade than you on the history test tomorrow."

The skeptical look in Sabrina's eyes didn't fade. "Really? How much you want to bet?"

"Another round of drinks?"

Sabrina rolled her eyes and shook her head. "Okay, but you'd better pay up."

"I won't be if you're the one buying," Nolan teased.

The comment only brought a dry, "Uh-huh," from Sabrina, but Nolan ignored it. He couldn't put his finger on it, but somehow he knew he was going to ace that test tomorrow. He could feel it in his gut.

4

The Intolerable Test

Nolan's mind was reeling. Somehow the history test was a lot harder than he expected it to be, and he could feel his confidence about beating Sabrina whittling away with each question he came across.

Subconsciously gnawing on the cap of his pen, he did his best to settle his nerves as he read over Question 16 again.

The French and Indian War was also known as:
A) The New World War
B) The Seven Year War
C) The War to End All Wars
D) The Huron Uprising

A quick glance at the clock indicated he only had about fifteen minutes to wrap this up before third period was over. Unfortunately, he still had nine more questions to go through, including three short answer questions.

Taking the pen out of his mouth, Nolan quickly crossed off A and C before decidedly circling Option B for The Seven Year War. He only vaguely remembered it from his notes but The Huron Uprising just didn't sound right.

Moving on, Nolan tensed up as soon as he read the next question.

All of the following are examples of laws formed under the Intolerable Acts, EXCEPT:
A) The Quartering of British soldiers in private homes
B) Prohibiting colonists from using the Port of Boston
C) Raising tea tariffs by 3% in the colonies
D) Criminal trials for colonists had to be held in Britain

The Intolerable Acts?

The term raced through Nolan's mind, but he couldn't remember it from his notes. He re-read the question over again, just in case it would somehow jog his memory. Unfortunately, reading the question for a second or even a third time didn't help. If anything, it only made things worse.

Nolan returned to biting the cap of his pen. In the back of his mind, he wondered if he'd been so distracted about wanting to do better on this test than Sabrina that he'd just read over his notes on autopilot last night. He prayed that wasn't the case.

Still, nothing about this question felt right. Even though part of him suspected it was just his nerves getting the best of him, he was almost certain he'd never seen anything about the Intolerable Acts in his notes or heard anything about it in Coach Grayson's class either.

Shaking his head, Nolan decided to skip the question for now and come back to it later. Thankfully, even though Question 18 was a fill-in-the-blank question, it was one Nolan knew right off the bat.

Why did the Boston Tea Party happen?

Nolan quickly took the pen out of his mouth and started jotting down the answer. Unfortunately, the test didn't leave that much space for him to elaborate so he had to make it as concise as possible and hope the answer wasn't too short.

American colonists were protesting against taxation without representation.

After he was satisfied with his one-sentence answer, Nolan continued with the test. He made it through the next four questions fine before his resurging confidence came to a screeching halt on Question 23.

The colony hit hardest by the Intolerable Acts was:
A) Georgia
B) Pennsylvania
C) New York
D) Massachusetts

Then, glancing ahead to the last question on the test, Question 25, he spotted another troubling fill-in-the-blank question.

> What event led to the passage of the Intolerable Acts?

By now, Nolan was almost positive the Intolerable Acts were never covered in their class.

Biting his lip, he glanced up at Coach Grayson. The large, balding man was sitting at his desk, browsing through something on his laptop. Since this was a Pre-AP class, he'd always discouraged them from asking questions during a test. The only exception was when they didn't understand the phrasing of a question.

Nolan chewed on the cap of his pen some more. Technically, he figured his issue with Questions 17, 23, and 25 could fall under that category. Unfortunately, it was in a bit of a gray area so he realized he might have to find a way to convince Coach Grayson.

After letting out an apprehensive sigh, Nolan got out of his seat and stepped over to the coach's desk, trying to ignore the way everyone was looking at him. His heart almost skipped a beat when he saw Coach Grayson's intense glare shift from his smudgy computer screen to him.

"Um, Coach Grayson?" Nolan asked in a whisper as soon as he was next to the teacher.

"Yeah, Leere?" was Grayson's annoyed response. Nolan hated how Coach Grayson never used his first name in class.

"Yes. Um, I just had a question about three of the questions."

"What about them?"

"Well," Nolan began, lowering his voice even more, "I don't remember anything about the Intolerable Acts in our notes. Did we even cover that?"

"Odds are we did," Coach Grayson's grumbled. "You should have studied more. Go back to your seat."

Nolan's heart sank. Just then, a soft voice from the row next to the coach's desk cut through the silence.

"Actually, I was kind of thinking the same thing–about the Intolerable Acts questions."

Coach Grayson and Nolan turned their attention to the petite girl sitting in front of the coach's desk. Brynlee Gigori. The girl had barely said two words all year, and that was only when Coach Grayson called on her in class.

"Me either," came another voice over the classroom. A few others coughed up the same chorus.

Nolan's eyes glanced back to Coach Grayson. The man took in a deep breath and raked his massive palms across his face before saying anything.

"Look, we went over the Intolerable Acts in class," Coach Grayson insisted to everyone as soon as he realized a lot of them had the same bewildered expression on their faces. "If it's on the test, we covered it. That's it. Make your best guess if you don't know it."

With a few reserved groans, everyone returned to their test. However, Nolan couldn't pull himself away from Coach Grayson's desk just yet.

"But, sir," he began, motioning toward the test with his hand, "I'm sure there was nothing in our notes about—"

"Do you want ten points taken off your test right now, Leere?" Coach Grayson cut in sharply.

Nolan stammered for a second, unable to cough up his rebuttal. He could feel everyone's eyes bearing down on him again.

"You'd better give me an answer in the next five seconds," Grayson warned.

Nolan shook his head before he choked out, "No. No, sir, I don't."

"Good. Then get back to your seat and finish your test. This is supposed to be a college-level class," he seemed to announce to everyone. "It'll be treated like one."

Nolan nodded and retreated to his desk. He let out a defeated sigh as soon as he took his seat and looked down at the test in front of him. Question 17 was staring back at him, demanding an answer Nolan couldn't come up with. Trying to ignore the frustration welling up in his stomach, knowing he probably wouldn't beat Sabrina now, he took the pen out of his mouth and circled option D.

An instant later, he couldn't stop himself from glaring at Coach Grayson. He was already back to focusing on whatever was on his laptop, hardly caring that at least half of the class didn't know anything about this subject.

As he was staring down Coach Grayson, Nolan noticed Brynlee had glanced up from her test and was looking back at him with a pair of sympathetic eyes. When she realized Nolan had seen her, she gave him a thin smile and shrugged before getting back to her test.

Nolan scowled and tried to re-focus again. Unfortunately, the bitterness still lingered. Brynlee might have been able to shrug it off, but he doubted he'd be able to.

Nothing about this felt right.

5

The Panicked Prankster

The rest of the morning passed by in a blur. As much as Nolan tried to get over it, he couldn't stop thinking about whether or not Coach Grayson even mentioned the Intolerable Acts before today's test. He certainly didn't remember anything about it.

Unfortunately, even if Coach Grayson did forget to cover the subject, Nolan still couldn't prove it. He didn't get a chance to look through his history notes before English class started last period, and now he was tempted to cut his lunch short just to get that done.

Of course, he knew there was always the chance Coach Grayson had said something about the Intolerable Acts during class and he just forgot to put it in his notes, but Nolan quickly dismissed the idea. If that was the case, it wouldn't explain why most of the class didn't know anything about it either.

There had to be something else he was missing.

Nolan was so preoccupied with trying to figure it out he barely even acknowledged Eli when he sat down across from him at their usual table in the cafeteria. But as much as he'd been dreading Eli's habitual greeting of, 'How's it hangin',' it never came.

After overturning the plastic tub of salad onto his hamburger patty to give it a hint of flavor, Nolan glanced back at his friend. Eli was still sitting in front of him with a blank expression on his face. He had a half-eaten curly fry in his hand and his eyes seemed to be glued to the opposite edge of their cafeteria table.

"Something on your mind?" Nolan finally asked when

he still didn't say anything, causing Eli to jolt with a start. He glanced back at Nolan for a split second before his eyes darted down to the carton of curly fries in front of him.

"No. Just feeling kind of burned out right now," he said drearily before eating the rest of the curly fry in his hand. "It's been kind of a rough morning."

Nolan laughed under his breath and took a bite out of his hamburger. "Well, I guess that makes two of us. I swear, the test I took in Coach Grayson's today was definitely a lot harder than I thought it would be–or should have been."

Eli looked back up at Nolan with a quizzical glint in his eyes. "Wait, you had a hard time with a test?"

"Hey, it happens to the best of us," Nolan said as casually as he could, hoping Eli wouldn't make that big of a deal out of it. Unfortunately, a malicious grin was already spreading across his friend's lips.

"Why? You didn't forget to study, did you?"

"No, I didn't forget to study," Nolan argued, giving Eli a dirty look. The skeptical look in his friend's eyes didn't change, though.

"As a matter of fact," Nolan added, "I spent a few hours doing that this weekend and Monday night, not to mention looking over my notes again during athletic study hall this morning. So, yeah, I'm pretty sure I was ready for it. It's just too bad Coach Grayson wasn't."

"Oh, yeah. Because it's totally the teacher's fault," Eli snipped with a roll of his eyes.

"Dude, there were, like, three questions on the test about something called the Intolerable Acts that no one knew anything about!" Nolan said before taking a sip of his lemonade. Across from him, Eli shrugged a little.

"And I'd probably be one of them."

"Yeah, well, it might have been something just for the Pre-AP classes," Nolan suggested almost instinctively. "Either way, since I definitely didn't know anything about it, it kind of made me think that he forgot to cover it, you know? So, I asked Coach Grayson about it."

"Yeah? And how'd that go?" Eli asked with a knowing smile.

"About like you'd expect," Nolan spat. "Even when everyone else started saying they didn't know anything about the Intolerable Acts either, he still acted like it was our fault for some reason."

Eli shook his head a little. "Figures. That guy's a joke, man. Remember how he was in football last year?"

"Yeah, I remember," Nolan agreed sourly. Both of them had been on Coach Grayson's football team last year and neither had fond memories of it or their losing season.

"It still kind of ticks me off, though," Nolan continued. "I probably screwed up on that test today because of him and he doesn't even have the guts to admit it."

"And by 'screwed up' I'm sure you mean getting something like a B-plus, right?"

Nolan glanced off to the side. "Yeah. Probably."

"Then why are you making such a big deal about it?"

"Because it wasn't my fault!" Nolan snapped, drawing a few looks from the people sitting around them.

"Okay, okay," Eli said, raising both palms for emphasis. "I get it. I'm just saying I wouldn't be that mad if I got a B-plus, you know? I mean, take it from me. I've had a hard time with tests for a while now. As far as I'm concerned, the best thing you can do is just forget about it and move on. Who knows? Maybe it won't be as bad as you think."

"Yeah, maybe," Nolan said. He absently picked at the tater tots on his tray and tried to settle down. "You really think I'm making too big of a deal out of it, though?"

Eli shrugged. "Well, it's sort of different today if Coach Grayson screwed it up and all that, but, for the most part, you're definitely cooler about it than Eric is."

Nolan gave Eli a curious look. "Your brother?"

"Who else? He's so freakin' obsessed about being the valedictorian or whatever this year that it's starting to drive him crazy. Well, crazier, anyway. He went off the freakin' rails the other night during supper just because he found out one of his friends or classmates or whatever got a ninety-seven on their calculus test and he got a ninety-four. And, yeah, I remember those were the exact grades because that's all he was talking about!"

"Dang! That sucks, dude," Nolan gasped. Deep down, though, he knew he could relate to Eric to some extent, especially after losing to Sabrina yesterday, but he pushed it to the back of his mind.

"I swear," Eli said curtly, "some people just need to realize that grades aren't everything, you know? A guy's got to get out there and enjoy himself every now and then. Like I did yesterday."

Nolan saw his friend's eyes go wide for a split second before he quickly glanced off to the side. He'd known Eli long enough to recognize his guilty look.

"So what did you do yesterday?" Nolan asked as a malicious grin started to snake across his lips.

Eli made a quick glance at the area around him. As usual, he and Nolan were just two of the students packed in tight, shoulder-to-shoulder, along one of the narrow tables lining the cafeteria.

"Nothing," Eli said a little too evasively. Trying to smooth it out, he added, "Nothing interesting, anyway."

Unfortunately, Nolan didn't buy into it and he already had an idea about what Eli was trying to hide. "You pulled a prank again, didn't you?"

Eli swore he felt his heart skip a beat. He could even feel the hairs on the back of his neck standing on end, too.

"No," he shot back, hardly believing his own voice.

"Oh, come on," Nolan insisted. "What'd you do? It can't be any worse than the time you put superglue on Ronny Cooper's glasses, can it?"

"Actually…" Eli started to say before he could stop himself. Across the table, Nolan watched on expectantly.

"Actually, what?" he pried, nearly grinning from ear-to-ear now.

"Look, just forget about it, alright? I really don't want to talk about it. Especially not here."

"Whatever," Nolan said with a roll of his eyes. He reached down and took another bite out of his hamburger. "Still, I think this is the first time you've been tight-lipped about something you pulled. If I didn't know any better, I'd almost say you're the one that messed with the PA sys—"

Suddenly, Nolan stopped chewing on his hamburger and looked back at Eli. He could already see the dread sweeping over his friend's face.

"No way! That was you?"

"Not another word, man," Eli snarled through gnashed teeth. Nolan hadn't said it that loud, or, at least, it didn't register very high over the clamor hanging over the cafeteria, but to Eli it seemed like Nolan had announced it over a megaphone.

"Okay, okay. But, seriously: you?"

Eli pulled his lips in tight and checked his surroundings again. By some miracle, no one seemed to be paying attention.

"Yeah. But keep a lid on it, alright? I just found out in third period that I'm in pretty hot water here."

"No kidding!" Nolan scoffed. "From what Sabrina told me last night, Superintendent Richter's probably one of the last people you'd want to tick off."

"Yeah, I'm starting to see that now," Eli acknowledged morosely. Nolan watched on as he took a deep, shaky breath and stared down at the table for a few seconds.

"Man, you really are freaking out about this, aren't you?" Nolan said. The grave look Eli shot him when he did look back up sent chills racing down his neck.

"You don't know the half of it, man."

"Why? What's going on?"

Eli pulled his lips in tight and tapped his thumb against the table a few times. He almost wondered if he should even tell Nolan, but, more than that, he didn't want to say anything about it right now. There were too many ears around.

"Not here," he finally choked out while glancing off to the side.

"What?"

"I don't want to talk about it here," Eli hissed, meeting eyes with Nolan again.

Nolan whisked his hands up in frustration. "Okay, so what do you want to do?" He glanced over his shoulder at the clock mounted above the second entrée line. It was just a little after 12:45. "We've only got about ten minutes before lunch is over," he reported, nudging his head at the clock.

Eli looked back down at his curly fries. He really wasn't

that hungry before and the fries looked even less appetizing now. A quick glance at Nolan's tray showed he still had about a quarter of his hamburger to finish and hadn't even touched the overcooked tater tots yet.

"You think we could go outside?" he asked reluctantly. His voice was shaking now.

Nolan wasn't too hungry either and quickly nodded in response. He took one last sip of his lemonade before stepping away from the table and taking his tray to one of the trash cans. Eli quickly followed suit, and, before long, both had retrieved their backpacks at the drop-off area near the doors and were walking out of the cafeteria.

Even though neither said anything they both knew where they were going. There was a porch area outside, wedged between the cafeteria and the band hall, where students could go if they finished their lunch early. The school officially called it Mountaineers' Hollow, but most of the students just called it The Nook.

As soon as they were outside, the two found an isolated area under a tree near the edge of The Nook, away from some seventh-graders playing hacky sack. Eli still looked like he couldn't decide if he wanted to talk or not, so Nolan tried to get the ball rolling.

"Okay. So what's going on?" he asked. "I'm guessing no one else knows, right?"

Eli shook his head. Through it all, his eyes remained focused on a crack in the concrete in front of him.

"No. No one else knows. At least not right now," he began warily. Even though they were out of earshot of anyone else he still kept his voice down. "But if anyone does find out, I'm pretty much screwed at this point."

"Well, you did play that song during Superintendent Richter's speech," Nolan suggested. "I'd say that probably has a lot to do with it."

Eli looked back at him. "Yeah, I know. But I found out this morning there's more to it than that now. Apparently, Superintendent Richter thinks I'm, like, some kind of hacker or something."

Nolan's head jerked back in surprise. "Seriously? I mean, no offense or anything, but I don't get why he'd think that. It was just some prank, right?"

"Yeah, but I kind of screwed up when I was doing it," Eli said shamefully.

"What do you mean?"

A trembling sigh rattled through Eli's lips. "Okay. So, when I, um, pulled my prank yesterday, I accidentally took some USB drive from the office with me."

"You mean you stole it?" Nolan blurted out, giving Eli a stern look.

"No, it was an accident," Eli stressed. When the skeptical look in Nolan's eyes didn't fade, he added, "I had to unplug it from the PA system in order to plug my aunt's old MP3 player into it, alright? I guess I was in a hurry to get out of there and forgot I put it in my pocket or something."

Nolan kept staring Eli down for a second or two before he shook his head in resignation.

"Okay, whatever," Nolan grunted. He made a rolling gesture with his right hand a second later to get Eli to continue with his story.

"So, basically," Eli began, "I didn't know I still had it in my pocket until I got to the assembly and I kind of panicked. So, I did the only thing I could think of. On the way out of the gym, I dropped it on the floor near the exit since everyone kind of gets jumbled up there. I didn't think anyone would notice."

"Did they?"

Eli shook his head. "No. Well, at least, I don't think so. But when I was in PE this morning, I heard one of the sixth-graders talking about the same USB drive. Apparently, he found it in the gym and went to the office to turn it into the lost and found."

Nolan shifted his weight onto his left foot. "So? It sounds like they don't even know who took the drive, then. And you know me, Eli, I'm not going to tell anyone."

Eli sucked his lips in tight and nodded. "Yeah, I know you wouldn't, Nolan, but there's more to it than that. A lot more, actually.

"The thing is, the sixth-grader said that when he went to the office to drop off the USB drive, the secretary recognized it and then he got called into the principal's office. Then Principal

Espinoza, Superintendent Richter, and some other guy from, like, Central Office or some crap like that started asking him questions about how he got the drive and all that stuff. Apparently, Superintendent Richter was freakin' pissed–and it wasn't *just because* I played 'Baby Got Back' over the PA system," Eli insisted with a raised finger.

"Fair enough," Nolan said, trying not to laugh. "So, what else happened?"

"Alright, so the way he talked, it sounds like they think I was trying to steal data from the school."

"All because you accidentally took the USB drive with you?"

"Exactly!" Eli exclaimed. Nolan was less excitable, though.

"And you're sure that's what you heard? Maybe that sixth-grader was just blowing it way out of proportion."

Eli quickly shook his head. "Oh, no. That's definitely what I heard, man. That kid was asking people in PE if they knew who did it, too. Apparently, Superintendent Richter really wants to find out who it was."

"And that's why you're so worried about getting caught now?" Nolan asked.

"Well, yeah!" Eli cried. "Think about it, Nolan. If I get caught, Superintendent Richter might throw me in jail or something."

"Oh, come on. I don't think he'd do that," Nolan scoffed.

"Yeah, but what if he does?"

Nolan bit his lip for a second. "Look, it's not like you haven't been busted for a prank before. Why don't you just go ahead and turn yourself in and tell them that taking the USB drive was an accident?"

Eli shook his head. "No way. I'm not doing that, man."

"Why not?"

"It's just not that easy," Eli insisted. "This isn't like the time I poured ice down Amy Dockins' shirt or put the dissected frog parts in Mrs. Ortiz's purse, alright? I actually took a USB drive out of the office. Do you even know how that looks? Even if I go in there and tell them this was just another one of my stupid pranks, there's no way they're going to believe me. They'll lock me up and throw away the freakin' key!"

Eli breathed shakily and looked down at the ground. "I

just don't know what to do, man."

Nolan pulled his lips in tight and he peered out across the teachers' parking lot. There was no denying it. Eli had definitely gotten himself into a mess this time. Unfortunately, Nolan could only think of one way out for his friend.

"Well, if you're not going to turn yourself in, I guess all you can do is keep quiet about it. Who knows? Maybe this will all blow over in a few weeks and Principal Espinoza will find something else to worry about or Superintendent Richter will just give up looking."

Eli shook his head and dipped his hands into his pockets. "I don't think that's going to work this time, man. I've got this feeling, you know? Like I'm not going to get away from this one. I just wish there was something else I could do."

Nolan reached out and put his hand on Eli's shoulder. He could actually feel him shaking.

"Look. I wish I had better news for you, but it's not like you can run off to Mexico or something. You haven't even taken Spanish yet."

A nervous laugh sputtered out of Eli's lips. "Yeah, that'd make things kind of hard, wouldn't it?"

"Totally," Nolan said with a thin smile. "The only other thing I can think of is to fake being sick for a couple of weeks, but I don't think you'd be able to pull that off. Plus, it would probably make Principal Espinoza really suspicious."

Eli shook his head. "No, that definitely wouldn't work. Plus, I don't think I'd want to do that, anyway. Even if I could pull it off, I'd be cooped up in my house all the time and I'd have to use that stupid sick day streaming service again."

"Yeah, I guess that kind of takes the fun out of it," Nolan grumbled.

"No, it's not that," Eli said. "It's just that the last time I tried to use the streaming service a few weeks ago I had a lot of problems with it. The thing would always disconnect and spend a few minutes buffering before I could do anything. The sound sync-up was way off, too. Honestly, I think I had a harder time staying focused on that thing than I normally do *in* school."

"And that's saying something," Nolan quipped.

"Oh, shut up!" Eli snarled playfully. A sharp buzzing

behind them caused the two to glance over their shoulders. The bell had rung. Lunch was over.

"And here we go again," Eli droned. "You mean it, though, right? Your lips are sealed?"

Nolan slid a pair of pinched fingers across his lips. "As always. Have I ever let you down?"

"Only about a million times," Eli grumbled as they started making their way back into school.

"Like when?" Nolan demanded.

Eli glanced over his shoulder as the two passed through the doors. "Gee, I don't know. Like when you told Mrs. Ortiz I was the one that put the frog parts in her purse."

"Dude, it was gross!" Nolan protested. "Besides, she suspected you from the start."

Eli just rolled his eyes and shook his head. "Whatever. Anyway, I've still got to get to my locker and head to English. Where are you headed?"

Nolan nudged his head off to the right. "Science."

"Yeah, that sounds like a blast," Eli grunted. "Talk to you later?"

"Yeah. Later, dude," Nolan said, exchanging a fist bump with his friend before the two went in different directions. It still took Nolan about a minute of weaving his way through the masses cluttering the halls before he arrived at his locker.

After unlocking it, he slid his backpack off and knelt down to have better access to the bottom shelf where he kept his books. No sooner had he unzipped his backpack than he spotted the green spiral he used for history inside.

"Dang it!" Nolan hissed under his breath, realizing he'd forgotten to cut his lunch short so he could look through his history notes. Now he wouldn't have a chance to do that before science started, and, worst of all, he'd probably be distracted by it for the rest of the day, too.

Going through English on autopilot was bad enough. He definitely couldn't afford to go through science and algebra like that.

"I might as well go ahead and buy the next round of drinks," Nolan grumbled as he started switching out his morning materials with the ones he needed for the afternoon.

Then it dawned on him. Even though Sabrina went to a different school, she would be taking the same test today since the district's tests were all alike now. If she knew what the Intolerable Acts were or had any notes on them, it might help him figure out if Coach Grayson covered the subject or not.

He'd definitely have to give her a call later that afternoon.

6

After School Anxiety

"Why don't you just relax for a bit?" Sabrina's mom suggested, sensing Sabrina's building frustration with every bump or curve the car took. "We'll be home in a few minutes."

Sabrina hardly gave her mom a glance out of the corner of her eye as a determined grimace formed over her lips and she turned her attention back to the Spanish worksheet in her lap. If there was one thing she wished she could do better, it was doing her homework in the car.

"I can't. I've got too much homework tonight," Sabrina finally said. Unfortunately, it didn't get the response she was hoping for.

"Yeah? How much?"

Without giving it much thought, Sabrina rattled off the things she had on the docket with a snippy tone in her voice. "Oh, just algebra, science, history, English, and, wouldn't you know it, Spanish," she said, capping off her statement by whisking a hand at the worksheet in front of her.

"Yeah, that's pretty intense, alright," her mom said, hardly sounding impressed. "You want to hear what I've got on tap after we get home?"

"What?" Sabrina asked, knowing she was expected to. She could already tell where this was going.

"Cooking supper, organizing my lesson plan for tomorrow, then uploading that to the streaming service, double-checking Lance's math homework, and grading about sixty chemistry quizzes. And in spite of all that, what am I not doing right now?"

Sabrina rolled her eyes. "I would say you're not working

on any of that, but, you've got to admit, it'd be pretty hard to do that while you're driving."

"Okay, well, all logic aside," her mom began with a wry grin, "the point I'm trying to make is that I'm finding time to relax whenever I can. You'd be amazed at how much it helps."

"Great. I'll keep that in mind, Mom," Sabrina said, immediately turning her attention back to her Spanish worksheet. She almost cringed when her mom kept talking.

"So are you going to put the homework away or did you want me to take the long way home? I might even stop at the grocery store first and you'll *have* to leave your homework in the car and come in with me."

"Do I have to?" Sabrina whined.

"Just give it a shot today," her mom insisted. "I promise I won't pester you about it tomorrow."

"Fine," Sabrina snorted, leaving her Spanish homework in the book as she slammed it shut and slid it into her backpack. Unfortunately, even as silence settled in, Sabrina's irritated mood lingered. It was still there when her mom pulled into the driveway a few minutes later.

"Feel better?" her mom asked optimistically.

"Sure. Why not?" Sabrina grunted. As soon as the car slowed down enough, she stepped out with her backpack slung over one shoulder and ducked underneath the rising garage door. After getting into the house, she grabbed a pack of raspberry Pop Tarts out of the cabinet on her way through the kitchen and quickly stepped into the living room, heading for the stairs.

Her younger brother, Lance, was sitting in his usual reading spot against the wall next to their mom's rocking chair. His eyes were glued to the latest edition of *Secret Agent Samurai* he'd picked up on Saturday and he didn't even bother to glance up as Sabrina passed by.

"Hey, Sabrina," he called out distantly. "Tons of homework tonight?"

Lance knew his sister's determined walk when he heard it. The crackling of the Pop Tarts wrapper just about confirmed it, too.

"Enjoy fifth grade while you can," was all she said before he heard the rhythmic thumping of his sister jogging up the stairs. The stern clack of Sabrina pushing her door shut echoed down the stairwell a few seconds later.

"That I will," Lance hummed as he got back to reading his book. He'd been aching to try and finish it ever since he got off the bus about an hour ago.

Upstairs, Sabrina sat her backpack down on top of her bed and took her phone out of her pocket. She turned the sound back on and placed it on the dresser next to her Pop Tarts, glancing at the clock as she did so. It was nearly five-fifteen.

That gave her about an hour to get started on something before supper was ready. Considering the hour-long break she'd probably have while she ate supper and helped with the mandatory dishwashing afterwards, that left her with about four hours to finish her homework from algebra and Spanish and then do her reading assignments for English and history before going to bed.

Sabrina was just glad she'd managed to finish most of the reading for science at school before her mom picked her up. If she ran out of time tonight, she could probably wrap up the rest tomorrow morning.

Shaking her head in frustration, Sabrina pulled out her algebra textbook first, knowing the homework for that class would probably take the most time to go through. She brought it over to her desk, retrieved a couple pages of notebook paper, and opened the book to the questions on Page 96.

Grabbing a pencil out of her desk, she ran it through the sharpener first before flicking her lamp on and writing a two with a circle around it for Question 2. Her class had been assigned all the even-numbered questions up to Question 28 tonight. Glancing ahead, it looked like the last six of the fourteen questions would be word problems, too.

"Great," she huffed, suppressing the urge to put this off until later.

Sabrina took a deep breath and started looking over the first question. She'd just started reading over the problem when she was interrupted by a shrill series of chirps from her phone. It was Nolan's ring.

Setting her pencil down in exasperation, Sabrina got out of the chair and grabbed the phone. She was half-tempted to let it go to voicemail but opted to answer it instead. Nolan rarely called her like this, so it must have been important enough. Still, she hoped it didn't take too long.

"Hey, Nolan," she answered halfheartedly.

"Oh. Hey, Sabrina," Nolan responded in a bit of a shaky voice. "Rough day?"

Sabrina scoffed and sat down on her bed. She took her glasses off and started rubbing the bridge of her nose. "Oh, not really. Just busy. Got a lot of homework tonight. So, what's on your mind?"

"The history test," Nolan said bluntly. "Did you have any problems with it today?"

Sabrina paused for a second and stared out her window while she thought back to fifth period. "Not that I can remember. Honestly, I thought it was pretty easy." Just then, a thin smile started to creep across her lips. "Why? Are you already worried about having to buy the next round of drinks?"

"No," Nolan answered unconvincingly. "There was just one section on it that I didn't remember from my notes. It was over the Intolerable Acts. Did you have anything like that on your test?"

Sabrina put her glasses back on. "Well, considering we probably took the same test today, I'm sure I did. I don't exactly remember it, though."

"But it sounds familiar?"

Sabrina shrugged. "Yeah, I guess. I really don't know, though. I'm feeling kind of fried right now."

Her eyes drifted back over to her desk and her open algebra book. Nolan still hadn't said anything back.

"So, is that all you wanted to know?"

"Sort of," Nolan answered, sounding hesitant. "Actually, I was just wondering if you could look through your notes real quick and see if you had anything about the Intolerable Acts in there."

Sabrina's shoulders sagged. "I can't right now, Nolan. I've really got to get started on my homework. Why do you want to know if that was in my history notes, anyway? The test is already over."

"Yeah, I know. It's just been bothering me all day. I went

through my notes a couple of times after I got home from school, but I still can't find anything about the Intolerable Acts in there."

"Well, maybe you forgot to write them down," Sabrina suggested. She tried to hide it, but there was still plenty of impatience riding on her voice. Nolan continued anyway.

"No. I don't think so. A couple of other people in my class even said the same thing– about not remembering the Intolerable Acts, anyway. I'm starting to think Coach Grayson forgot to teach us about it."

Suddenly Sabrina knew what Nolan was getting at. Ever since Superintendent Richter implemented the consolidated testing syllabus, teachers were expected to teach everything Central Office printed on the tests before they got distributed to the schools on the testing date. There could be big problems for a teacher if they slipped up and forgot to cover something. It was an aspect of the new system her mom absolutely hated.

Still, Sabrina almost wondered if Nolan was just letting his nerves get the bet of him thanks to the bet he'd made yesterday.

"So, do you think you could look through your notes real quick?" Nolan asked when she didn't answer.

Sabrina shook her head to jolt herself out of the trance she'd fallen into. An instant later her eyes drifted back to her desk. "Look, I'm not trying to be rude, but I really don't have time for it tonight, Nolan."

A shrill, "Crap!" hissed through her phone.

Biting her lip, Sabrina added, "But we should be getting our tests back tomorrow, so I guess we could compare our notes at Fryer Tuck's when we meet up to see who got the best grade. Is that okay?"

"Yes. Yeah, that would be great," Nolan responded, sounding relieved.

"Okay. Well, I guess I'll see you then," Sabrina said hurriedly as she stared at the algebra homework that was on standby. Nolan seemed to read her thoughts over the phone.

"How much homework do you have tonight, anyway?" he asked, making Sabrina grit her teeth.

"Algebra and Spanish. Plus some reading for history and English, too."

"Holy crap!" Nolan exclaimed. "No wonder you're in such a

rush."

"Yeah, totally," Sabrina chuckled dryly. "Well, anyway, I better get with it, you know?"

"Oh, right. Sorry!" Nolan blurted out. "Good luck with that homework."

"Yeah, thanks," Sabrina said back. She quickly said bye to Nolan and hung up before he got a chance to prolong the conversation even more.

With that, Sabrina put the phone on silent, sat it on her dresser, and stepped back over to her desk to get started on Question 2. Even though she tried to clear her mind to focus on the algebra homework, part of her was still trying to think back to the history test she'd taken earlier that afternoon. She was starting to think there had been a few questions about the Intolerable Acts on it, but didn't remember going over that subject when she was studying last night either.

Impulsively, Sabrina swiveled around and glanced at her backpack, knowing her history spiral was in there. Part of her realized it wouldn't take too long to glance through her notes and satisfy her own curiosity, but she quickly shook her head at the idea and turned away.

She could deal with Nolan's problems later.

7

Uncovered

The shrill ringing of the school bell pulled Nolan back to reality. Second period had just ended, but he barely remembered anything from the last fifty-five minutes. But as bad as he felt for spacing out during Spanish, he felt even worse knowing he had to go to history next. He'd been dreading the class all morning.

A tired look was plastered over Nolan's face as he slid his Spanish book into his backpack and filtered out of the classroom behind everyone else. So far, the morning had been a complete washout. The frustration he'd been feeling about yesterday's history test had festered into an obsession overnight, making it nearly impossible for him to concentrate on much else today.

At this point, Nolan was almost positive Coach Grayson had forgotten to go over the Intolerable Acts in class. Unfortunately, he couldn't be sure until he met up with Sabrina after school and that was still seven hours off.

As grueling as today had been, though, he was starting to wonder if he'd even make it to seventh period, let alone Fryer Tuck's, before he lost his mind.

The thoughts were still weighing heavily on him when he passed into Room 115 a short time later. He half-expected Coach Grayson to give him a dirty look when he entered, but, like most other times before class, Nolan's old coach was just slouched in front of his laptop when he came in.

Brynlee Gigori was nice enough to give Nolan an encouraging smile on the way to his desk, which he only partially returned, but most everyone else seemed to be minding their own business or talking to their neighbors. It bugged the heck out of him.

"Has anyone said anything about the test yet?" Nolan asked just loud enough for anyone sitting nearby to hear.

In front of him, Ryan Ocilby stopped doodling in the margins of his spiral just long enough to say, "Not that I've noticed. Why?"

Nolan shook his head. "I don't know. I guess I just thought people would still be upset about it or something."

"Why? You want to get up in front of everyone and ask Coach Grayson about it again?" Ryan suggested. Even though he didn't look back, Nolan could practically hear the smirk on Ryan's lips when he said it.

"Dude, put a sock in it," Nolan grumbled before he started to pull his history spiral out of his backpack.

The bell rang again a minute or two later and ushered in third period. As always, Coach Grayson waddled over to shut the door to the hallway before he flicked off half the lights and got the room ready for the projector.

"Did you finish grading our tests yet?" one of Nolan's classmates squeaked out as Coach Grayson walked by her desk. A sour look quickly contorted the coach's lips.

"I did. And I'll be getting those back to you in a bit. But before I can do that, or even get started with today's class, I've been instructed to show you a special announcement from Central Office," Coach Grayson said bitterly.

After syncing up his laptop to the projector from the cart in the middle of the room, Coach Grayson transferred the display onto the projector screen and moved the mouse over a minimized image on the taskbar.

"Okay. So, as I'm sure all of you remember, some wise-guy decided to play a dirty song over the PA system during the assembly on Monday," he began.

Nolan's breath got stuck in his throat.

"And even though this might seem like a harmless prank, sneaking into the office and messing with the computer equipment is a pretty big deal. So, with that in mind, our superintendent has asked the teachers to show you this picture and see if any of you recognize the person in the photo."

A chill raced down Nolan's back as soon as Coach Grayson opened the file and a grainy, off-color security camera photo appeared on the screen. It showed someone wearing a gray hoodie near the reception counter in the office. The person appeared to be walking and the hood obscured the top half of their face from the security camera's vantage point.

Of course, Nolan already knew who it was, but if Eli hadn't spilled his guts about it yesterday he doubted he would have even recognized his friend in the picture. Based on the perplexed looks from everyone else in the room, Nolan guessed they were in the same boat.

Before they could study over it any more, however, Coach Grayson abruptly closed the photo and got to work at opening his slideshow presentation for the lecture.

"Alright, enough of that. But, seriously, if any of you know who the kid in the picture is, let Principal Espinoza know. Central Office is actually offering a cash reward to anyone that can point the guy out."

"A cash reward?" one of Nolan's classmates echoed.

"Didn't I say it was a big deal?" Coach Grayson grunted. "Anyway, we'll be talking about the start of the Revolutionary War today. But first, I have an announcement of my own."

An uneasy silence fell over the class as they watched Coach Grayson move back over to his desk.

"So, I know several of you complained about not knowing about the Intolerable Acts on yesterday's test, and, as it turns out, students in my other Pre-AP class said the same thing during fifth period. So, I looked over my testing syllabus from Central Office after school yesterday and came across something interesting."

Nolan was still reeling from the security photo but watched on intently with the rest of the class as Coach Grayson picked the stack of tests up off his desk.

"As it turns out, the Intolerable Acts weren't on the testing syllabus either," their teacher announced.

A few excited gasps whispered across the classroom.

"So, I brought the matter up with Principal Espinoza, who then contacted Central Office about it, and guess what? Those questions weren't even supposed to be on the test since they were part of last year's syllabus. Because of that, Central Office told us we could omit them."

More delighted gasps rose over the classroom, and a sense of relief washed over Nolan.

"Now, before you get too excited," Coach Grayson warned as he started handing out the tests, "since we had to take out three questions that leaves just twenty-two on the test, so your answers count five points apiece now instead of four. Other than that, most of you did very well."

Nolan waited anxiously as Coach Grayson weaved through the rows, distributing the tests. It wasn't long before he stepped by and put Nolan's test face down on his desk. He didn't waste a second to turn it over and look at his grade. There, in red ink on the top of the page, was a 95.

A mixture of relief and anxiety raced through Nolan's mind. He'd made a much better grade than he'd expected, but he'd obviously missed a question, too. Scanning over the test, he quickly found a red X next to Question 7.

What piece of literature helped rally support for the revolution?
A) The Bill of Rights
B) The Magna Carta
C) The Federalist Papers
D) Common Sense

Thanks to reading over his notes several times since yesterday, Nolan realized he should have circled D on this question instead of C.

Still, he figured a 95 wasn't too bad, all considering, and a further review of the test showed that Questions 17, 23, and 25 were all crossed out with a black marker, followed by an annotation of, "Omitted per C.O.," with Coach Grayson's initials listed below.

A smile started to creep over Nolan's lips. For the first time since he had taken the test yesterday, he realized there was a chance Sabrina could actually be buying the drinks tonight instead of him. Then again, he'd still missed one question, so that wasn't a sure thing yet either.

His thoughts were interrupted when Coach Grayson finished returning the tests and moved back to the cart he'd left his laptop on. "Alright, now that we have all that out of the way, let's get back to business."

No sooner had he pressed the button on his laptop to show the first slide in the presentation than the class quickly got to work at copying the information into their notes. Nolan did his best to try and listen to what Coach Grayson was saying, but, after a few slides, his already muddled focus started to waver and drifted back onto the security photo.

Unfortunately, as unsettling as it was for Central Office to ask the teachers to show the security photo to their classes, that was just the tip of the iceberg.

"You're serious? You actually think I should turn myself in now?" Eli snapped, glaring back at Nolan.

Their lunch period had just started, but they were already standing under the tree in The Nook again. Considering how animated Eli was right now, Nolan was kind of glad they had the place to themselves for the moment. Then again, he could hardly blame his friend for the way he was acting.

Bright red flyers exhibiting the same picture he'd seen in Coach Grayson's class had been posted above every water fountain, on every restroom door, and at the front of every entrée line in the cafeteria during third period. Each flyer contained the same chilling message.

Do you recognize the person in this picture? If so, please alert your principal or assistant principal immediately and receive a CASH REWARD.

Thank you for your cooperation.
-Dr. Lars Richter, Superintendent

Both of them knew Eli was in over his head now.

"Well, it's just a thought," Nolan shot back. "I mean, you've seen the pictures. It's just like what you were telling me yesterday. They think you were trying to hack into the system or something. You need to come forward and tell them it was just a prank."

Eli shook his head. "No way, man. No way. I'm not doing it, alright? I mean, yeah, if all I did was play that song over the PA system, then I'd do it. But this wasn't just some prank."

A curious look crossed Nolan's face. "It wasn't?"

Eli whisked his hand back at the school. "Not to them, it wasn't! As far as they care, I stole a USB drive out of the office. That's the only reason they're making such a big deal about this."

"Then tell them it was an accident," Nolan argued.

"Yeah," Eli coughed, "like they'd believe that."

"Well, I did, didn't I?" Nolan said sincerely. "Look, it's only going to get worse the longer you wait."

Eli glared back at the school and raked his fingers through his straggly brown hair. Without looking back, he pointed a finger at Nolan as if it was an extension of the thought that had just crossed his mind. "Or maybe they'll forget about it after a while–like what you said yesterday."

"Dude, they've practically got wanted posters put up all over school," Nolan said. "I don't think they're going to be forgetting about it any time soon."

"Oh, for crap's sake!" Eli hissed, looking dejected. After letting out a shaky breath, he finally turned his eyes back to Nolan and said, "You think someone's going to recognize me in those pictures?"

Nolan stared back at Eli for a second while trying to form his own mental image of the security camera picture. Eventually, he just shook his head. "I don't know. I just know that *I* couldn't. That doesn't mean someone else might, though. Seriously, why don't you just turn yourself in before this gets any worse?"

"Because I can't," Eli stressed. "I mean, what if I get detention for a year or get grounded until I'm old enough to drive or something?"

"Well," Nolan began slowly, "it's still better than ending up in juvenile hall, isn't it?"

"I thought you said that wasn't going to happen."

"Well, yeah, but that was before they started putting up all those flyers," Nolan said. "If you don't do something about it now, they're probably going to think you took the drive on purpose when they catch you."

An injured look filled Eli's eyes. "What do you mean *when*

they catch me? You're not going to rat me out, are you?"

"No, of course not," Nolan assured him. "I'm just saying you're going to get caught eventually, okay? You always do. Either someone's going to tie you to the prank or you'll slip up and say something that gives yourself away like you did at lunch yesterday. You've got to get ahead of this thing."

Nolan watched as Eli let out a terse laugh and shook his head before he turned his anxious gaze towards the ground. He didn't say anything else for a few seconds.

"Eli?"

"I don't know, Nolan. Maybe you're right, but—"

The clacking sound of the door to the school opening made them glance over their shoulders. The same seventh-graders they'd seen yesterday were back to continue their hacky sack game. It reminded Nolan that they probably didn't have much time to eat their own lunches now.

"Look, why don't we go in and get some food and you can think about it over lunch?" Noland suggested.

Eli kept staring at the ground, but eventually shrugged and nodded his head. "Alright. Sure," he said sullenly before following Nolan back into the school.

For what felt like the millionth time since he'd overheard the sixth-grader during PE yesterday, Eli found himself wondering if he'd even be in this mess if he'd just dropped the USB drive in the trash can outside of the gym instead of dropping it on the floor. It had been the first thing to cross his mind at the time, but so had the possibility of someone seeing him do it.

Unfortunately, there was no way to know now.

8

Questionable Questions

Sabrina couldn't believe how tired she was getting. The walk to Fryer Tuck's hadn't seemed that long or exhausting on Monday, but she hadn't been speed-walking because she was running late either.

She rounded the corner at the end of the block and finally saw Fryer Tuck's boxy, pale green building straight ahead. She was supposed to meet Nolan at five-thirty, but, thanks to her mom getting held up in traffic, she was running nearly fifteen minutes behind.

Of course, she'd texted Nolan about ten minutes ago to let him know, but she never heard a reply chime over her phone on the way there. In the back of her mind, she hoped he wouldn't make a big deal about it.

By the time she walked through the door, she found Nolan slouched in their usual spot with a scornful look on his face. He hadn't seen her yet since he was busy texting someone on his phone, but Sabrina guessed the message would be heading her way soon enough.

"If that's for me, I'm finally here," she apologized breathlessly as she took her backpack off and slid into the booth seat across from him. "Sorry. My mom was kind of late picking me up today."

Nolan quickly waved it off. "No, it's alright. I'm just dealing with some of Eli's crap right now," he grunted, barely even looking up from his phone.

"Why? He didn't get you in trouble again, did he?"

"No, but it's just about as annoying," Nolan said. While he kept it to himself, he was getting tired of the way Eli hadn't stopped texting him poorly thought out alternatives to turning himself in.

Trying to avoid getting deeper into that subject, he gestured at the half-empty carton of tater tots on the table between them. "Anyway, I was kind of hungry so I went ahead and bought some Bullseye Tots. You can have some too if you want."

Sabrina rolled her eyes and shook her head like Nolan should know better. "Thanks, but I definitely try to stay away from stuff like that."

"Seriously?"

"Oh, yeah. Deep-fried food is the worst. I think I read somewhere that it's like eating poison or something. Plus, my mom's fixing spaghetti tonight, so I probably shouldn't eat yet."

"Well, I guess that leaves more poison for me, then," Nolan said blissfully as he plucked another tater tot out of the carton and popped it into his mouth.

"So," Sabrina began with a haughty smile, "you ready to see who'll be buying the drinks today?"

"Yeah, sure. Just give me a second here," Nolan said distantly as he wrapped up his text message. He didn't start rummaging through his backpack until he'd turned the phone off and slid it into his pocket.

"Of course, you could always save yourself some trouble and just go ahead and buy me a cream soda," Sabrina cooed after she retrieved her test from her backpack.

Nolan hadn't found his test yet but stopped to glare back at her. "Hey, you may have beaten me plenty of times before but that doesn't mean I'm going to start expecting it," he chided. "One of these days your luck's going to run out."

Sabrina grinned and sat her test down on the tabletop. She made sure to turn it around so it would be facing Nolan right-side-up and then tapped her finger on the red 92 at the top of the page.

"Well, unless you did better than that, I'd say my luck's not running out anytime soon."

Nolan had just pulled his test out of his backpack when he glanced down at the grade. Sabrina's stomach sank as soon as she saw a jubilant look in his eyes.

"Okay, what'd you get?" she groaned.

"What did I get? Oh, just a ninety-five!" he exclaimed as he slapped the test down next to hers. "And you know what, Ms. Chambers? I think I'll have a Cherry Coke today."

"Oh, that's just great," Sabrina grumbled as she slouched back in her seat. "And here I thought I had this in the bag after your meltdown last night."

Across the table, Nolan laughed under his breath and rolled his eyes.

"Yeah, well, thankfully, what happened today definitely changed all that," he said with a shrug, causing Sabrina to squint her eyes in confusion. It was almost like he was trying to include her on an inside joke she'd never been a part of.

Unfortunately, before she could ask him about it, he leaned over the table and looked straight back at her. "Now, about that Cherry Coke…"

"Okay, okay. I'll get you your stupid Cherry Coke," Sabrina huffed before she pulled herself out of the booth and went to stand in line at the front counter. The person ahead of her was busy making a large order, so she could tell she was going to be there for a while.

As she waited, her mind drifted back to their history test. Something about it just didn't feel right, and it wasn't because Nolan had beaten her either.

Sabrina knew she'd only missed two questions on her test, giving her the ninety-two. That meant the questions had been four points apiece. But if that was the case, there was no way their test scores could be three points apart.

Something wasn't adding up.

"Ready to order yet?" the clerk behind the counter asked, jarring Sabrina out of her thoughts.

"Actually, not right now," she said bluntly before heading back to the table. Without saying a word, she slid into her side of the booth and pulled both tests over to her, focusing on Nolan's first.

"Still can't believe it?" Nolan asked quizzically when he realized she hadn't returned with his drink. Sabrina didn't say anything, though, and just studied over the front of his test for a few seconds.

"How many questions did you miss?" she finally asked, flipping Nolan's test open.

"Just one. Well, technically just one," he added as he dipped another tater tot into his mustard and ketchup cocktail.

Sabrina glanced up at him. "Technically?"

"Yeah. After they took the questions about the Intolerable Acts off, I only missed one. Of course, considering *your* grade, I'm guessing you still missed more than that," Nolan jabbed playfully. Sabrina wasn't in the mood, though.

"What in the world are you talking about? Who's they?" she demanded. The perplexed look in her eyes was growing. By now, Nolan was starting to look confused, too.

"Who else? Central Office," he said knowingly. "Didn't your teacher tell you about that today?"

Sabrina just shook her head and glanced back down at Nolan's test with a sour look in her eyes. She found the crossed-out questions a second later. When Nolan realized what she was looking at, he decided to add on to his explanation.

"So, yeah, the Intolerable Acts weren't on the testing syllabus, so Central Office took them off. That's why no one in my class knew anything about them and why Coach Grayson never talked about them either."

Sabrina scowled as she pulled her test over and flipped it to the second and third pages. "And you're sure the Intolerable Acts weren't on the syllabus?" she asked without looking up from the tests.

"Well, it's not like we got to look for ourselves, but that's what Coach Grayson said. Apparently he didn't figure it out until the other Pre-AP class had issues with it, too. Why? What's the big deal?"

Sabrina abruptly pulled the tests up off the table and exhibited both to Nolan. "The big deal is that mine doesn't have any omitted questions on it and I still got all the questions about the Intolerable Acts right."

"Wait, what?" Nolan coughed, snatching the tests out of Sabrina's hands. He felt a twinge of embarrassment when he realized his greasy fingertips were leaving circular smudges on the paper. He quickly took to holding the tests by pinching the bottom edge to minimize the damage.

Sure enough, Questions 17, 23, and 25 were the same on Sabrina's test as they were on his. The only difference was that each one had a green checkmark next to it, including the last one where Sabrina had simply filled in, *The Boston Tea Party*, in response to the question about what led to the creation of the Intolerable Acts.

"That's so weird," Nolan murmured as he handed Sabrina's test back to her, secretly hoping she wouldn't notice the greasy fingerprints. "Did your teacher accidentally go over the Intolerable Acts in class or something?"

"I don't know," Sabrina said as she sat the test down on the tabletop. She started digging through her backpack a second later. "It kind of sounds familiar, but Mrs. Tiller's not exactly the type to overlook something like that. I mean, she's a great teacher and all, but she's not going to go out of her way to do extra work, you know?"

"Yeah," Nolan agreed absently. "So, do you have any notes on it?"

"I'll tell you in a bit," Sabrina said as she pulled out her history spiral and thumbed over to the section their test had covered.

Nolan ate a few more tater tots while he waited. A few minutes later, he cocked his eyebrows when Sabrina let out a confused hum and started reading over her notes again.

"Something wrong?"

After skimming over her notes for a few more seconds, Sabrina shook her head. Eventually, her eyes drifted back over to Nolan's.

"Nothing," she said distantly.

"There's nothing wrong?"

"No. I mean there's nothing in my notes about the Intolerable Acts," she said, gesturing back at the spiral.

"So, what does that mean?" Nolan asked. "Like, how did you get those questions right when no one at my school even knew anything about them?"

Sabrina stared at her spiral and the tests for a few seconds. "Well, I guess it means that my teacher somehow went over the Intolerable Acts in class and yours didn't. It's just weird that I didn't take any notes on it," she added with a hint of concern in her voice.

"Hey, it's never bothered Eli."

"Yeah, well I'm not Eli," Sabrina grumbled, glaring back at Nolan. She knew he was just messing with her, but she still didn't like being compared to that guy. Nolan seemed to take the hint and didn't egg it on.

"Still," she began, "it almost seems like..."

"What?"

Sabrina bit her lip for a second or two before spitting it out. "I don't know. It's like, I know how much trouble a teacher can get into if they forget to cover something that's going to be on a test, alright?"

"Okay," Nolan agreed.

"So, since I'm the only one here that got them right, what if that means the Intolerable Acts really were on the syllabus and your teacher just made up that story to try and get out of it? I mean, I know that's a bad thing to say, but do you think they'd do something like that?"

Nolan didn't have to think twice about it.

"Coach Grayson? Oh, my gosh! In a heartbeat."

"Seriously?" Sabrina gasped. She kept looking for a hint of sarcasm in Nolan's eyes, but it wasn't there.

"Hey, we're talking about the guy that rounded down some guy's weight by a whole five pounds in wrestling last year just to get him into a lower weight class and win some more matches."

"Wow! That's insane," Sabrina exclaimed. "Did he get caught?"

"Oh, yeah! Well, obviously he didn't get fired for it since he's still there, but he's the reason Meade's not going to have a seventh grade wrestling team this year."

"Jeez! What a sleazeball," Sabrina snarled. A broad smile crossed Nolan's lips briefly before it faded.

"Still," he began in a more somber tone, "I'm not so sure he'd try and pull something as big as this, you know? From what I know of him, it's kind out of his league. Plus, I think he said that he talked to our principal about the syllabus issue before Principal Espinoza talked to Central Office about it."

"But are you sure about that?" Sabrina asked. "What if

your history teacher's making that up, too?"

Nolan glanced off to the side. "Well, I guess he could have, but I don't think that he would. It just seems like it'd be really risky, especially if anyone started asking around."

Sabrina thought about it for a second before she said, "Well, since he was pretty much giving everyone better grades, maybe he wasn't *counting* on anyone asking around."

Nolan could already tell what she was getting at and his shoulders slouched down in response.

"Do I really have to ask Principal Espinoza about this?" he groaned, secretly praying Sabrina would say otherwise. Unfortunately, the firm look in her eyes didn't change.

"Yes, you do. I would if this happened at my school."

"But what if your history teacher just forgot to tell you about the omitted questions?" Nolan bartered. "You know, maybe they just didn't get the memo or something like that."

"Then I'll ask her about that, too," Sabrina said sternly. "Seriously, this could be a really big deal, Nolan. We need to find out what's going on."

Nolan still looked hesitant, though. "But what if it's nothing?"

"Then it's nothing, and everything's fine," Sabrina said with a shrug. "Either way, we definitely need to know for sure. There could be a lot more to this than you think."

"How?" Nolan spat. "It's just one test."

Sabrina glanced off to the side and shook her head. "I don't know. It just could," she insisted with a slight hitch in her voice. A few seconds later, she added, "I mean, that's how things got started a few years ago."

Suddenly, Nolan realized why she was making such a big deal out of this. Without thinking, he rolled his eyes as he said, "I'm sure it's not like the cash-for-grades thing, Sabrina. I mean, I know what happened to your dad sucked, b—"

"Nolan..." Sabrina growled slowly, shooting him an icy stare. He quickly pulled his lips in tight and raised his palms in submission.

"Sorry," he said sheepishly. After glancing away briefly, he carefully added, "Look, all I'm saying is that it's probably not going to be that bad, okay? Sure, maybe Coach Grayson forgot to tell us about the Intolerable Acts and tried to cover it up, but that's it."

Sabrina took in a deep breath and nodded her head. Her mind was still reeling from the person Nolan mentioned a bit ago.

"Just promise me you'll ask your principal about it tomorrow," she choked out, partially glaring at Nolan through the corners of her eyes.

Nolan sighed and stared back at Sabrina for a few seconds. Eventually, he gave her the answer he knew he had to give her.

"Okay. I'll look into it."

9

Haunts of the Past

The constant babble coming out of Lance's mouth was driving Sabrina nuts. Through it all, she wondered if she talked this much when she was in second grade. She certainly hoped she didn't, but it seemed like a regular thing with Lance every time they walked home from Batts.

"What's grandmother doing here?" Lance thought aloud as they cut across their front yard.

"I don't know," Sabrina said, feeling a shiver race down her spine. Sabrina hadn't even noticed their grandmother's old sedan in the driveway until just then.

No sooner had she opened the front door than they found their grandmother waiting for them at the dining room table. The eerie silence hanging over the house and the grave look in their grandmother's eyes was more than enough to tell Sabrina something was wrong.

"Hey, kiddos," their grandmother finally choked out. "Why don't you two take a seat?"

"What's going on?" Sabrina said as she slid her backpack off her shoulders and let it fall to the floor behind the sofa. "Where's mom and dad?"

"It's your father," was her grandmother's chilled response. "He's been arrested."

"Did something happen between you and Nolan today?"

Sabrina blinked her eyes and realized she was still sitting at the dinner table. Lance had already left and she was the only one that still had a plate full of food in front of her. Her mom was at the other end of the table, looking at her inquisitively.

"Hmm? Oh. Um, no. No, nothing's wrong," Sabrina

stammered. When she noticed the concerned tone in her mom's eyes hadn't faded, she added with a thin smile, "Just thinking about school stuff."

"Got a lot of homework again?"

Sabrina looked down and used her fork to aimlessly scrape a few strands of cold spaghetti around her plate. As much as she tried to hide it, she was still jittery from the memory she'd been replaying in her mind. It didn't help that her mom was sitting in the same spot where her grandmother had been sitting three years ago either.

"No. Just algebra," she said dryly, still keeping her eyes diverted from her mom's. Unfortunately, she'd already given too much away.

"Okay. What is it?" her mom said firmly.

"Nothing!" Sabrina insisted, still not making eye contact with her mom.

"Sabrina, you and I both know that's not the case. Now, tell me what's bothering you."

For a while, Sabrina kept her eyes down on her plate, hoping her mom would just give up. But she could still feel her mom's gaze bearing down on her. Finally, she caved.

"Mom, do you ever get the feeling the school district is just as crooked as it was a couple of years ago?"

Her mom slouched back in her chair. "Sometimes. Why? Did you see or hear something today? If you did, you need to tell me."

"And you're not involved in anything, right? Not like dad was?"

"Never in a million years," her mom said resolutely.

Sabrina took in a deep breath. Her eyes drifted down to her plate again. "Okay. So, as crazy as this probably sounds, I'm starting to think Nolan's school might be messing with their test grades."

Even though Sabrina half-expected her mom to tell her how ridiculous that was, it never came. Instead, the look in her mom's eyes was cold and unwavering.

"Alright. What makes you think that?"

"You remember that history test I had yesterday?"

"Yeah. I thought you said you got an A on it," he mom

replied, remembering asking Sabrina about it on the ride back home.

"Yeah, I did, but a couple of weird things happened on Nolan's test."

"Such as?"

"Well, for one, Nolan's test had some omitted questions on it and mine didn't," Sabrina said with a hint of aggravation riding on her voice.

That made her mom pause for a second. After taking a sip of water out of her glass, she asked, "You mean he had questions on his test that you didn't have, or some of his test questions were omitted when yours weren't?"

"The last one. There were about three questions that Central Office apparently omitted because they weren't on the testing syllabus."

Her mom didn't seem too concerned. "Well, it happens every now and then. Did you get the answers wrong, too? Maybe your teacher just doesn't know yet."

Sabrina shook her head. "No, and that's what's so weird about this. I actually got the questions right and Nolan didn't, even though neither of us had any notes about it. I think Nolan said several of his classmates didn't have any notes on it either."

A puzzled look swept over her mom's face. "And you're sure you didn't have any notes? Maybe you just overlooked it or something."

Sabrina quickly shook her head again. "No. I went over my notes several times when I met up with Nolan earlier. He said he's gone over his notes a lot, too. Neither of us has anything about the Intolerable Acts."

"Is that what these questions were about?"

"Yeah. I mean, I kind of remember hearing about it in class somewhere, but I guess Nolan didn't. From what he told me today, no one at Meade knew anything about it either."

Sabrina watched as her mom frowned and glanced off to the side.

"What is it?"

"Okay, this better not leave this house," her mom stressed, "but it almost sounds like Nolan's history teacher forgot to cover something that was on the test."

"Yeah, and that's exactly what I thought. But I think it goes deeper than that," Sabrina blurted out before she could stop herself. Just as she feared, it caught her mom's attention.

"What do you mean?"

Sabrina's breath trembled for a second as tried to think of a way out. Unfortunately, she knew there wasn't one and choked out what she had to say.

"I'm starting to think there's a lot more to this than just Nolan's history test."

"Okay. Like what?"

Sabrina paused again. She probably wouldn't have even thought about this if Nolan hadn't mentioned it earlier, but it had been bugging her ever since she started walking back home from Fryer Tuck's.

"Do you remember Eli Reznik?" she finally asked.

Her mom squinted her eyes and slowly repeated the name. "Eli Reznik?"

"Yeah. He used to go to Batts with me," Sabrina explained.

Sabrina's mom thought about it for a second before she was able to put a face to the name. "Oh, yeah. I think I remember that kid. Why? What about him?"

"Okay, so even though he was, like, the worst student in our grade at Batts, Nolan says he's actually making A's on his tests now."

"Well, I'd hardly say that's a bad thing, wouldn't you?" her mom mused with a shrug.

"Yeah, except he's doing almost none of his homework and studying for his tests as little as possible," Sabrina shot back. "Nolan told me everything the other day. Apparently Eli will magically get an A-minus on tests he's barely even studied for."

Her mom stared back at Sabrina. "So, just because this Eli kid's been doing better at school you think that means Meade is tampering with their test scores?"

"Well, yeah. That and the whole thing about Nolan's history test."

Sabrina's mom pursed her lips as she thought about it. "Well, the omitted questions thing is a bit strange, but I'd hardly call Eli's improvement a smoking gun."

"What?" Sabrina nearly shrieked.

"It's something I've seen before," her mom explained. "Sometimes a low-performing student can make a big rebound in the right environment. Maybe Meade is the right environment for Eli."

"But this is Eli Reznik, Mom! He doesn't even study for his tests. If he's suddenly doing better without doing any of the work and Nolan's history teacher suddenly omits test questions that aren't supposed to be omitted, what else could it be?"

"Lots of different things," her mom cautioned. She even stared straight back at Sabrina for a second or two to drive her point home. "And at the end of the day, test fraud is a pretty big accusation to make. What makes you so sure that's what's going on?"

Sabrina slouched back in her seat. "I don't know. I've just got this feeling about it. That's all."

"No, that's not all," her mom said, glaring back at Sabrina. "I've seen that look on your face before and I know exactly what it means, so spit it out. What really makes you think Nolan's school is messing with their test grades?"

Sabrina took off her glasses and briefly massaged the bridge of her nose. "Okay," she said as she put her glasses back on. "Everything about this feels way too familiar."

Her mom shot a curious look back at Sabrina. "What do you mean by that?"

"I mean it kind of feels like it did right before dad got arrested–when he was getting all those teaching awards. Before we found out the guy was a complete fraud."

A heavy silence fell over the dining table. Patricia could still remember the unique but off-putting smell of the police station when she met her now ex-husband there. More than that, though, she remembered the different ways he tried to justify being part of the cash-for-grades racket.

Patricia bowed her head and glanced off to the side, unable to contain the shivering breath that rattled out of her mouth. Through it all, she could feel Sabrina's imposing glare seeping into her.

"I didn't realize that still bothered you so much," she finally choked out.

"Yeah, well why wouldn't it?" was her daughter's blunt response. "He flat out lied to us, Mom."

"Sabrina, that was three years ago. You can't let what he did define who you are, and you definitely can't let what he did cause you to think a school's up to something just because someone's getting better test grades."

A derisive scoff blurted out of Sabrina's lips and she fell into the backrest of her chair as noticeably as she could. "So nothing about what I've just said sounds suspicious to you?"

"I didn't say that," Patricia insisted, struggling to keep her voice down. The last thing she wanted right now was for Lance to get curious and see what they were arguing about. "All I'm saying is that you need to approach this with a cooler head. You can't let your emotions about what happened get the best of you."

Sabrina glared back at her mom. "Isn't there someone you can call, though? You know, see if they can look into what happened on Nolan's history test?"

Patricia hesitated. As sure as she was that Nolan's history teacher had probably forgotten to teach something and then tried to cover it up with some falsified omissions, she wasn't exactly comfortable ratting the guy out to someone like Superintendent Richter. If anything, she was tempted to turn a blind eye to it.

"Mom?" Sabrina cut in when she didn't say anything.

Jolting herself out of her thoughts, Patricia nodded and glanced back at Sabrina. "Okay. If it makes you feel better, I'll email someone at Central Office later. But, I'm serious, Sabrina. You need to keep quiet about this. The last thing your school or the district needs right now is a bunch of rumors flying around about test fraud–especially when we're not even sure if that's what's going on. Understand?"

"So, how long do you think it'll take to get an answer? Like, if you emailed them tonight?" Sabrina cut in. She hardly seemed to care about what her mom had just said.

"Sabrina, I don't have any way of knowing that. Not for sure, anyway. I seriously doubt they'd email me back tonight or even tomorrow morning, though."

The look in Sabrina's eyes was unsettling. "So, basically, we're just supposed to go around hoping Meade isn't messing with their tests until Central Office emails you back, if they ever do?"

"Well, I don't like it any more than you do, but, yes, that's exactly what we're going to have to do. We have to go through the proper channels, Sabrina.

"Now, is there anything else you want to talk about? Something that's bothering you perhaps?"

Much to Patricia's disappointment, Sabrina's bleary eyes darted over to the clock mounted on the wall next to the dining table. She could already tell the discussion was over before she said anything.

"Nope. I should probably get started on my algebra homework, anyway."

Patricia pulled her lips in tight and nodded, allowing her daughter to be excused from the table. She heard Sabrina's door slam shut a few seconds later. Even though her room was upstairs and on the other side of the house, Patricia could still hear the kitchen clock and some of the other wall decorations rattle from the impact.

Memories about everything that happened three years ago flooded into her thoughts as she sat alone in the dining room. It took her a few minutes before she was able to push it all to the back of her mind again.

Shaking her head on it, Patricia stood up and cleared Sabrina's plate off the table. As she raked the partially eaten spaghetti and garlic bread into the trash, she struggled to figure out how she would word her email to Central Office later.

10

The 75% Witness

Nolan wished he could hit the reset button on Thursday morning. So far, nothing had gone the way he'd wanted it to. He'd overslept by an hour, barely caught the bus on time, and, to top it all off, he'd left his English book sitting on the dining room table.

He still had an hour-and-a-half-long study hall coming up, though, so he was trying to make a mental list of everything he needed to do to make up for it on his way from the bus stop to the locker rooms. Unfortunately, there was quite a bit on the docket.

Setting up a meeting with Principal Espinoza was at the top of the list, but Nolan knew he was going to have to wait until first period to do that. Meade didn't open its doors until eight, and, for whatever reason, Coach Adams still expected him to be in study hall by the time the buses arrived at seven-thirty. He guessed the coach was just trying to be fair to all the other guys in athletics that had to be at practice by then, but Nolan still thought it was annoying.

Aside from following through with Sabrina's orders, Nolan had other things to catch up on, too. That included studying for a quiz in his computer class and finishing his reading assignments for science and history.

Nolan's mind was already buzzing once he rounded the northwestern corner of the school. After spending so much time trying to figure out how to ask Principal Espinoza about the test questions last night, he hadn't been able to get much else done. Nolan just hoped the next hour and a half would be different.

Trying to ignore the stress, Nolan strode up to the locker room door and reached for the handle. He was just about to open it when the door popped open and Landon Collins and Jonathan Reed, two of the linebackers from his team, stepped out. Landon's pudgy face lit up as soon as he saw him.

"Oh, cool. There he is now," he announced to Jonathan. "Hey, Leere, you got a second?"

Nolan groggily nodded his head. "Sure. What's up?"

Landon and Jonathan exchanged knowing glances before Landon cut to the chase. "So, we were wondering: Eli Reznik's not, like, a water boy or something, is he? You know, for athletics?"

The question caught Nolan completely off guard. Then again, so did the eager smile tugging at Landon's lips and the way Jonathan looked just as anxious to hear Nolan's response.

"Eli? No. Why would you think that?"

Before he could get an answer, Landon turned and batted Jonathan on the shoulder. "Ha! You see? I told you he wasn't in football this year!"

"So, what?" Jonathan snapped. "I'm telling you, man, I saw him in the locker room the other day. He walked right past me and everything."

A confused look swept over Nolan's face. "You saw Eli in the locker room?"

Landon chuckled under his breath and nudged his head back at Jonathan. "That's what he thinks. Of course, he also told me he's only about seventy-five percent sure of that, so I wouldn't count on it."

"Hey, the only reason I'm not a hundred percent sure is because the guy was wearing a hoodie, just like the guy in those posters was," Jonathan argued. When he saw the wide-eyed look plastered across Nolan's face, he added, "You know, the posters they put up around school yesterday?"

"Yeah. Yeah, I know," Nolan said, hoping he didn't sound too flustered. "You really think it was the same guy, though?"

"Oh, yeah. I'm positive. And I'm willing to bet it was Reznik, too."

"Even though you didn't really see his face and Leere just told us Reznik's not in athletics this year?" Landon pointed out. Jonathan still wasn't giving in, though.

"Dude, just because Reznik's not in athletics doesn't mean

squat! He still could have walked through the locker room or something. I mean, come on, jacking with the PA system even sounds like something that guy would do. Don't you think so, Leere?"

A nervous jolt shot down Nolan's spine. He had no idea what he should say, but Jonathan and Landon were already staring back at him, waiting for an answer.

"Yeah, I-I guess so," he finally stammered out.

"See, even Leere thinks so!" Jonathan said, whisking a hand back at Nolan. "I'm telling you, man, as soon as I tell Principal Espinoza about it, that reward money's as good as mine."

"Actually," Nolan cut in, "I was just saying that it sounds like something Eli *might* do. I don't really think he's the guy you saw in the locker room."

A haughty laugh burst out of Landon's lips. After glaring at him for it, Jonathan turned his intense gaze back to Nolan.

"Oh, yeah? How's that?"

"Well, you know," Nolan began tepidly, "he was at the assembly with me." He could already tell he'd said that in a less-than-convincing tone, so he quickly added, "So, it's not like he could have been in the locker room at the same time, right?"

"Yeah, maybe not," Jonathan grumbled, though he was still eying Nolan suspiciously. His thoughts were interrupted when Landon batted him on the shoulder again and pointed towards the practice field.

"Hey, everyone's starting to line up for stretches. We'd better get over there before Coach Adams makes us run tardy laps."

"Yeah, yeah," he grumbled as the two of them slid their helmets on.

Before jogging off with Landon, Jonathan stopped and looked back at Nolan. "I think I'm still going to tell Principal Espinoza about it," he announced. "You know, just in case it's important."

Nolan felt an anxious twinge rattle down his back again but managed to nod nonchalantly. "Alright. Whatever," he droned, not knowing what else to say. As soon as Jonathan started jogging off to the practice field, Nolan turned and quickly stepped into the locker room.

He needed to get in touch with Eli. Unfortunately, he wasn't entirely sure how to do that yet. Eli wouldn't be coming in until eight, if he was on time at all, and that was still about thirty minutes off. Plus, if one of the assistant coaches gave him a bunch of busy work to do again, there was a chance Nolan could be stuck in athletic study hall the whole time, too.

Of course, he knew he could have just texted or emailed Eli, but Nolan doubted he'd be able to explain everything through a quick message. Besides, he thought he remembered Eli telling him before that his parents didn't even let him take his cell phone to school.

He was going to have to meet with Eli in person.

Nolan was racing through the options in his head the best he could by the time he made it to the athletic's film room for study hall and took his seat. If he didn't figure out a way to warn Eli before Principal Espinoza or Jonathan got to him, their stories wouldn't match up and then they'd both be in trouble.

As the first thirty minutes of study hall were coming to a close, though, Nolan had only come up with one possible idea to meet up with Eli. He just hoped his friend would get there on time.

The revving of the engine and the jolt of the compact car scooting forward forced Eli's eyes open again. After passing through the intersection, the car took a sharp right on the next street and Eli sulked into his seat even more as soon as he saw the two-story structure of Meade Middle School looming ahead. It was the last thing he wanted to see right now, especially since he'd just pulled himself out of bed about thirty minutes ago.

"So, did you ever get your English homework done last night?" his mom asked impatiently from the driver's seat, glaring at Eli as they entered the school zone. Eli slowly realized he must have nodded off when she asked the question the first time around.

"Yeah, I read most of the next chapter," he said, feeling his mom's insistent gaze drilling into his temple.

"But not all of it," his mom huffed in frustration. "Eli,

you need to get off those video games and start putting more effort into your homework! I'm tired of getting notes from your teachers saying you're just scraping by in their classes."

"Yeah, well I am getting A's on their tests, right? What if I'm just one of those people that's smart enough they don't need to do their homework?"

A frustrated tisk slipped out of his mom's lips as she pulled over to an empty spot that had just opened up in front of the school. She sat silently for a second or two before she managed to say anything.

"Eli, you know I'm proud of you for how you've been doing on your tests. I am. But your father and me just wonder how much better you'd be doing if your homework grades were better. You know, if you really put some heart into your schoolwork."

"What's the point? I'm never going to be as good as Eric," Eli sneered as he started to get out of the car. His mom reached out and grabbed him by the shoulder before he could open the door.

"You don't have to be. I'm not saying that. All your father and me are asking is that you try harder. Just think, with a little bit more effort and less gaming, you could probably have straight A's on your next report card–just like your brother."

An impatient honk behind them gave Eli the excuse he needed to unbuckle his seat belt, grab his backpack, and pop the car door open.

"Just promise me you'll start trying harder," his mom called from the driver's seat.

Eli sighed and slung his backpack over his shoulder. His mom was still staring at him, giving him the look that told him she wasn't leaving until she got an answer.

"Okay," he finally conceded.

"Okay, what?"

Another honk came from the car behind them, but his mom ignored it.

Scowling, Eli looked back down at his mom with one hand on the car door. After rolling his eyes, he finally answered with an unenthusiastic, "Okay. I'll try harder. I promise." He was a bit unnerved when it didn't even get a hopeful smile out of her.

"Alright. Have a good day at school, then. Love you!" she

called back to him.

A simple, "Yeah," was all she got before he shut the car door and started walking towards the school, scanning the crowds around him to be sure no one had heard that. Luckily, nobody seemed to be paying attention.

Trying to ignore the burning in his cheeks, Eli worked his way through the crowds and headed to the main entrance, the one closest to his locker. He'd just passed by the flagpole when he heard the 7:55 bell ring and everyone that had been milling around outside started filing into the school. Grudgingly, Eli did the same.

No sooner had he passed through the double set of doors with everyone else than Eli took a right at the first intersection. It was already jam-packed with other students, and, even though his locker was only a quarter of the way down the hall, he could tell it was going to take a little while to get there.

Eli really wished he could have just stayed in bed today, especially when he stepped past a water fountain and got a glimpse of one of the bright red flyers hanging above it. He didn't dare look at it, but the reminder still sent an anxious jolt searing down his back. It had been four days since he pulled his prank and Superintendent Richter was still looking for him.

He'd played video games until two in the morning hoping to get it off his mind, but he couldn't stop thinking about it or what would happen if he got caught. Now he was going to have to try and make it through Mrs. Fulton's algebra class on just a couple hours of sleep, and he knew that was never a good thing.

Shaking his head, Eli looked down and started dialing in the combination to his locker. He'd just unlatched it when someone stepped in and leaned against the locker next to him. Just from his peripheral vision, Eli could tell it was Nolan from the lanky build, the yellow cast, and the short, bleached-blonde hair highlighting his head.

"Hey, we've got to talk," he said in a hurried whisper.

"Dude, what are you doing here?" Eli asked, glaring back at Nolan. "Aren't you supposed to be in athletics right now?"

"Yeah, but I told Assistant Coach Pitman I needed to grab my history book real quick," Nolan explained. When the confused look on Eli's face remained, he cut to the chase. "Alright, here's the thing. Jonathan Reed saw you in the locker room the other day."

The color drained from Eli's face.

"He saw me?"

"Yeah, and he's almost positive you're the guy on the flyers, too. He said he was going to tell Principal Espinoza later."

"And you're just going to let him, aren't you?" Eli growled. The frustration about the way Nolan had suddenly stopped answering his texts last night was resurfacing. Nolan just glared back at him, though.

"Hey, I tried to tell him it wasn't you, alright? I mean, I even told him you were at the assembly with me."

"Really? You did that?" Eli gasped, instantly feeling a pang of guilt.

"Yeah," Nolan shot back. "Unfortunately, I don't think he believed me. Or maybe he did. I don't know. Either way, we're in kind of a sticky situation here, man."

Eli looked back at Nolan like he'd just been stabbed in the gut. "So, what am I supposed to do? Turn myself in?"

Nolan quickly shook his head. "No. Don't do that. Just remember I told Jonathan that you were at the assembly with me in case he asks or something. If you do that, maybe we can get out of this. Got it?"

Eli's mind was still swimming, but he managed to slowly nod his head. Nolan patted him on the shoulder in response.

"Good. So, where you headed now?"

"Huh?" Eli grunted absently before his mind was able to catch up. "Oh, um, algebra."

"Yikes! And first thing in the morning, too. That's rough, man."

"You're telling me," Eli grumbled awkwardly. "Anyway, guess I'll see you at lunch or something, right?"

Nolan nodded and habitually held out his hand for their usual parting fist bump.

"Yeah. Later, man. And remember," he stressed with a point of his finger, "if anyone asks, you were at the assembly with me."

"Got it," Eli grunted, pointing back at Nolan in acknowledgment. A second later, they parted ways and strode off through the thinning crowds.

11

A Familiar Pattern

Sabrina could barely keep her eyes open by the time third period rolled around. She hoped lunch would give her a boost later, but she still had to make it through algebra and half of her computer class and she wasn't sure she'd be able to do that without completely falling asleep.

In a lot of ways, she was still surprised she hadn't passed out at her desk during English earlier, or that Mrs. Faridae hadn't called her out for nodding off a few times. Sabrina was pretty sure her English teacher had caught her doing it, too.

All the same, Sabrina found herself rushing through the crowded, teal-carpeted hallways on the way to Room 133 once she got out of English. It seemed farfetched, but she thought she might be able to get a power nap in before Mrs. Sidney's algebra class started if she got there soon enough. With that goal in mind, Sabrina managed to get there in a little over a minute.

Panting slightly as she stepped through the door, Sabrina quickly found her way to her seat and slouched into it. Her heavy eyes slid shut an instant later and she was trying to settle her mind down when a soft voice interrupted her.

"Are you feeling okay, Sabrina?"

Her eyes reluctantly cracked open to glance at the source of the comment. Sabrina's stomach sank when she found the face of Chelsea Waters staring back at her. She was one of the most talkative people Sabrina knew.

"Yeah, I'm just feeling kind of drained right now," Sabrina said, letting her eyes slide shut again. She hoped keeping it simple would end the conversation right there, but it didn't work.

"I know what you mean," Chelsea said, half chuckling. "We played Woodridge Middle School last night, and then I had to work on my homework after the game. I swear, I think I was up until midnight or something! Were you at the game, too?"

"No, I wasn't," Sabrina said, hardly caring to hear about her classmate's volleyball game. She nearly cringed when Chelsea opened her mouth again.

"Well, you definitely missed a good one. Actually, okay, we didn't get off to a good start so we lost the first set, but, luckily, Maritza made a few saves in the second set when we really needed it, so we were barely able to win that one."

"Yeah, that's nice," Sabrina hummed, sounding just as disinterested as she looked. Chelsea kept going, though.

"You know, I think winning the second set really helped us out, too, because then we managed to win the third one pretty easy. So, yeah, even though we got off to a bad start, we actually won the whole match!" Chelsea concluded with a beaming smile.

"Well, I'm sorry I missed it," Sabrina grunted. She didn't mean to sound so sarcastic about it, but the tone was clearly riding on her voice. Chelsea noticed.

"Boy, you sure are grumpy today! Did somebody wake up on the wrong side of the bed this morning?" she asked in a motherly tone that made Sabrina's skin crawl in more ways than one. Sabrina stopped trying to be so subtle.

"Chelsea, I'm running on about two hours of sleep right now and I'm trying to get a little bit of rest before this class starts up. So, yeah, I'm probably not in the best mood right now."

Chelsea's eyes went wide and her tone changed in an instant. Unfortunately, it wasn't because she'd gotten the point. "Oh, my gosh! You only got two hours of sleep last night?"

"Something around that," Sabrina said in resignation as she took her glasses off, sat them on the table in front of her, and rested her forehead against her palms.

"So, are you, like, going to go home early or something?"

"Not if I can help it," Sabrina said without taking her palms off her face. "I haven't missed a day of school since second grade and I'm not about to start now, especially since I'm not even sick. Plus, my mom's a chemistry teacher at Basin High

School, so it's not like she can come and pick me up either."

"What about your dad?"

A sharp twinge shot down Sabrina's back, making the drowsiness turn to rage for a second. "He's not available either," she choked out, hoping her racing heart would slow down.

"You still might want to think about going to the nurse's office for a while and getting a nap or something, if they even allow that," Chelsea said with genuine concern seeping through her voice. "I definitely learned my lesson last month."

Sabrina sat up and put her glasses back on. "Why? What happened last month?"

Chelsea hesitated for a second and glanced at the digital clock at the front of the classroom. She was a bit disappointed when she realized they still had about a minute to go before third period started.

"You remember how David broke up with me last month?" she finally squeaked out.

"Yeah, kind of," Sabrina said nonchalantly, trying to hide the fact that she didn't. Chelsea still picked up on it, though.

"Well, anyway, after he broke up with me, I had a really hard time getting to sleep after that–for a couple of days, actually. I guess I liked him more than I thought," she said with a slight flutter in her voice.

After biting her lip and glancing away from Sabrina, half-hoping for a word of consolation that never came, Chelsea continued.

"Anyway, I was pretty upset about it, and maybe even a bit embarrassed since he kind of dumped me in front of everyone between passing periods. So, just to try and make it look like it didn't bother me that much, I still went to school a couple of times even though I didn't get any sleep the night before. That totally turned out to be a bad idea."

"Why? Because you couldn't stay awake in class?"

Chelsea shook her head. "Not just that. I couldn't stay focused either. Or, at least, I guess that's what it was." She glanced down at the floor. "My grades kind of took a hit."

Sabrina perked up. She wasn't sure how she'd missed this happening to her classmate last month, but she'd never known Chelsea was having grade problems.

"Really? How bad was it?"

"Pretty bad," Chelsea admitted sheepishly. She lowered her voice a bit more and leaned in closer to Sabrina. "Just between us, I'm actually on academic probation in volleyball right now. Well, actually, I guess it's more like the coach has warned me that I *will be* on academic probation if I don't get my grades up halfway through this six weeks, but it still *feels* like I'm on probation, you know?"

Sabrina's eyes went wide. "No way!" she exclaimed before she could stop herself. Chelsea sucked her lips in tight and her eyes darted around the classroom to make sure no one had overheard.

"Yeah. I kind of realized I'd messed up when I started seeing questions on my tests that weren't even in my notes."

Even though she still felt exhausted, Sabrina swore her temples constricted a little from what Chelsea just said. "Wait. Did you say that you didn't have any notes for some of your test questions?"

Chelsea nodded and kept her shame-filled eyes diverted from Sabrina. "Some of them, yeah. I think I was the only one that got them wrong, though, so I guess I forgot to write down that stuff."

Sabrina couldn't believe it. It almost sounded like Chelsea had come across the same thing she and Nolan found on their history test last night, except there weren't any omitted questions involved. She wondered just how isolated the issue was.

"So, was that just in this class?" Sabrina asked, looking and sounding a bit intrigued. It unnerved her classmate a little.

"No, it was kind of like that in all my classes. Like I said, I was having a hard time sleeping then, so I think I missed a few things my teachers said."

The weariness Sabrina had been feeling all morning was fading fast. Her mind was reeling as she suddenly unzipped her backpack and retrieved her algebra materials. She needed to find out what questions Chelsea had missing notes on from their last algebra test.

Unfortunately, a sharp ringing cut through the air right before she could ask Chelsea about it and third period started.

As usual, Mrs. Sidney promptly stood up from behind her desk, turned off the lights, and flicked the switch against the wall to turn on the overhead projector that was bolted to the ceiling.

"Seriously, though," Chelsea whispered before Sabrina could say anything. "Think about going home early if you can and using the streaming service. You'll be glad you did later."

Sabrina quickly shrugged it off and started to ask Chelsea about her missing notes anyway, but was interrupted by Mrs. Sidney this time.

"Okay, you know the drill," she announced lethargically. "Fold your homework in half and pass it up to the front. After you've done that, go ahead and open your books to Chapter 8. We'll be learning how to solve problems with variables on both sides of the equation today."

Sabrina pulled out her algebra folder to retrieve her homework from last night. Next to her, she could tell Chelsea was busy retrieving her own homework. If she didn't have time to ask her about the test questions now, she needed to find a compromise.

"So, what time do you have lunch today?" Sabrina whispered.

Chelsea shot a confused look back at her. "What?"

"What time's your lunch?" Sabrina asked again, but Chelsea was still giving her a puzzled look.

"Right after this class. Why?"

Sabrina frowned. Just as she suspected, they didn't have the same lunch period.

"Is there some other time we could meet up later today?" she asked. "You know, so we can compare notes, or tests, or maybe even both?"

Chelsea felt someone tapping their folded homework against her shoulder and blindly took it from the person behind her to pass up to the front. "I don't know. Why do you want to do that?"

A nervous jolt shot down Sabrina's back. She suddenly realized she hadn't thought this through very well, so she blurted out the first thing that came to her mind. "Oh, you know," she said with a shrug, "just trying to help you out."

"Help me out?" Chelsea echoed skeptically. Even though

Sabrina could feel her cheeks starting to tingle, she kept pushing it.

"Sure. I take pretty good notes. Maybe I can help you fill in what you missed. That way you can be ready for anything that comes up on the midterms at the end of the semester."

Even though Sabrina hoped Chelsea would agree to it right off the bat, she was still staring her down like she wasn't sure if Sabrina was being totally honest. The desperate look in Sabrina's eyes probably wasn't helping much either.

"I don't know, Sabrina," Chelsea began just as the guy behind Sabrina impatiently tapped his stack of folded homework against her shoulder. "I've got volleyball practice right after school, so I don't know when we could do that."

Biting her lip, Sabrina snatched the homework out of her neighbor's hand and sat it on her desk. Out of the corner of her eye, she could see Mrs. Sidney starting to go row-to-row, collecting the homework.

"Okay, well, maybe just let me borrow your last test in here tonight," she suggested sternly. "That way I can copy the notes I have on the things you missed and get it back to you."

"Do we really have to do it today, though?" Chelsea whined. She was even more shocked when Sabrina quickly nodded her head in response.

"Yeah, if we can. You know, just so I can get started on it while it's on my mind."

"Ms. Chambers? If you and Ms. Waters are done talking, do you think you could hand the homework assignments up to the front like I've asked you to?" Mrs. Sidney hissed from the end of her row, interrupting Sabrina's thoughts for a second.

"Yeah, hang on," she grumbled before handing the stack of homework to the person in front of her so they could get it to Mrs. Sidney. Through it all, Sabrina was still staring straight back at Chelsea.

"So, you think we could do that?"

Chelsea frowned. She really didn't feel comfortable giving out her test, but, at the same time, she didn't like the idea of tackling the midterms with incomplete notes either.

"Okay. Sure," she conceded as she retrieved her last test out of the folder. She reluctantly handed it over to Sabrina face down a second later. "Just try and get it back to me by tomorrow."

Even though she was considerate enough not to turn the test over right then, a wry grin still slid across Sabrina's lips as she slipped the test into her folder.

"Hey, I can definitely do that," she assured Chelsea.

12

The Permission Slip

Even as he stepped into the office, Nolan wasn't sure if he was doing the right thing. No one ever made it a point to meet with the principal on purpose, but he was about to do it anyway. Of course, he knew he wouldn't even be there if Sabrina wasn't expecting him to do this, but it still didn't make him feel any better about it.

"Can I help you?" the secretary asked once Nolan stepped up to the counter.

"Um, yeah. I'm here to see Principal Espinoza. I've got an appointment with him at one-thirty." It was actually a few minutes before, but Nolan decided to head straight to the office after science instead of going on to sixth period. As far as he was concerned, the less his classmates knew about this, the better.

"Your name?"

"Oh. Um, Nolan Leere."

The secretary looked at the schedule on her computer before she nodded and glanced at Nolan out of the corner of her eye. "Alright. I see that the principal's expecting you. So, if you'll go ahead and sign in here," she said, tapping one of her long, red nails on a clipboard containing a spreadsheet, "I'll make sure the principal's ready."

A second later, the secretary stepped into the administrative hallway and poked her head into Principal Espinoza's office. By the time she came back, Nolan had finished filling out his name, time of visit, and purpose of visit on the spreadsheet.

"All signed in?" she asked expectantly. Even though Nolan indicated he was, the secretary still examined the spreadsheet before nudging her head towards Espinoza's office. "Okay. You're welcome to go ahead and see him now, Mr. Leere."

"Thanks," Nolan said as he rounded the counter and walked to the office. Once at the doorway, the principal ushered him in with a wave of his hand, not even bothering to get out of his chair.

"And close the door behind you, if you would please," he asked as soon as Nolan entered his office. Nolan instantly complied.

"So, what brings you here today, Mr. Leere?" Principal Espinoza asked after gesturing towards the chair in front of his desk. "I'm guessing it's because you know who messed with the PA system, isn't it?"

Nolan stopped in his tracks and stared back at Principal Espinoza. "What?" he gasped, feeling his heart beating a little faster. He wondered if Jonathan had already told Principal Espinoza about his seventy-five percent suspicion.

"Well, you know: the guy–or girl–that pulled the prank the other day," Principal Espinoza clarified. "I'm sure you've seen the flyers."

"Hmm? Oh, yeah. Right," Nolan grumbled, struggling to settle his mind down. "Actually, this was about something else."

Principal Espinoza looked a little disappointed, but went ahead and gestured toward the chair in front of his desk again. "Okay, well never mind I said it. So, what's this about, Mr. Leere?"

Nolan sat his backpack down next to the chair and did his best to swallow the frog in his throat. "Well, it's about Coach Grayson," he said as he took his seat.

"Okay," Principal Espinoza hummed. "Do you have a complaint or something?"

"Not exactly," Nolan choked out, doing his best to keep his eyes diverted from Principal Espinoza's sleepy stare. "I was sort of going over a history test with a friend of mine from a different school yesterday and we found something kind of strange."

"Such as?"

Nolan still hesitated before he managed to spit it out. "Alright. So, basically, the test I took in Coach Grayson's class earlier this week ended up having three questions omitted on it.

Coach Grayson said it was because those questions weren't on the syllabus or something, but my friend said her test didn't have any omitted questions on it and she still got the same questions right."

Principal Espinoza sat in silence for a few seconds and stared back at Nolan as he processed what he'd just said. "What school does your friend go to?"

"Oh, um, River View Middle School. You know, the magnet school across town?" Nolan blurted out as if Principal Espinoza didn't realize the district had other middle schools in it. He tried to stifle his embarrassment, but he could still feel his cheeks starting to warm up.

"And I'm guessing you found this odd because the tests are consolidated now?" Principal Espinoza said flatly.

Nolan nodded.

"Okay," Principal Espinoza hummed, "so what does this have to do with Coach Grayson?"

"Well," Nolan began unsteadily, "since my friend got the questions right and everything, and even thinks that her teacher went over the stuff in class, it kind of has us wondering if Coach Grayson might have, you know, forgotten to teach us something and just made up the thing about the omitted questions to cover it up."

A surprised scoff escaped Principal Espinoza's lips and he shot a disappointed look back at Nolan. "Well, that's quite an accusation. Are you always this suspicious of your teachers, Mr. Leere?"

Nolan promptly shook his head. "No, sir. Not usually. It's just, I don't know, after everything that happened a few years ago, I think my friend's a bit paranoid." He diverted his eyes away from Principal Espinoza's and scratched the back of his head before he added, "I mean, her dad *was* one of the teachers that got caught in the cash-for-grades thing."

Principal Espinoza let out a morose sigh. "Yeah, that could have a lot to do with it. I take it you don't necessarily share your friend's opinion, though?"

"Not really, but my friend did make a couple of good points. Plus, neither of us had any notes on the stuff–which was weird–and Coach Grayson did get in trouble for rounding down someone's weight in wrestling last year, so I thought that maybe she could have been onto something, you know?"

The edges of Principal Espinoza's lips tugged upward slightly. "Well, all considering, I guess I can see how someone might think Coach Grayson could have done something like that. But if you and your friend are worried about this, Mr. Leere, I can assure you Coach Grayson did nothing wrong."

"Seriously?" Nolan blurted out. Across from him, Principal Espinoza simply shrugged and continued with his explanation.

"Absolutely. After Coach Grayson brought the issues with the test to my attention, I'm actually the one that called Central Office to see if we could omit those questions. They confirmed the questions about the–what was it–Insufferable Laws?"

"Um, the Intolerable Acts," Nolan corrected him reluctantly.

"Right, the Intolerable Acts," he exclaimed, pointing back at Nolan. "Either way, Central Office confirmed that those questions shouldn't have been on the test because they weren't on the testing syllabus, so they gave us permission to omit them."

Nolan nodded and looked off to the side for a second. Even though he was satisfied with the answer, he got the feeling Sabrina would want more than that.

"So, do you have, like, a note or something about that from Central Office?" Nolan asked.

The principal's lips contorted into a slight scowl. "Of course. I could show you the fax I got from Central Office the other day if you want."

The sharp ringing of the sixth period bell slicing through the air made Nolan jolt with a start. "If you don't mind," he said, trying not to sound as jumpy as he felt. "I mean, it's not like I don't trust you, but..."

Principal Espinoza silenced him with a wave of his hand as he got out of the leather chair and stepped over to a filing cabinet behind his desk. "Don't worry about it. Just give me a bit and I'll have it for you."

After digging through the cabinet for a few seconds, Principal Espinoza turned back around with a single sheet of paper in his hand.

"Here you are," he announced as he placed it down on his desk, spun it around so it would be facing Nolan right-side-up, and slid it over to him. Nolan picked up the piece of paper and began reading over it as Principal Espinoza watched on.

Principal Hector Espinoza:

Regarding your concerns about the Intolerable Acts being included on the consolidated testing syllabus for 8th grade American History (Pre-AP), it has been confirmed that this subject was included on the test in error as it was part of last year's syllabus, not this year's.

Corrective actions, such as question omissions, have been approved to correct the mistake and adjust the test scores as needed. A memo will be sent to other middle schools alerting them to this issue.

I would personally like to thank you and Mike Grayson for bringing this matter to our attention.

Sincerely,

Dr. Lars Richter, Superintendent

"Convinced?" the principal asked once it looked like Nolan had finished studying over the letter.

"I guess so. I just can't figure out why my friend's teacher went ahead and taught her class about it if the Intolerable Acts weren't even on the testing syllabus."

"Yeah, I'm not sure why they would have done that either," Principal Espinoza said as Nolan handed the fax back to him and he returned it to the filing cabinet. "The only thing I can think of is that your friend's teacher taught it out of habit since it used to be on the testing syllabus. Trust me: it's easy to do if you've been teaching the same subject for a while."

"Yeah, I guess so," Nolan said distantly. He stared at the edge of Principal Espinoza's desk for a bit as he continued to mull over the issue.

"So, is there anything else you needed?" the principal

asked a short time later.

Nolan drummed his fingers across his knees before looking back up. "No, sir. I guess not."

"Okay. Well, if you think of anything else, please feel free to let me know. Otherwise, I'd recommend just moving on. As I said, Coach Grayson did nothing wrong, and, if you missed any of those questions, they've been taken off the test. No harm, no foul, right?"

"Right," Nolan droned.

"Okay, then," Principal Espinoza announced. "I'm sure you need to get on to sixth period. You can get a pass from the receptionist on the way out."

"Alright, I guess that just about covers it, anyway," Nolan said as he got out of the chair and picked his backpack up off the floor. "Thanks for clearing everything up, sir."

Principal Espinoza stood up and shook Nolan's hand from behind the desk. Nolan tried not to flinch under the tight grip. "Don't mention it. After everything that happened a few years ago, I'm glad to see students taking an interest in what goes on at their school."

The comment only brought a subtle nod from Nolan before he turned and headed out the door with his backpack slung over his shoulder.

Once he was gone, Principal Espinoza softly slid the door to his office shut and stepped back over to his desk. He stared at the phone for a second or two before he picked up the receiver and dialed the number for Central Office. A receptionist picked it up on the second ring.

"Yes, this is Principal Hector Espinoza at Meade Middle School. Get me over to Superintendent Richter, if you could, please."

13

Irregularities

A series of shrill chirps jarred Sabrina awake. Once her eyes cracked open, she noticed her room was a lot darker than she remembered and her cell phone was ringing at the edge of her desk.

Nolan was trying to call her.

Yawning, she turned her desk lamp on and glanced at the clock on the nightstand behind her. It was a little after eight in the evening. Sabrina guessed she must have dozed off at her desk for a while, but she didn't know how long she'd been out or what she'd been doing beforehand. She vaguely remembered doing something with Chelsea's test, which was still lying on top of the desk next to her own, but that was it.

The phone rang again. Shaking her head on it, Sabrina grabbed the phone and answered it before it could go to voicemail. "Hey, Nolan," she said drearily.

"Hey. You busy right now or anything?"

Sabrina shook her head and tried to ignore the test full of red marks in front of her. "No. Just a bit tired is all. What's going on?"

"Well, I just thought you should know, but I talked to my principal about the omitted questions today."

The drowsiness hanging over Sabrina evaporated.

"You did? What'd he say?" she asked eagerly. Nolan seemed to hesitate before he answered.

"Basically, he said they weren't doing anything wrong," Nolan reported in a quiet but firm voice. Sabrina scoffed out loud and slouched back in her chair.

"Well, if they were doing something wrong, I don't think

they'd just come out and say it, Nolan! I mean, come on, what did you expect them to say?"

"Yeah, I know, but there's a bit more to it than that."

"Yeah? Like what?"

"Like the fact that Principal Espinoza showed me a letter he got from Central Office," Nolan responded dryly. "Superintendent Richter actually gave them permission to omit the test questions."

"Seriously?"

"Yeah. Well, I guess it was more of a fax than a letter, but Principal Espinoza still showed it to me. It was signed by Superintendent Richter and everything."

"So what'd it say?" Sabrina demanded. "You actually read it, didn't you?"

"Yeah, I read it. It didn't say much, but it did say the Intolerable Acts weren't supposed to be on the test because they weren't on the syllabus or whatever–just like my history teacher told us the other day. They *were* on last year's syllabus, though. I think the letter said that, too."

Sabrina's eyes narrowed. "What's that got to do with anything?"

"Well, you know," Nolan began, "maybe that's why your teacher taught your class about it but Coach Grayson didn't. Like she was just doing it out of habit or something."

"Yeah, maybe," Sabrina grumbled, still sounding unconvinced.

"So, I guess your history teacher had a memo about it, too?" Nolan asked expectantly. "The fax I saw today also said something about that–that Superintendent Richter was going to send out memos to everyone, I mean."

A guilty twinge rattled around in Sabrina's stomach. "Actually, I think I forgot to ask her about it."

"Seriously?" Nolan exclaimed, sounding more shocked than upset. "How'd you forget to do something like that? You were making such a big deal about it yesterday."

Sabrina ran a hand through her hair and glared at the tests in front of her. "I don't know. I guess I had a lot on my mind today."

"Yeah, well I did, too," Nolan shot back. An instant later, he seemed to calm down some. "Look, either way, at least we know they weren't doing anything wrong now, right?"

Sabrina pulled her lips in a little and slouched deeper into her chair. She glanced at Chelsea's test again. Before she'd nodded off, she'd been going over it just to see if the questions corresponded to everything in her notes.

Then it hit her. They hadn't.

"That can't be right," she mused aloud, catching Nolan off guard.

"What do you mean? I told you: your teacher probably went over the stuff by mistake."

"No, it's not that," Sabrina cut in quickly. "It's just that I think I ran into the same problem on a different test. You know, with test questions that aren't in our notes."

"On one of my tests?"

Sabrina shook her head, eyeing the tests in front of her again. "No, on one of my classmate's algebra tests. I started going over it earlier."

"And you're doing this because..."

"It's kind of a long story," Sabrina began evasively, "but we were talking before algebra started this morning and she mentioned that she went through a rough patch on her tests a few weeks ago. She said she was having trouble sleeping back then, too."

"Alright. So, what? I think that's a problem anyone would have if they weren't getting enough sleep, don't you?"

"Yeah, I know, but she also said something about having questions on her tests that she didn't remember from her notes."

"Oh, great," Nolan grunted. "So, what, you just told her that you think the school's messing with the grades and asked to see her tests?"

"Well, not like that. I mean, I did ask her if I could borrow her tests, but I told her I was trying to help her fill in her notes so she'd be ready for the semester finals in a few months."

"And she believed you?"

Sabrina shrugged and glanced off to the side. "More or less. It took a bit of convincing, but she still let me borrow one of her tests."

"Great," Nolan grumbled coldly. "So, how many of these

questions did you come across on your friend's test, anyway?"

Sabrina pulled herself closer to the desk and looked back over Chelsea's test. The number of red marks on it was staggering, but she'd already made a small list in the back of her algebra spiral for the questions that caught her attention the most.

"So far, I've found about two questions she missed that I got right even though I didn't have any notes to back it up. It's just like what happened on our history test."

"And you're sure your classmate doesn't have any notes on it?" Nolan asked.

"I doubt it. She's a good student and everything, but she didn't even show any problem-solving steps with those two questions. It's like she didn't even know what to do. Of course, whether or not her lack of sleep had anything to do with it is anyone's guess.

"You weren't having the same problem too, were you?" Sabrina asked Nolan abruptly. "Maybe your teacher did go over the Intolerable Acts in class and you were just out of it or something."

"No, I don't think that's it," Nolan said quickly. "Plus, pretty much everyone in my class and the other Pre-AP class didn't know anything about it either."

"Oh, right. I forgot about that. Crap!" Sabrina hissed, glaring back at Chelsea's test.

"Hey, don't get worked up about it," Nolan warned her. Even over the phone, he could tell what she was thinking.

Sabrina leaned back in her chair. "Yeah, well how else am I supposed to feel about it? Even if your principal said he got permission from Richter and showed you a note and all that, it still doesn't explain what happened on our tests. Or on Chelsea's."

"Chelsea's?"

"Sorry. The classmate at my school I was telling you about," Sabrina added. "Still, how do you explain all that? It's like I keep getting the same questions right that other people miss, even though neither of us have any notes on it."

"Maybe you're just that smart," Nolan suggested in a way that made Sabrina wonder if he was being sarcastic or sincere. Either way, it caused a thin smile to snake across her lips.

"It would be nice if I was, but I think that's a stretch. Plus, if I was that smart, I could probably come up with a better explanation to all of this instead of grasping at wild ideas."

"Well, maybe that's it," Nolan said, causing Sabrina to cock her eyebrows in confusion.

"That's what?"

"Maybe you can't explain it because there's nothing going on with our tests. I mean, sure, you've already looked at two tests and, yeah, they both have something weird going on with them, but that's about it. The tests are from two different schools, two different subjects, and Coach Grayson had absolutely nothing to do with your friend's test. If you ask me, it's probably just a coincidence."

Sabrina looked back at Chelsea's test. Even though she knew Nolan was probably right, she couldn't shake the feeling that there was something else going on. Something she just couldn't put her finger on. Suddenly, an idea jolted through her mind.

"So, basically, you're saying that if I got some questions right on my tests when you or Chelsea didn't, it's only a coincidence, right?"

"Yeah," Nolan said.

"So what if it happened on more than just two tests? Would you still say it was a coincidence then?"

"Well, no. I guess that'd be different," he admitted reluctantly. "Why?"

A devious grin crept across Sabrina's lips. "You think you could look at something for me?"

14

Rude Awakenings

Nolan couldn't believe how many times Sabrina had asked him to look over one of his tests last night. She'd even texted him before he left for school that morning. Still, every time she asked, he gave her the same response.

No.

He wasn't sure if it was the right thing to do when Sabrina was getting this worked up about it, but he knew it was the only way out of this mess. If he didn't find any weird questions on the first test, Sabrina would've begged him to look at another, and another, until something finally showed up that at least partially backed up her crazy ideas. After that, the obsessing and the speculating would start all over again.

Trying not to dwell on it, he let out a frustrated sigh as he rounded the next corner in the hallway. He made it to Coach Grayson's class a few seconds later and was still pondering over the situation when something jolted him out of his thoughts.

The doorknob wouldn't turn.

"What the…?" Nolan grunted. He twisted the doorknob again just to be sure he wasn't turning it the wrong way, but he wasn't. The door was locked and the lights inside the room were off, too.

Nolan stared at his perplexed reflection in the darkened window for a second before he spotted the yellow post-it note taped to the door.

American History will be held in Rm. 202 today.

\- *Asst. Principal Horne*

"Okay, then," Nolan grumbled under his breath before doing an about-face and heading back in the direction he'd come from. He didn't remember anything about a special presentation today, and he almost wondered if a water pipe had burst in the ceiling like it did in Mrs. Ortiz's class when he was in sixth grade. If that was the case, they could be having history in Room 202 for weeks.

Nolan was still rummaging over the possibilities when he saw Brynlee heading to class herself.

"History's in Room 202 today," he warned her. The small girl stopped in her tracks and glanced up at Nolan with a confused look in her eyes.

"Really?" she squeaked to the point Nolan barely heard her in the crowded hallway. "But isn't that one of the seventh grade science classes?"

"Search me," he grunted as Brynlee took up step next to him. "The note didn't say why."

"Maybe we're watching a video or something."

"Yeah, maybe," Nolan hummed. Considering the note had been signed by their assistant principal, though, he seriously doubted that was the case. Something else was going on.

As soon as Nolan and Brynlee walked into Room 202, they found Assistant Principal Horne waiting at the front of the class. As usual, a heavy aroma of freshly smoked cigarettes lingered in the air around her and her frizzled, graying hair looked like it needed to be brushed again. Some other man Nolan hadn't seen before was sitting at the desk behind her, but Coach Grayson was nowhere to be seen.

Both he and Brynlee were still processing the sight when the firm look in Horne's sagging eyes directed them to take their seats. The silence hanging over the classroom suggested enough.

"Yeah. This can't be good," Nolan grumbled under his breath as he took his seat near the back edge of the class. The process was the same for other students coming in until the bell rang and third period started a few minutes later. He watched on with the rest of the class as Assistant Principal Horne nodded at the substitute teacher, who stood up from behind the desk to shut the door.

"Okay," Assistant Principal Horne began in her raspy voice as soon as the door clicked shut. "I'm sure you're wondering why you're having history in here today. Well, there's no easy way to say this, so I'll just give it to you straight. Mr. Grayson won't be here for a while. He and Principal Espinoza have been put on administrative leave pending an investigation."

A sullen hush fell over the classroom.

"An investigation into what?" one of the students blurted out.

Horne's beady eyes glanced down at the beige tile lining Room 202. "Based on the legal nature of the investigation I can't tell you everything, but I can tell you Mr. Grayson and Mr. Espinoza are both suspected of conspiring to commit test fraud."

The announcement shot through Nolan's mind like a dart and he was fully aware of the quivering breath that trickled through his lips.

Sensing the confusion sweeping over the class, Assistant Principal Horne added, "I'm sure all of you remember the issues you had on your history test the other day?"

A few silent nods from the class was all the affirmation she needed.

"Okay. Well, the simple truth is Mr. Grayson forgot to cover something that was on the syllabus, and, instead of facing his mistake, we think he talked Principal Espinoza into forging a letter from Central Office authorizing the school to omit the questions. Obviously, Central Office takes that sort of thing pretty seriously."

"So, the Intolerable Acts really were on the syllabus?" Nolan croaked out. His mind was still swimming in shock.

"They were," was Assistant Principal Horne's blunt response. "And while forging the note was bad enough, we have reason to believe Mr. Grayson and/or Mr. Espinoza took it a step further and got the student that pulled the prank on Monday to help them remove the Intolerable Acts from the district's syllabus, too."

A panicked twinge raced down Nolan's spine and the classroom seemed to shrink around him. He was barely even aware of one of his classmates speaking up.

"How would they do that, though? Remove the Intolerable Acts from the syllabus, I mean?"

Assistant Principal Horne took a deep breath. "We'd been withholding this information while we were trying to track them down, but I guess I might as well tell y'all about it now. When the student messed with the PA system on Monday, they took a USB drive from the office with them. That USB drive contained a link to the syllabus.

"With that in mind, Central Office wanted me to let you know they'll actually be doubling the cash reward for anyone that comes forward with information about our prankster. With everything going on, they need to know if they were involved in this, too."

Another short, quaking breath rustled through Nolan's lips. His mind was buzzing and he couldn't help but wonder if this was why Eli had been so hesitant to turn himself in for the last few days.

"Anyway, you'll be having history in here until investigators from Central Office can complete their evidence sweep of Coach Grayson's classroom. I'll be Meade's acting principal during the investigation and Mr. Garth here is going to be your substitute teacher during the interim as well."

"What about our grades?" Brynlee asked after raising her hand.

"They'll stay the same. Central Office decided it wasn't right to punish you for something your teacher didn't cover. Anything else?"

Assistant Principal Horne paused for a few seconds to make sure there weren't any more questions before continuing. From the looks of things, the class was too stunned to think straight.

"Okay. So, I just want to say that I'm sorry I let this get by me, especially since I've been at a conference for the past few days, but I assure you we're taking steps to make sure we don't have any other questionable staff members here. If any of you know anything, or if you have any questions, please feel free to stop by my office. I'll let Mr. Garth take it from here."

With that, Assistant Principal Horne strode out of the classroom and shut the door behind her. As soon as she was gone, a wiry grin crossed the lips of the thin, balding man Nolan guessed was just out of his thirties.

"Very well then," he began in a nasally voice that made Nolan's skin crawl. "So, as your assistant principal indicated, my name is Mr. Garth–which really is my last name and not my first!" he said with a series of snickers. No one else laughed. "And if memory serves me right, I believe you're working on the Revolutionary War. So, let's get started, shall we?"

Even though he tried to pay attention to the substitute's lecture, it was nearly impossible for Nolan to do so. Granted, he suspected everyone else was having the same problem just by glancing around the room, but he doubted it was because they knew who the prankster was.

As much as Nolan wanted to deny it, he couldn't ignore the feeling that Eli's involvement in all this made too much sense.

For one, his friend almost always stuck to simple pranks, so sneaking into the office to mess with the PA system and then sneaking into the gym through the boys' locker room was a big change for him. But more than that, Eli usually liked to brag about his pranks, so the fact that he was keeping quiet about this one was unusual, too.

For the first time since he found out Eli was the prankster, Nolan started to wonder if he should rat him out. Eli wasn't going to turn himself in, and, considering how bad this could get if Eli really did help Espinoza and Grayson erase something from the system, Nolan didn't want to get in trouble for not coming forward sooner.

Then again, if he said anything it would be all too easy for Jonathan Reed or Landon Collins to tell Assistant Principal Horne that he lied to them about being at the assembly with Eli, too. Then they'd probably think he and Eli were in on this together.

A knot started to grow in the pit of Nolan's stomach as the weight of the situation bore down on him. Ultimately, he knew there was only one thing he could do.

15

Guilt by Association

The scent of stagnant cafeteria food greeted Eli as soon as he stepped out of shop class. The food had never been that appealing to him, but he was so hungry today he hardly cared what it smelled like.

Quickly filtering into the masses clogging the hallway, Eli started to make his way to the cafeteria. He was just about to step through the main entrance when a familiar voice stopped him in his tracks.

"Hey, Eli! Hold up a second."

Eli glanced to the right in time to see Nolan emerging from the crowd. He had a frantic look in his eyes.

"Hey, man. What's going on?"

Before Nolan said anything he grabbed Eli by the shoulder and started ushering him away from the cafeteria. "We need to head to The Nook. Now," he commanded somewhat breathlessly.

"What? Now?" Eli sputtered. "Can't it wait until after lunch?"

"No," Nolan insisted as he continued to urge Eli onward. "We've got to talk now, man."

"Why? What's the rush?" Eli asked as he reluctantly took up step next to Nolan.

"It's about your prank," Nolan said firmly, though softly enough it wouldn't carry over the crowded hallway. "I need to know something about it."

"Okay, like what?"

"I'll tell you when we're outside," Nolan grumbled.

After what felt like hours, the two passed through the

double set of doors halfway down the hallway and stepped out into The Nook. Eli's eyes had barely adjusted to the bright sunlight before Nolan stepped right in front of him and stopped him from continuing on to their usual spot by the tree.

"Okay, man. Give me one good reason why I shouldn't turn you in right now," he growled. Eli's eyes went wide.

"Wait. What? I thought you said you weren't going to do that."

"I wasn't, but that was before Assistant Principal Horne told my history class that the guy that messed with the PA system on Monday might have helped Coach Grayson or Principal Espinoza take something off the syllabus. You wouldn't know anything about that, would you?"

"Dude, what are you talking about?" Eli gasped. "I didn't help Principal Espinoza or Coach Grayson with anything. I don't even like those guys!"

"But you did take that USB drive with you the other day, didn't you?" Nolan reminded him. Eli quickly diverted his eyes from his friend's accusatory stare.

"Well, yeah, but—"

"And no one told you what to do or how to get it?"

"What? No. I just sort of did it. Dude, seriously, why're you making such a big deal about this all of a sudden?"

The rage in Nolan's eyes faded a little when he noticed the fearful look in Eli's. He could tell it wasn't because his friend was trying to keep the truth from him either.

With a guilty twinge, Nolan took a deep breath and stepped back from him. "Sorry. It's just that Assistant Principal Horne said a few things during my history class that kind of got me thinking."

"Yeah? About what?" Eli demanded.

Nolan hesitated for a second before he choked it out. "She said that the USB drive you took out of the office had a link to the syllabus on it. You didn't know that when you took it, did you?"

Eli quickly shook his head. "No. Not at all, man."

"And you didn't really mean to take the USB drive with you either. It was just an accident, right?"

"Yeah," Eli said with a slight nod. "I didn't even know I had it in my pocket until I got to the gym. Why?"

Nolan glared back at Eli for a few seconds. Eventually, he told Eli the same thing Assistant Principal Horne told his class that morning.

"Principal Espinoza and Coach Grayson got fired today," he said bluntly. His friend's eyes went wide a split second later.

"Holy crap! Are you serious?"

Nolan slowly nodded his head. "Yeah. Apparently, Central Office thinks they were messing with test grades and that they took the Intolerable Acts off the syllabus. That's the thing my history class was having a hard time with the other day."

It only took Eli a second or two to put the pieces together. "And, what, you actually thought I helped them do something like that?"

"Well, I was starting to wonder," Nolan said sheepishly. "I mean, something about your prank just seemed kind of…"

"What?"

"Out of place," Nolan conceded.

Eli glared back at him. "Out of place? What's that supposed to mean?"

Nolan started to glance away but forced himself to make eye contact with Eli again. "Alright, don't take this the wrong way or anything, but this prank was way more complicated than the ones you usually pull."

"Dude, all I did was plug an MP3 player into the PA system," Eli argued.

"Yeah, I know. But how did you know how to do that?" Nolan asked. "I mean, how did you even know that'd work or where to find the PA terminal?"

Eli shrugged and glanced off to the side. "I don't know. I think I just sort of came up with the idea a few weeks ago. I guess I've been sent to the office so many times I just kind of knew where most of the stuff was."

"What about sneaking into the office and then cutting through the locker room to sneak into the gym, though?" Nolan pointed out. "I know you told me how you thought of the locker room thing yesterday, but how'd you figure out how to get into the office?"

Again, Eli shrugged. "Beats me. I think it just sort of came to me one day, too. Probably when I heard that Superintendent

Richter was going to be coming. As big of a deal as everyone was making about it, I guess I figured that'd make it easier for me to sneak into the office."

Nolan could hardly believe it. In a lot of ways, he was impressed Eli had come up with all of this on his own. He doubted he would have been able to, even if he'd planned it out for a month.

"So, what was your plan for getting out of this?" Nolan asked. Eli's eyes dipped away in shame a second later.

"Um, yeah, I didn't exactly have one," he said, forcing a smile. "Honestly, I didn't think they'd make such a big deal out of this. Then again, I wasn't counting on ending up with that USB drive in my pocket either."

"Yeah, that probably changed things up a bit," Nolan chuckled.

"Yep. But I swear someone's trying extra hard to catch me," Eli said. With a shrug, he added, "Maybe harder than they should be."

"What do you mean?"

"It's like when Sally Gardner blamed me for getting ink all over her backpack a few years ago," Eli explained. He pointed a finger back at himself a second later. "I had nothing to do with it, but, since everyone knows I'm the practical joker around here, they just decided it was my fault because it was easier than figuring out what actually happened."

Nolan shot a quizzical look back at Eli. "So you're saying someone's trying to frame you for this? I mean, you already kind of told me that you pulled this prank."

"Yeah, I know I did *that*," Eli shot back in annoyance. "But I keep getting the feeling like someone's trying to pin all this other stuff on me, you know? And they're trying to make me look like the bad guy, too."

"You mean with all the flyers they put up?"

"Yeah! Exactly!" Eli cried, pointing his finger back at Nolan. "All I did was pull a prank that wasn't even meant for Superintendent Richter and people act like I'm Jesse James or something. The whole thing's nuts!"

"Well, nuts or not, Assistant Principal Horne and maybe even Superintendent Richter think you might have been working with Coach Grayson and Principal Espinoza now, and they're probably not going to take the flyers down any time soon either."

"Great!" Eli hissed. "So, what are we going to do about it?"

Nolan shook his head. "I don't know. But we'd probably better think of something quick."

"Why's that?"

"Because Assistant Principal Horne told us something else this morning," Nolan began ominously. "They're offering more reward money now, too."

"You really think that'll matter?"

Nolan paused and stared back at Eli. His conversation with Jonathan Reed and Landon Collins yesterday quickly crossed his mind.

"It might to someone, but let's hope not," he said before motioning for Eli to follow him back to the cafeteria. He doubted either of them had much of an appetite, though.

16

The Common Denominator

Sabrina checked the time on her phone again. As ready as she was for four o'clock to roll around, she was a little disappointed when she realized it was only 3:52. It had just been three minutes since the last time she'd checked.

A frustrated grimace pulled at her lips as she set the phone down and turned her attention back to the spiral notebook sitting on the cafeteria table in front of her. She'd made a lot of notes since she started waiting for her mom to pick her up, but she didn't feel like she was any closer to sorting things out than she had been twenty minutes ago.

Of course, it had been a pretty eventful day, too.

As of now, she'd found a total of eighteen questions on her tests that didn't correspond to something in her notes–and that included two more on her history test that had nothing to do with the Intolerable Acts.

But as alarming as that was, the fact that she'd gotten every single one of them right was somehow even worse. Unfortunately, that wasn't the only thing bothering her.

Sabrina finally asked her history teacher, Mrs. Tiller, about the omitted questions during fifth period. Even though the fax Nolan saw yesterday said Superintendent Richter was going to send out a memo to the history teachers telling them to omit the Intolerable Acts questions, Mrs. Tiller said she never got anything like that from Central Office.

In fact, Mrs. Tiller was pretty sure she'd gone over the Intolerable Acts in class, too.

After hearing that, Sabrina wasn't sure what to believe anymore. On one hand, it looked like Nolan's school was lying about getting permission to omit the questions, but, on the other, she couldn't ignore the fact that she'd uncovered an unsettling amount of undocumented questions on her tests either.

No matter what Nolan said last night, she was sure it couldn't just be a coincidence anymore.

Sabrina tapped her pen against the cafeteria table a few times before reaching for her phone to check the time. She was anxious to ask Nolan about it just to see what he thought, but she didn't want to be too hasty. After all, part of her wondered if she was just being paranoid about all this and she didn't want anyone overhearing.

But even though the after-school crowd in the cafeteria had thinned out considerably since she first got there, Sabrina figured Nolan probably wouldn't be back home and away from all the prying ears on the bus until about four. Unfortunately, the time on her phone indicated it was only 3:56.

Close enough, Sabrina decided impatiently.

An instant later she pulled up Nolan's name in her contacts and initiated the call. As the phone started to ring, Sabrina glanced back at her notes to be sure she hadn't overlooked anything. Just as before, though, she was sure that she'd reached a dead end.

"Hey, Sabrina," Nolan greeted indifferently after the fourth ring. "You calling to say, 'I told you so?'"

The comment caught Sabrina completely off guard and her mind snapped to the first thing she could think of. "What? About the test questions?"

"Well, sort of," Nolan began unsteadily. "You are talking about the thing with my history teacher and my principal getting fired, right?"

Sabrina's heart skipped a beat. "Wait, they got fired?"

"Yeah. Well, actually, I guess they got put on leave or something, but it's been all over the news. You seriously didn't know?"

Sabrina shook her head. "No. I'm still waiting for my mom to pick me up from school and was kind of busy working on something else. What happened?"

"You remember the fax Principal Espinoza showed me yesterday?"

The hairs on the back of Sabrina's neck stood up. "Yeah."

"Well, apparently he and my history teacher made the whole thing up. They even faked the superintendent's signature and took the Intolerable Acts off the syllabus to cover their tracks."

"Oh, my God! That's insane," Sabrina gasped as she slouched back in her chair.

"You're telling me!" Nolan grunted. "Anyway, I guess it proves that you were right all along, you know? My history teacher really did screw up on that test and tried to hide it."

"Well, you know, everything kind of pointed in that direction," Sabrina crowed, even though she felt guilty taking pride in what had happened. All the same, something about this situation still didn't feel right to her.

Nolan had already started talking about what happened in his history class that morning when her eyes drifted onto the notes sitting on the cafeteria table in front of her. Just then, a troubling thought sent her mind into a frenzy.

"Hey! Do you still have your last science test?" she asked abruptly, interrupting Nolan mid-sentence. Based on the pause that followed, she could tell the question caught him by surprise.

"Wh- My last science test? Yeah, I think so. Why?"

"Alright, look over it and see if you can find any questions that aren't in your notes. Then meet me at Fryer Tuck's around five-thirty."

"Okay, but what's the point?" Nolan grumbled. "Don't we already know my principal was lying about getting permission to omit the questions now?"

"Maybe," Sabrina said coolly. "But maybe he wasn't lying either."

The inside of Fryer Tuck's was bustling with activity. The line at the counter was a lot longer than Sabrina had seen on the other days she'd met Nolan there and most of the tables were already taken, too. She guessed the burger joint's proximity to one of the high school football stadiums had a lot to do with that.

All the same, she was already halfway through her bottle

of cream soda by the time Nolan slid into the booth seat across from her. It looked like he'd rather be somewhere else.

"You know, I'm going to go broke before long if we keep meeting like this," he said, exhibiting the fountain drink he'd just bought.

"Yeah, well, it was the best thing I could think of," Sabrina snipped. Her eyes quickly settled on the backpack Nolan brought with him. "So, did you go over your last science test?"

Nolan took a quick sip from his drink before he started unzipping his backpack. "Yeah, I did. And I found a few questions that weren't in my notes, too."

"Awesome! Which ones?" Sabrina said excitedly. She was already taking her test out of the folder she'd had sitting on the tabletop for the last few minutes.

Nolan surveyed his test for a second before he said anything. "Um, looks like 9, 14, 17, and 21."

After glancing at her test, Sabrina quickly confirmed they were the same undocumented questions she'd found.

"Good, good. I didn't have any notes on those questions either. Now, tell me what you got for them."

Nolan cocked his eyebrows and glared at her warily before he glanced back down at his test. "Yeah. Let's see: I put C on 9, A on 14, wrote in, 'Shield Volcano,' for 17, and put B on 21."

A chill ran down Sabrina's back. They were the same as the answers she'd gotten on her test. Her heart raced as she asked the next and possibly most important question.

"And did you get them right?"

Nolan continued to give her a strange look but slowly nodded his head. "Yeah. Why? Didn't you?"

Instead of answering, a grin spread across Sabrina's lips and she slouched back into her seat. As much as she was expecting it, she could hardly believe what had just happened.

"Um, is something wrong, Sabrina?" Nolan asked slowly. Sabrina barely seemed to come out of the trance she'd fallen into, though.

"Is something wrong? Do you know what this means, Nolan?" she finally said.

"Um... That we got a few test questions right?"

A haughty laugh cackled out of Sabrina's mouth and she

shook her head. "Oh, no. It's way more than that! These were questions that neither of us had any notes on, and, yet, by some miracle, we still got them right."

Nolan shot a confused look back at her and shrugged. "So? You got the answers about the Intolerable Acts right without any notes the other day."

"Yeah, but this is different," Sabrina stressed. "What happened on the history test made it look like your teacher messed up. This doesn't."

Nolan glared back at her for a second or two. He still didn't get where she was going with this. "You mean because we got the answers right?"

"Yes! And on questions we shouldn't even know about," Sabrina insisted. "Come on, don't you think that's weird?"

"Not as much as some things," Nolan grunted under his breath while giving her a strange look. He took a sip out of his Cherry Coke to try and wash down the uneasiness settling over him, but it didn't have much effect. Reluctantly, he added, "Maybe these were just easy questions or something."

"Easy?" Sabrina spat. "You think everyone just knows that-that… Iceland sits over a hot spot in the earth's crust like Hawaii?" she stammered, citing Question 14.

"Well, they weren't as hard as the Intolerable Acts questions were. Or, you know, at least not for me," he argued. "I mean, I might have taken this test about two weeks ago, but I don't remember having any problems with them. Did you?"

Sabrina glanced at Question 14 again and felt a brief sinking feeling in her stomach. "No, I guess not. But, come on, this isn't just some run of the mill question like, 'Is the sky blue?'" she said, pointing down at her test. "Somehow both of us just sort of knew some random geologic factoid about Iceland."

"And we probably heard it in class," Nolan suggested sternly. "Look, you might have been right about what happened on my history test, but this is totally unrelated. You can't just keep looking for connections that aren't there, Sabrina."

The eagerness in Sabrina's face fell flat. "You don't believe me?"

Nolan quickly tried to back-peddle out of it. "I didn't say that. I'm just saying they already got the guys that messed with the tests, you know? You don't have to keep doing this."

Sabrina pulled her lips in tight and nodded her head. She glanced out at Crescent Avenue for a few seconds before she said, "So how do you explain what happened on Chelsea's algebra test?"

The question caught Nolan a little by surprise, but he still managed to come up with a viable response. "I don't know. Didn't you say she was running on, like, zero sleep at the time? I'm pretty good at math, but I don't think I could even come close to passing an algebra test if I didn't get much sleep the night before. I'll bet your friend Chelsea was the same way."

"Maybe, but that's not the point," Sabrina insisted. "Algebra's not something you can just walk into and start doing just because you heard something in class. You've got to know how to solve the problems. So, if that's the case, how was I able to get some answers right on the algebra test without any notes but Chelsea couldn't?"

"Well, maybe it was on your homework?" Nolan suggested with a little annoyance riding on his voice. Sabrina quickly shook her head.

"It wasn't, I checked. Plus, if the concepts weren't in my notes and we didn't go over it in class, how would I have been able to do the homework?"

Nolan paused and looked down at the table. After a few seconds, he shrugged in concession.

"Okay, you got me. I don't know."

"Exactly!" Sabrina beamed. "And that's what's so weird about this. As far as I can tell, I had absolutely no idea how to solve division problems with more than one variable going into that test, but I still aced them like there was nothing to it. Do you remember those questions from your algebra test?"

Nolan contemplated it for a second or two before he shook his head. "Not really. I mean, it's probably on there, I just need to look at it again to be sure. Do you think anyone else in your class had a problem with them?"

"I don't think so," Sabrina said after taking another sip of her cream soda. "At least, I don't remember anyone complaining about it. Still, doesn't it sound at least a little bit like our history test the other day?"

"You mean except for the fact that my entire class didn't know anything about the Intolerable Acts and, so far, your friend's the only one that didn't know anything about those division problems?"

"Well, yeah. Basically. But, still, wouldn't you say it's pretty much the same thing, just reversed?"

Nolan shrugged and glanced off to the side. "I don't know. Maybe."

"You seriously don't see a connection?" Sabrina snipped. Nolan glared at her as if it was obvious.

"You do remember the little thing about my history teacher and my principal getting fired today because one of them forgot to teach us about the Intolerable Acts, don't you?"

"Yeah, I do," Sabrina cooed. "But what if the only reason they're saying that is *because* they got caught?"

A thin smile creased across her lips when she noticed the confused look in Nolan's eyes.

"What do you mean?"

"Just think about it," Sabrina said. "I've found the same pattern on just about every test I've looked at so far. They all have a few questions that aren't in my notes, and, since every school's taking the same tests now, there's probably a good chance you don't have any notes on those questions either."

Nolan took a deep breath and continued to glare back at her. "Okay? So what's your point?"

Sabrina leaned in closer to Nolan. "What if the only reason your history teacher and your principal got accused of messing with the syllabus is because no one actually noticed this problem *until* that thing happened with your history test? Maybe someone's trying to cover it up by pinning the blame on them and making it look like the whole thing is only happening at your school."

"Why would they do that, though?" Nolan asked skeptically. Across from him, Sabrina shrugged knowingly.

"Why wouldn't they? If every test has undocumented questions on it the whole district could be committing test fraud, not just Meade."

"Okay, but how're they doing it?" Nolan asked. "You said it yourself. Outside of my class not knowing about the

Intolerable Acts and your friend not knowing anything about the stuff on your algebra test, both of us have basically just known the answers to these questions like it was nothing. How do you explain that?"

Sabrina slouched back into her seat and lightly drummed her fingers on the table. "I don't know. I'm kind of still trying to figure that out."

When Nolan didn't say anything in response, Sabrina took another sip out of her cream soda and stared at her science test for a few seconds. Suddenly, she stopped drinking and sat the soda bottle down again.

"Or maybe I've been looking at this the wrong way."

"What do you mean?"

Sabrina glanced back at Nolan. "I've already proven that a lot of our tests have undocumented questions on them, but I never thought to ask myself what really sets your history test and how Chelsea did on her algebra test apart from the rest."

"And we already figured that out," Nolan said. "Coach Grayson's teaching mistake and your friend's lack of sleep. That's all there is to it."

"But what if it isn't?" Sabrina insisted. "Let's just talk about the history test for a second. Your school was the only one that had problems with the Intolerable Acts even though none of us had any notes on it. So, since I don't remember my history teacher telling us about the Intolerable Acts either, what really sets your school and my school apart?"

"Well, lots of things," Nolan said with a shrug. "Your school's on the other side of town; Meade's not a magnet school like yours is; we've got different mascots..."

"Yeah, but besides all that," Sabrina huffed, glaring at Nolan. He just grinned back at her, though.

"Seriously, what do you want me to say? There could be a ton of differences."

"Just try and think of something that happened within the last week," Sabrina said impatiently.

Nolan gave her a slight eye roll before he took a deep breath and did his best to think it over. Unfortunately, only one thing came to mind.

"Well, someone did mess with the PA system the other

day."

A derisive glint instantly filled Sabrina's eyes. "I don't think that's going to matter that much here, Nolan."

"Hey, I'm just saying," he argued back. "Plus, it was actually a pretty big deal at Meade this week. They put up wanted posters trying to find out who did it and everything."

"Just because someone messed with the PA system?" Sabrina asked skeptically.

"Well, yeah. Basically," Nolan said when he realized she was still expecting an answer. He didn't want to slip up and tell her it was Eli.

"Seems kind of excessive, don't you think?"

"Well," Nolan began hesitantly, "the guy did play the big butts song during Superintendent Richter's speech."

"Oh, yeah. That thing," Sabrina grumbled, remembering Nolan telling her about it the other day. "Guess Superintendent Richter really flipped his lid on that one, didn't he?"

"Yeah," Nolan laughed nervously. His voice was teetering on reluctance when he added, "Plus, they kind of think that the guy that pulled the prank might have helped Coach Grayson and Principal Espinoza take the Intolerable Acts off the syllabus."

Sabrina shot a curious look straight back at him. "Why would they think that?"

Nolan felt his breath quiver and hoped Sabrina didn't notice.

"Because from what I heard, the guy that pulled the prank also took some USB drive off the terminal in the office. Supposedly, it had a link to the syllabus on it."

Sabrina dipped her head down and glared back at Nolan through the tops of her eyes. "So, they had a link to the syllabus on a USB drive that was hooked up to a server in the office?" Across from her, Nolan nodded.

"Yeah. Look, that's just what our assistant principal told my class this morning, alright? I thought it was kind of weird, too."

"And you wouldn't be the only one," Sabrina scoffed. Her eyes drifted back down to her science test as she mulled over it for a second. "Still, if that drive really did contain a link to the syllabus, it kind of makes me wonder if other schools are set up that way."

Nolan shrugged. "I don't know. I guess they could be."

"And if they are," Sabrina began, "then maybe that prank really is the biggest thing that sets our schools apart. That prank happened on Monday, right?"

"Yeah. It was the day before our history test. That's probably why our assistant principal thinks the prank had something to do with it."

Sabrina glanced away and took a sip out of her cream soda bottle. She sat silently for a few seconds before she started to nod her head.

"Then that's got to be it. Taking whatever was on that drive off the server must have brought up a much bigger issue and someone's trying to keep it under wraps. Did they ever catch who did it?"

"What? The, um, guy that messed with the PA system?" Nolan replied clumsily.

"Yeah."

Nolan quickly shook his head. "No. No, they haven't caught him yet. Why?"

Sabrina shrugged. "I don't know. I guess I just figured it'd be nice if we could talk to them, you know? Maybe find out what they know about the drive. I'd bet you money that if we can figure out what's really on there, we can figure out what's going on with our tests. Maybe even prove that your history teacher and your principal didn't actually mess with the syllabus."

Nolan's mind raced. "You really think so?"

Sabrina glared at him like it should have been obvious. "Oh, yeah! I don't care what they say. If the thing was plugged into a server in the office, there's got to be more on there than just some syllabus. They're probably just using those guys at your school as scapegoats."

Nolan bit his lip and glanced off to the side. Every bit of him was telling him not to do it, but, even after taking a sip out of his Cherry Coke, he still couldn't shake his gut instinct. He had to tell her.

"Actually," he began in a cracked voice, "I think I might know who did it."

17

Special Offers

Eli could tell he was in trouble the second he glanced behind him and saw the cold look in his mom's eyes when she stepped into the living room.

"So, do you have much homework this weekend?" she asked as she came up behind the couch. She'd just gotten back from work and was still wearing the black and green polo shirt the TV station made its employees wear on Fridays. Eli only got a glimpse of it before his focus drifted back onto the gameshow he was watching.

"Yeah, I've got some," he said distantly. To his right, Eric snickered and shook his head.

"Which is his way of saying, 'More than I want to admit,'" he chided from their dad's recliner. He quickly looked back at the tablet in his lap when his mom shot him a dirty look for the comment. It didn't take long for her gaze to shift back to Eli, though.

"So?" she demanded expectantly.

Eli forced himself to tear his eyes away from the TV. "Okay, I've got to write out definitions for about twenty science terms," he grumbled.

"And do his algebra homework," Eric added. Eli quickly glared back at him for bringing that up, but a malicious grin was already smeared across his brother's thin lips.

"Hey, you're the one that was griping about it earlier," he pointed out.

Eli was still glaring at his older brother and wishing the guy wasn't so much bigger than he was so he could smack him in the face when he slowly choked out a response to his mom. "And, yeah, there's that, too," he conceded as he turned to look back at her. His mom still didn't seem to be too impressed with the confession, though.

"Eli, do you remember what we talked about before school yesterday?"

"Well, yeah. But, come on, it's Friday night. Can't I at least chill out for a little bit?" he said. He knew he was pleading his case with his eyes as much as his voice, but, as always, it didn't seem to have much of an effect.

Instead of arguing back with him, though, his mom took a deep breath and glanced back to the TV. The game show had gone into its final commercial break.

"Has your father called or anything to say when he'll be back from the shop?" she asked bluntly. He worked as a mechanic at a garage across town and usually didn't get back from work until seven or seven-thirty. It was currently a quarter after six.

Eric shook his head. "No, not yet. Why?"

Instead of answering, their mom bit her lip and nodded her head. "Okay, how about this?" she began, clearly directing what she was about to say towards Eli. "If you get at least ten of those vocabulary words done before he gets back, I'll order us a stuffed crust pizza tonight."

The reaction from Eli was swift. "Seriously? A stuffed crust pizza?"

"Seriously," his mom affirmed a second later. She tried to hide it, but the hint of a smile was still tugging at her lips.

Across the living room, Eric let out a scoff that was begging to be noticed.

"Wait a second. He's getting a stuffed crust pizza just for doing *half* of an easy assignment? That's ridiculous! I'm already trying to figure out what to do my research paper on for anatomy and physiology, and no one told *me* I should go ahead and get started on it."

"I'm getting all of us a stuffed crust pizza," their mom corrected him sharply. "But only if Eli does his part. He's been getting better test grades and we need to recognize that, but I want to be sure he's working hard like the rest of us. Because if he does, we might just get more rewards like this later on down the road. Fair enough?"

Eric still looked disgusted by the offer but did his best to ignore it. He knew there wasn't much of a point in arguing back with his mom, anyway.

Back on the couch, Eli couldn't believe this was happening. His mom had never really rewarded him for anything before. Of course, when it came to school, she'd never had much of a reason to either.

"Okay. Sure," he said with an eager smile.

"Good," his mom hummed. For a second, Eli even caught a slight glint of pride gleaming in her eyes, but she quickly nudged her head back at the TV. "Just remember, though, your father could be coming back in the next twenty or thirty minutes, so you might want to make the best use of your time."

Eli followed her gaze back to the TV where the gameshow he'd been watching had just started up again. Aside from the not-so-subtle hint, he could also feel Eric's cold stare drilling into his right temple from out of the corner of his eye. It gave him enough reason to grab the remote and turn off the TV.

He had just gotten off the couch when his cell phone started going off in his room. Eric rolled his eyes and groaned a little.

"Well, so much for that," he grumbled. Turning to look back at their mom, he asked, "I guess that means we're having leftovers, then?"

Eli just gave him a dirty look before heading to his room. Luckily, he was able to get to the phone before it stopped ringing to see whose name was showing up in the caller ID. It was Nolan.

Eli hesitated. He knew he probably shouldn't take the call right now, but, after his conversation with Nolan during lunch, he felt like he needed to. Setting the hesitation aside for a second, Eli grabbed the hand-me-down phone with the cracked screen and answered the call.

"Hey, Nolan," he said. At first, all he could hear was Nolan's breath on the other end of the line. Eli could hear the sound of wind whistling over the phone, too.

"Hey," his friend answered back a little breathlessly.

"Are you out jogging or something?" Eli asked.

"No. Just walking back from Fryer Tuck's. I met up with Sabrina."

Eli's brows furrowed in confusion. "Oh, okay. So, what, you're not going to a game tonight?" he asked, knowing Nolan almost always went to the Rosenburg High School football games on Friday nights.

"No, they're playing out of town this week," he explained hurriedly. "Look, I needed to ask you something."

Eli could already feel his stomach sinking. Somehow the way Nolan said that sounded a little too much like when he told him to head to The Nook earlier that afternoon.

"What is it?" Eli asked.

"You remember how you told me you thought someone was trying to pin all this stuff about the syllabus on you?"

"Yeah."

"I kind of had to fill her in on a few things, but I think Sabrina figured out what's going on there," Nolan announced shakily. The sinking feeling in Eli's stomach bottomed out.

"Oh, for God's sake, Nolan. Tell me you didn't..."

Eli stopped himself short and made sure to shut his bedroom door before saying, "Tell me you didn't tell Sabrina-freakin'-Chambers I was the guy."

The pause at the other end of the line was more than enough of an answer, but Eli still heard what he'd been dreading a second or two later.

"Yeah, sorry, but I kind of did."

Eli's free hand involuntarily clenched into a fist hard enough to make his knuckles turn white and he struggled to hold back the words he really wanted to say right then and there. Luckily, Nolan cut in before they could escape his lips.

"Look, we've found something weird on our tests," Nolan said. "It's kind of hard to explain right now, but we think someone is definitely trying to make it look like Coach Grayson, Principal Espinoza, and even you took something off the syllabus. They're trying to keep anyone from finding out that there's something going on with the tests all over the district."

"And that's why you told her it was me?" Eli growled. "Come on, dude! Sabrina's nuts. Don't you realize how stupid that sounds?"

"It's not stupid," Nolan shot back. "I mean, I almost thought it was at first, too, but now I think Sabrina's onto something." He hesitated before he added, "We think that that USB drive you took out of the office has a lot to do with it."

For a second, Eli's anger faded a little. "The USB drive?"

"Yeah. As soon as you unplugged it, everything went haywire. We think they've got something on there that they don't want anyone to find out about. You don't remember anything about the drive from the other day, do you?"

Eli still felt a bit rattled after Nolan brought up the USB drive, though he wasn't entirely sure why. He shook his head and took a seat on the hardwood floor in front of his bed.

"Not really. Like I said, I didn't even know I had it in my pocket until I got to the gym on Monday."

"But what about when you were in the office? Did you see or notice anything unusual about it then?" Nolan asked. Eli quickly shook his head, though.

"No. It was too dark to really see much. Seriously, man, outside of the thing being plugged into the PA terminal, I don't remember much about it. That sixth-grader might, though."

"Sixth-grader? What sixth-grader?" Nolan asked.

"Conrad. Or, at least, I think that's what his name is. He's the dorky sixth-grader in my PE class I told you about the other day. You know, the guy that found the USB drive in the gym? I'm guessing he probably got a better look at it than I did."

"Alright," Nolan said. "I guess I'll have to ask him about it on Monday, then."

"Seriously?" Eli spat.

"Well, if you don't know anything about the drive, I guess I sort have to, don't I?"

A wry grin played at the edge of Eli's lips. "So, do you even know who Conrad is? Or does he know who you are?"

"No, I don't think so," Nolan answered flatly. "Why?"

"Well, don't you think I would be kind of weird if some eighth-grader just showed up out of nowhere and started asking him about the USB drive? What if he freaks out and tells someone?"

"Oh, yeah. I guess I didn't think about that," Nolan admitted shamefully. "So, do you think you could ask him for me? You said you have PE with him, right?"

A short laugh burst out of Eli's lips. "Yeah, that's

definitely not going to happen."

"Why not?"

"Let's just say that Conrad probably won't want to talk to me that much," Eli said. Even though he was grinning at the remark, he still felt a stab of guilt in the back of his mind.

"Because..."

"Dude, he's a pudgy and short sixth-grader and a complete dork on top of that. Let's just say he's one of my favorite targets when we play dodgeball and stuff."

"Great," Nolan huffed. "I wonder if anyone else I know is friends with him."

"I doubt it," Eli said with a slight cock of his head. "Seriously, though, why's asking him about the drive so important?"

"Because if we can find out more about that drive we might be able to prove that Coach Grayson and Principal Espinoza didn't take something off the syllabus," Nolan explained. "And if we can prove that, then it'd mean you didn't help them take anything off the syllabus either."

A sudden jolt snapped through Eli's mind. "So, you prove that and I'm off the hook?"

"Well, not for messing with the PA system, obviously, but, yeah, you probably wouldn't have to worry about people thinking you were in cahoots with Coach Grayson and Principal Espinoza anymore."

Eli pulled his lips in tight and tapped his fingers against the hardwood floor a few times. "So, you and Sabrina are trying to get to the bottom of this, right? She's not just going to rat me out for the reward money?"

"Nope. She's definitely not going to rat you out, and, yeah, that's the gist of it," Nolan said.

Eli wasn't sure if it was from the anxiety or a sense that he could finally clear his name, but a confident grin slid across his lips.

"Any chance I could get in on that?"

18

The Watermark

After tossing and turning most of the night a single thought pulled Sabrina out of bed early Saturday morning.

What if the undocumented questions follow a pattern?

Ignoring how tired she felt, Sabrina slid her glasses on and staggered over to her desk. She flicked on the lamp and started rummaging through the tests she'd left stacked on top of it overnight, looking for something recent.

Even though she suspected the USB drive probably had something to do with it, Sabrina still went over some of her tests from last year after she got back from Fryer Tuck's last night. She kept hoping she'd come across something that would help her figure out how she was getting the undocumented questions right, but, as expected, she didn't find anything useful outside of a few more undocumented questions.

If anything, it only proved that whatever was happening this year had also been happening during seventh grade, too.

Sabrina let out a fatigued sigh as she pulled her science, English, and history tests out of the stack and set them on the desk in front of her. She took her seat and, after scraping away some crust that had built up in the corners of her eyes, started looking over her science test first.

Since she'd taken it with her to Fryer Tuck's yesterday, Sabrina's eyes quickly settled on Question 9, the test's first undocumented question. She put a finger on it and was just about to keep skimming over her test when she realized she needed to be writing these down.

Biting her lip, Sabrina grabbed one of the spirals she'd used for taking notes in English last year and flipped it over to one of the blank pages near the back. She wrote an underlined heading of, 'Science,' at the top of the page, and then started filling in the undocumented questions she'd found below that, along with the answers she'd put in for them.

Science
9 - C
14 - A
17 - 'shield volcano'
21 - B

Once she'd finished, she moved on to the next test: English. As before, the compulsive test review she'd done yesterday was still fresh on her mind and it didn't take her long to spot the undocumented questions she'd discovered there.

Unlike her science test, though, the English test wasn't a simple mixture of multiple choice and fill in the blank questions. In addition to those, there were also a few questions where she'd had to correctly diagram a sentence.

Considering half of the undocumented questions on this test were over that, Sabrina quickly realized finding a pattern within the test answers might not be possible. But at the same time, she didn't want to give up on the theory either.

Ultimately, she decided to notate it accordingly.

English
2 - D
9 - Sentence Diagram
12 - B
21 - Sentence Diagram

Sabrina's eyes started to light up when she compared the undocumented questions on her English test to her science test. Both tests had a total of four undocumented questions, and, in both cases, undocumented questions appeared on Questions 9 and 21.

She started to wonder if that was the pattern but stopped that train of thought and moved on to her history test before she could get ahead of herself. After all, she'd only gone over two tests so far.

As many times as she'd gone over her history test in the

last week, it didn't take Sabrina long to find the questions about the Intolerable Acts. However, she also jotted down the other two undocumented questions she'd found yesterday during lunch.

History
5 - A
10 - C
17 - C
23 - D
25 - 'The Boston Tea Party'

Sabrina's heart sank as soon as she finished filling in what she'd put for the last answer. Questions 9 and 21 weren't undocumented questions on this test, so, according to her list, that meant the pattern hadn't held up.

Sabrina tapped her pen on top of the spiral a few times in frustration. Between three tests the answers were different, the question numbers were different, and the total number of undocumented questions varied from test-to-test, too.

She tried to see if there was some kind of mathematical correlation, but, as much as she wanted it to happen, the pattern still wasn't there. Everything about the undocumented questions seemed to be completely random.

The reality came crashing down on her. She was no closer to cracking this riddle than she had been last night!

Cursing under her breath, Sabrina tossed her pen down and started to reach around the desk for the switch to her desk lamp. Before she could turn it off, though, she spotted something on her history test she hadn't noticed before.

A series of faint circles were clustered around the center and along the bottom edge of the paper. They were only half an inch across at the most, and just a little bit darker than the rest of the paper, but they were there.

A scowl started to form on Sabrina's lips. She hated having any extra folds or wrinkles in her tests, and finding these smudges just made her morning that much more frustrating. All the same, she pulled the test up off the desk to get a better look.

She could partially see through the circles, so whatever caused the marks had bled through the paper. The faint but squiggly lines of someone's fingerprints were visible on them, too.

Even though her mind was still a little dazed from the restless night, Sabrina quickly remembered that she'd handed the test over to Nolan to look at the other day when they were at Fryer Tuck's. He'd been eating tater tots at the time.

The scowl on Sabrina's lips deepened. These were grease-prints! Thanks to Nolan, her test wasn't nice and clean anymore.

But just as quickly as it had come, her scowl started to diminish when she noticed something else about the smudges. A faint red mark could be seen within one of the thumbprints at the bottom center of the page.

Sabrina pulled her lips in tight and held the piece of paper in front of her lamp. Light shot through the greasy fingerprints like wax paper, but the once indistinct lines inside became clearer. Even though it had nearly faded away, possibly from the grease reacting to the ink, Sabrina was just able to make out a simple logo after straining her eyes a little.

$|N2]^{c}$

"IN2?" Sabrina thought aloud, not sure what to make of it. She almost wondered if the first character could have been a lowercase L, but something about it didn't fit. Sabrina wasn't sure what to make of the closed bracket or the lowercase C on the right either.

With a sudden jolt of curiosity, she grabbed her English test and held the bottom edge of the paper up to the lamp. This time, the watermark was much easier to read. Instead of an IN2 with a lower case C at the end, she could clearly see it was an N and a 2 enclosed in brackets with a small circle above the right bracket.

$[N2]^{\circ}$

Sabrina still didn't understand what it meant, but a quick check of her science and algebra tests revealed the same watermark. Impulsively, she started looking through the rest of the tests she had stacked on her desk. Every one of them carried the same marking, even the seventh grade tests she'd looked at last night.

Setting last year's tests aside, Sabrina slouched into her chair and tried to wrap her mind around this latest discovery. She briefly wondered if the number after the N was some sort of chronological indicator since her history test had been taken during the second six weeks of the school year. However, that idea was quickly pushed aside when she remembered the same marking had been found on her seventh grade tests, and those spanned several different six week periods.

Sabrina pulled her lips in tight. She knew the watermark had to mean something else, but couldn't figure it out. Unfortunately, the shrill call of her mom's voice from the bottom of the stairwell broke her concentration.

"Okay, guys! Saturday breakfast is almost ready. Time to get out of bed!"

Sabrina couldn't help but smile a little. She'd been so absorbed in looking over her tests that she didn't even hear or smell her mom making breakfast downstairs. Now that Sabrina had pulled herself back to reality, though, it was almost impossible for her not to catch the scent of scrambled eggs, sautéing peppers and onions, and sizzling sausage drifting through her partially cracked bedroom door.

It all added up to one thing: her mom was making breakfast burritos again!

Deciding to shelve the watermark situation, Sabrina went ahead and stood up out of her chair. She was about to turn off the lamp on her desk when a thought struck her.

She might not know what the watermarks on her tests were, but there was a chance her mom would. She just hoped her mom wouldn't ask her why she was looking over her tests on a Saturday morning.

After biting her lip, Sabrina grabbed her history test, turned off the lamp, and opened the blinds before heading out the door. She was nearly at the stairs when she looked towards Lance's room and noticed the light streaming in through the crack underneath his door. She obviously wouldn't have to worry about telling him to get up this time.

A thin haze hung over the bottom floor of the house by

the time Sabrina made it downstairs. Looking ahead towards the kitchen and dining room, Sabrina could see her mom busy trying to get everything cooked just right.

"Need any help?" she asked almost instinctively. Her mom was turning over the sausages on the skillet with a set of tongs, and, even though she looked a little surprised at first, quickly nudged her head towards the griddle where the scrambled eggs and sautéed veggies were cooking.

"Turn that off and put the eggs and the peppers in their bowls. They should be ready," her mom commanded hurriedly. A second later, she added, "Didn't expect to see you up already."

Sabrina shrugged and sat her history test down on the island in the middle of the kitchen as she stepped over to the griddle. "Eh, I was already kind of up, anyway," she said as she turned off the griddle and used the spatula to start filling the large bowl her mom had already set out with the scrambled eggs.

Her back was still turned to her mom, so she didn't see the peculiar look she got for that answer. But instead of holding it on Sabrina, her mom's gaze shifted to the test Sabrina had left on the island. Even from where she was standing she could tell it had already been graded.

"Does that have anything to do with it?" she asked, nudging her head towards the test. Sabrina still didn't turn around until after she had finished raking the eggs into the bowl.

"What?" Sabrina asked as she looked back at her mom. She nudged her head towards the test again.

"Oh, yeah. Sort of," Sabrina began a little shakily. She quickly gestured to the bowl of scrambled eggs next to her. "Need me to go ahead and put this on the table?"

"Yeah, that'll be fine," her mom said. An instant later, she clicked off the burner for the skillet and used the tongs to start transferring the sausage links to the plate with the paper towel over it. "So, what's bothering you about the test?"

Sabrina placed the bowl of scrambled eggs next to the tortilla container and the assorted hot sauces on the table and quickly headed back to the griddle to load up the sautéed peppers. On her way, she grabbed the history test and showed it to her mom, pointing out the grease stains on the bottom edge.

"I found this on my test when I was reviewing it last night.

You know, just to see what I failed to study up on."

Her mom looked perplexed, and it wasn't just because of her daughter's devotion to reviewing a test she'd made a 92 on.

"How'd you get these splotches on your test?"

"I think it was when I showed it to Nolan at Fryer Tuck's the other night when we were comparing our grades. But I'm not talking about that. I'm talking about this," she said, pointing directly at the faint watermark. "Do you know what this is? I just noticed it this, um, last night."

Her mom's lips dipped into a bitter frown the second she saw the logo. "Oh. That's to remind everyone that Intuitive Degrees gets paid to make our tests now instead of the teachers," she said bitterly. She looked a little rattled, but quickly nudged her head at the griddle before Sabrina could say anything.

"Why don't you go ahead and get the peppers and the onions, hmm?" she asked as she took the plate full of sausage links to the dining room table.

Sabrina gave her mom a curious look, but eventually sat the test back down on the island and stepped over to the griddle again.

"So, what's Intuitive Degrees?" she asked warily over her shoulder.

When she didn't get an answer right off, she looked back in time to see her mom glancing out of the dining room and into the living room, towards the stairs. Sabrina knew her mom was checking to be sure Lance wasn't coming down the steps before she said anything.

"It's an education consulting firm," she began bluntly, heading back into the kitchen. "Superintendent Richter has been working pretty closely with them ever since he took over. A lot of us think they're the ones that came up with the consolidated testing idea. The sick day streaming service is probably theirs, too."

"So, that's all their stuff?"

"We think so. He's never actually come out and said it, but, considering they're the ones that write and print our tests now, everything seems to point to it. We think they're paying him under the table to use their systems, too."

Sabrina couldn't hide the shocked look on her face. "That's

crazy! Has anyone said anything about it?"

A shrill grunt slipped out of her mom's lips as she wiped the splattered grease off the countertop next to the range with a wet rag. "No one that still works for the district. It's amazing how anyone that tries to point out how messed up all this is winds up getting demoted or replaced with a teacher from a district Richter used to…"

Her mom suddenly trailed off and clenched her eyes shut. She let out a couple of aggravated chuckles and raised her palm to Sabrina as if to shut herself off.

"Anyway, I probably shouldn't be saying much about it. And neither should you," she suggested sternly. "That's just how things are in this district these days, and, all considering, I guess we should just feel lucky that we have jobs right now."

Sabrina swore it sounded like her mom was just repeating something someone else had told her. She was about to say something when her little brother's pleasant voice cut through the silence hanging over the kitchen.

"Good morning!" he announced as he stepped into the dining room. Unlike Sabrina, who was still wearing her pajama bottoms and a nightshirt, he was already dressed in his jeans and Spider-Man T-shirt. "What were you guys talking about?"

"Oh, nothing much. Just school stuff," their mom said with a forced smile as Lance took his seat at the table. "What did you want to drink?"

"I'll have some orange juice, please," Lance said. Their mom quickly stepped over to the refrigerator in response.

"Okay. One OJ, coming up! Sabrina, do you want to get me a glass for his drink? And get you one for your drink, too," she said.

Sabrina did as she was told and stepped over to the cabinet next to the refrigerator to get the glasses. Right when she looked back at her mom to see what she wanted for her drink, she found her mom shooting an unnerving glare at her while the open refrigerator door was keeping her face hidden from Lance.

The look in her eyes sent chills running down Sabrina's spine, and she got the message loud and clear.

Her mom didn't want Lance to know anything about what they had just been talking about, and, for the rest of their breakfast, she complied. As soon as it was over and the dishes were done, though, Sabrina hurried back upstairs and shut her door. A few seconds later she started pulling up online searches for Intuitive Degrees.

19

The Same Enemy

A heavy sense of dread hung over Nolan's mind as he stepped across the street separating the houses from the park they formed a barrier around. Sabrina had suddenly decided they needed to meet up here around three, and, even though she didn't say much over the phone, he already guessed it had something to do with their tests again.

But as much as Nolan hated the idea of reviewing tests on a Saturday afternoon, he really wasn't looking forward to having to explain why Eli had come along with him. After all, Nolan had gone ahead and told him about the meeting without bothering to ask Sabrina first, and he didn't have to guess why. He knew her answer would have been no–and a big NO, at that!

As far as Nolan was concerned, though, this was the only way he could get Eli involved. He just hoped Sabrina wouldn't blow too much of a gasket when she found out.

"Is that her?" Eli asked. Nolan turned to glance back at Eli for a second before he was able to follow his friend's gaze to a covered picnic bench just behind the playground. They were still about fifty yards out, but Sabrina's short figure and long swept-back hair was unmistakable.

"Yep, that's her," he droned. Without giving it a second thought, Nolan stepped off the jogging track they'd been following and made a B-line for the picnic bench. Eli quickly took up step next to him.

"So, you think she'll still be mad at me for the thing I did back in fifth grade?" he asked. "You know, the thing where I snapped off the end of her pen and then put it in her backpack?"

Of course, Nolan easily remembered the week of detention

Eli got for that prank and the way Eli's parents had to buy replacement books for Sabrina after Eli got ink all over her original ones, but tried to humor him anyway.

"Well, that was about two-and-a-half years ago. Who knows, maybe she doesn't remember it."

"Maybe?" Eli echoed nervously.

Nolan pulled his lips in tight and glanced ahead of them. Even though they were only about twenty yards out, Sabrina seemed to be paying more attention to something on her phone than the park around her and hadn't seen them walking up yet.

"Look, just don't bring it up and maybe she won't either," he suggested sternly.

Eli was just about to say something back when Sabrina looked up from her phone and noticed them. Her posture slumped and her face darkened an instant later.

"Okay, what's he doing here?" she growled.

Even though Nolan was worried about how Eli might react, his friend just smirked back at her. "Well, it's nice to see you, too," he chided flatly. Sabrina ignored him, though, and kept her fiery eyes focused on Nolan.

"Hey, you wanted me to ask him about the drive after our meeting last night, didn't you?" he said almost apologetically as he took a seat across from her. Eli started to slide in next to him, but, as soon as he saw the look in Sabrina's eyes, he resigned to stepping off to the side and leaning against one of the brick pillars supporting the roof over the picnic table.

"Yeah, but that didn't mean bring him along," she sneered. "I mean, what, did you not understand that or something?"

Nolan looked embarrassed and briefly glanced back at Eli before pressing on. "No, I knew what you meant, but he's wrapped up in this just as much as we are. If there's something going on at our school, he wants to get to the bottom of it, too."

A baffled look swept over Sabrina's face. "Why? How does any of this even matter to him?"

"Maybe because I don't want to get sent to jail for something I didn't do?" Eli hummed. Based on the sour look contorting Sabrina's lips, Nolan could tell she was about to go off on Eli so he jumped in to try and kill the tension before it got any worse.

"Look, I'm sorry for not checking with you first, but they're trying to make it sound like whoever took the USB drive off the PA system the other day is in cahoots with Principal Espinoza and Coach Grayson," he explained. "If we can prove that they weren't messing with the syllabus, then it'd mean Eli didn't have anything to do with it either."

Sabrina could see Eli nodding in agreement, but she tried to ignore it. "Okay. So he wants to clear his name. That's fine. But for God's sake, let him do that on his own. Do you really think someone like him's actually going to help us figure this out anyway?"

Eli's eyes narrowed and he took a step towards the picnic table. "Hang on. What's that supposed to mean?"

Nolan lifted a hand to keep Eli from stepping any closer and shot a disapproving look at Sabrina. "I do. And, seriously, I wouldn't have told him what we're trying to do if I didn't think he could help us, alright? So, why don't you just give him a chance?"

"Maybe because I know he's not worth it," she snarled as she stared right back into Eli's enraged eyes. "And, come on, how's he going to help us out, Nolan? Does he know something about the USB drive that we don't?"

Both of them suddenly turned their attention at Eli, who seemed to melt back into the brick pillar he'd been leaning against.

"Well, no, not exactly," he admitted shamefully. Feeling compelled to bring it up, he impulsively added, "But I know someone in my PE class that probably does. He found the USB drive after I dropped it in the gym and Superintendent Richter ripped him a new one for turning it back in late or something. Either way, he definitely had it longer than I did, so I was thinking of asking him about it on Monday."

Sabrina tossed her hands up in frustration.

"Great. That way even more people can find out what we're trying to do. While you're at it, why don't you go ahead and see if this guy wants to join us for our next meeting? Maybe he can bring donuts."

"I'm just going to talk to him," Eli argued.

"And Nolan said he was just going to talk to you, too, but here you are!" she sneered.

"Well, how else are we supposed to find out about this drive if we don't ask this guy about it?" Nolan huffed. Sabrina sent a chilled glare back at him.

"Hey, I'm not saying we shouldn't ask him about it, alright? I'm just saying we've got to be careful about this." Looking back at Eli, she added, "Seriously, do you guys talk about lost USB drives in PE all the time or something?"

Eli hesitated and he cast a frantic glance at Nolan for a second. He could tell Nolan was thinking back to their own phone conversation last night where Eli basically told Nolan the same thing Sabrina had just told him.

Slowly, he grumbled, "Well, no. I guess I don't even talk to this guy that much, period."

"Then how were you going to pull this off without him thinking it's weird?" Sabrina demanded. She suddenly pointed at Nolan and said, "I mean, let's say Nolan's this guy in your PE class. What if *he* asks why *you're* asking about it? What are you going to do then?"

Eli and Nolan tried to come up with an answer, but neither could think of anything. Sabrina threw her head back and groaned a second later.

"Seriously, do either of you even know what's on the line here? Whoever's behind all this could really mess up our lives if they find out what we're doing. I mean, they were able to get your history teacher and your principal put on leave for test fraud, and, as far as I know, neither one of them has said a single word against it.

"We're not going up against some schoolyard bully here, guys. We're dealing with someone that means serious business."

"Really? Schoolyard bully?" Nolan echoed with a cocked eyebrow. As soon as he said it, a cynical grin crept across Eli's lips like he suddenly had permission to laugh about it, too.

"Hey, it was the first thing that came to mind," Sabrina grunted. "Either way, we can't take stupid risks like having Eli randomly ask someone in his PE class what they know about the drive–especially if Superintendent Richter's already chewed them out for it."

"You really think that'd make a difference?" Nolan asked. Sabrina adamantly nodded back at him.

"Oh, yeah. If Superintendent Richter put the fear of God into this guy, I'm guessing they'd be more likely to tell someone about something that's even remotely suspicious than someone that didn't get chewed out by him."

Sabrina suddenly turned her attention back at Eli. The look in her eyes was more curious than accusatory this time. "This guy in your PE class… Is he another eighth-grader?"

"What? Conrad?" Eli blurted out before shaking his head. "No. He's a sixth-grader."

Sabrina scoffed and rolled her eyes.

"Fantastic. That probably makes it even worse." She stared at the picnic table in front of her for a few seconds before she asked, "And you said his name was Conrad?"

"Yeah. Why?"

Instead of answering his question, Sabrina followed it up with another.

"Is he a short and kind of pudgy kid with spikey red hair?"

Eli's eyes narrowed and he chuckled lightly in surprise. "Yeah. You know him or something?"

"Or something," she said. "He's in our Sunday school class at church. My little brother's actually really good friends with him, too."

Sabrina suddenly paused and stared out towards the playground for a second. "That kind of makes me wonder if I could ask him about the drive tomorrow," she mused distantly.

Eli couldn't believe what he was hearing. "Wait a second. So, it's okay for you to ask him about it, but not me?"

Sabrina just looked back at him knowingly. "Only because I'm guessing he knows me a lot better than he knows you. Trust me, I wouldn't be doing this if he was just some guy in my Sunday school class."

"But wouldn't that also make it easier for him to get suspicious about it?" Nolan asked. Across from him, Sabrina shrugged.

"Maybe, but maybe not. Like I said, it'll probably work better if I'm the one asking about it instead of some random eighth-grader in his PE class. Unless you're good friends with Conrad, too."

Eli looked a little embarrassed and glanced off to the side.

"Yeah, not exactly," he said shamefully.

"Okay, then," Sabrina said with finality. "I'll ask Conrad about the drive during Sunday school tomorrow."

"Alright," Eli and Nolan mumbled in agreement.

Nolan bit his lip and took note of the backpack sitting on top of the picnic table in front of Sabrina. Bringing Eli with him unannounced had definitely taken them off subject for the last few minutes.

"So, why'd you want to meet out here instead of Fryer Tuck's anyway?" he asked. "I'm guessing it wasn't to figure out who needs to ask this sixth-grader about the USB drive."

"Oh, right," Sabrina said, feeling a slight stab of embarrassment. An instant later, she grabbed her backpack and started unzipping it. "I found something kind of interesting on our tests this morning and thought it might be better to talk about it here instead of with a bunch of other people around."

"You mean you're still looking at tests?" Nolan asked. "I thought we already figured out every test has undocumented questions on them."

"We did, but I found something else this morning when I was looking for patterns on those questions," Sabrina said as she withdrew a small stack of tests from her backpack. After thumbing through them for a bit, she pulled the history test out and handed it to Nolan. "Here. Check out the bottom of the page on this one."

Eli stepped up next to the picnic table and leaned over Nolan's shoulder to get a better look. Nolan felt a guilty twinge when he spotted the greasy fingerprints he'd left on it the other day.

"Yeah. Sorry about that," he said, pointing at the smudges. "I thought I'd wiped my hands off enough, but I guess I didn't."

Sabrina quickly shook her head. "Don't worry about it. If you hadn't done that, I don't think I would have noticed the thing I called you about. Look inside one of the grease marks near the center of the page. Hold it up to the light if you need to. There's actually something else there."

Following her instructions, Nolan turned around and held the test up against the sky, trying to keep the pages still against the light breeze. He squinted his eyes against the brightness, and, eventually, he was able to make out some faint red markings. Kneeling next to him, Eli saw them, too.

"Wait, is something written inside the paper?"

"Sort of," Sabrina said flatly. "It's a watermark. The government prints them on paper money to try and keep them from being counterfeited. Not that I think the school's worried about the tests being counterfeited or anything."

After she'd finished with her explanation, Nolan turned to look back at the symbol on the test again. "So, what's this a watermark of? I think I can make out an N or something, but that's about it."

"The N is part of it, but the rest of it is a number two and then there's a small circle for a degree symbol. It all stands for a company called Intuitive Degrees. The N-2 is their way of abbreviating the word '*In-tu*-itive,'" she explained, making sure to put extra emphasis on the first two syllables as she said it to demonstrate how the logo worked with the word.

Nolan stopped holding the test up against the sky and turned to look back at Sabrina. "They're using N-2 for the word Intuitive?"

"Hey, don't look at me! I'm not the one that came up with it," Sabrina said. "Either way, after I found their watermark on this test, I looked at my other tests and found them there, too, so I decided to ask my mom about it."

"Why'd you ask her?" Eli blurted out.

"Because her mom's a high school chemistry teacher," Nolan explained before Sabrina could. Looking back at her, he asked, "What'd she say about it?"

"Well, she's actually the one that told me what the N-2 symbol stands for. Apparently, Intuitive Degrees is an education consulting firm that does a lot of work with the district. They even write and print out all of our tests. That's why their watermark is on all of them."

"Sort of like a signature," Eli interjected.

"Yeah, sort of like that," Sabrina said with a little bit of annoyance dripping off her voice as Nolan handed the history test back to her.

"Anyway, my mom wasn't able to tell me much else before my little brother showed up and she kind of stopped talking about it, so I decided to try and look into Intuitive Degrees some more after breakfast. It's really kind of freaky. They're a national firm, but even though we live in a digital age they still set up shop in every district they've got a contract with. They're using the old Dayton Elementary School building as their district office here," Sabrina concluded with a slight hitch in her voice.

"Dayton Elementary?" Nolan echoed with raised eyebrows. He knew Sabrina's dad used to teach there before he got arrested.

Sabrina pulled her lips in tight and quickly nodded. "Yeah. Either way, since they at least make all the tests, I kind of get the feeling they're somehow behind the stuff going on with our tests. So, if we really want to figure out what's going on here, I think we're going to have to do two things."

"Yeah? What's that?" Eli asked.

"First, we need to figure out what exactly is on that USB drive. I'm the only one here that seems to know Conrad, and vice-versa, so I think I'm the best person to try and ask him about it during church tomorrow."

"And hope he doesn't get suspicious," Nolan added.

"Yeah," Sabrina agreed flatly. "But while I'm doing that, or around the time I'm doing that, I think I'm going to need you guys to help me with the second thing."

Nolan and Eli exchanged curious glances before turning their attention back to Sabrina. "What's that?" Nolan asked reluctantly.

Sabrina pressed her index finger down on the table next to her tests. "I think we need to find out more about the building Intuitive Degrees is using here."

"And what good would that do us?" Eli spat. He almost expected Sabrina to glare at him for it but she didn't.

"I found out as much as I could online today, but, even though I found out they're using the old Dayton Elementary building for their local office, I couldn't find out much more about that specifically. Even the Street View thing has pictures of the surrounding neighborhoods that are, like, a year old at the most, but the stuff right around the new Intuitive Degrees office hasn't been updated. It's still five or six years old."

"And that's weird to you?" Nolan asked. Sabrina glared back at him.

"Well, yeah! After talking to my mom this morning, it sounds like Intuitive Degrees pretty much runs a lot of the stuff around the district. The fact that the Street View images aren't updated just for the area around their building makes me wonder if they're trying to hide something."

"Like what?" Eli asked skeptically.

Sabrina shook her head. "I don't know, but that's where I was hoping you guys could help me out by getting some eyes on it. Maybe even snap a few pictures of the place with your phones, if you can."

"Oh, for the love of… Are you serious?" Eli snarled.

"Well, I was going to see if Nolan could help me do it when I asked him to meet me here, but since you're here now and since I'll be asking Conrad about the drive tomorrow…"

A nervous laugh sputtered out of Eli's lips. "Oh, that's great!" he sneered. Looking back at Nolan, he added, "And here I thought we were trying to get me out of trouble, not into even more of it."

"You're just going to be going out to some building and getting a few pictures, Eli," Sabrina argued. "If anything, what I'll be doing is going to be a lot riskier than that."

"Yeah, unless someone sees us and starts asking questions," Eli shot back. "And where is this place, anyway?"

Sabrina noticeably hesitated for a second. "You know where the old Action Theater is?"

Eli's eyes went wide. "The Action? That's, like, on the other side of town! How in the world are we supposed to get over there?"

"Well," Nolan began slowly, "I guess we could go to a movie out there."

"We could, but I wouldn't!" Eli scoffed. "Have you ever been to The Action? Their popcorn's always burnt and the place smells. I mean, it literally smells, man! Plus, you know that's on a bad side of town. Our parents would never drop us off there alone."

Nolan glanced back at Sabrina. He was hoping to find some speck of reluctance in her eyes, but it wasn't there. She still wanted them to do this.

"I don't guess there's anything else we could use as an

excuse, is there?"

Sabrina shook her head. "Not really. I kind of looked into it earlier today when I thought you and me might be going out there. The theater's about it."

Nolan still didn't look too thrilled but nodded his head in understanding. He looked back at Eli a second later.

"Got any movies you've been wanting to see?"

20

The Drive

The steady gurgle coming from the coffee machine in the church foyer was starting to grate on Sabrina's nerves. She and Lance had been waiting for their mom to finish digging through her purse for about as long as the coffee machine started brewing another pot and it was nearly halfway through by now.

Sabrina impulsively pulled her phone out to check the time. Even though her eyes were focused on her purse, her mom still noticed.

"Sabrina. Put your phone up while you're in church, please."

"I was just checking the time," she protested. Her mom shot a dirty look back at her before she returned to rifling through her purse.

"Well, first off, doing something like that while you're waiting on someone is extremely rude. Secondly, though, there's no need to check the time. We got here early today, so we don't have to be in a rush for once. Now, please, put up the phone."

"Okay," Sabrina groaned. She tried to ignore the smug look Lance was giving her as she pocketed the phone again. A second or two later, their mom finally retrieved the money she was going to give them for their weekly tithe.

"Okay, remember, this is for the offering. Not donuts," she stressed as she split the money between the two of them, making sure to spend a little more time glaring at Lance. Her ten-year-old son rolled his eyes in response.

"I know, I know. You don't have to tell me twice," he grumbled. He easily remembered how much his mom had gotten onto him for making that mistake last week.

"Good. Anyway, I'll see you two back here at the coffee bar after our services," their mom told them. "And please remember to pray for our schools today. Got it?"

"Got it, Mom," the two murmured before their mom slid her purse over her left shoulder and started walking towards the main sanctuary. She'd barely faded into the crowd before Sabrina batted Lance on the shoulder.

"Come on. Let's get downstairs," she said right as she started heading towards the stairwell at the other end of the foyer. It caught Lance off guard so much he had to hurry to catch up to her.

"Why are you in such a hurry today? Didn't Mom just say we've got plenty of time?"

"We do," Sabrina acknowledged right as they made it to the end of the foyer and stepped through the doorway leading to the stairs. She started jogging down them a second later. "But I still want to get to the youth service as soon as we can."

"Why?"

Sabrina stopped whenever she made it to the bottom of the stairs and looked back at him. Lance swore she looked like she had just swallowed a bug. "Well, you know," Sabrina began uneasily. "I've got a lot of homework to do after this."

"And walking fast is supposed to help? We're still going to be here for, like, an hour-and-a-half," he pointed out. He could tell Sabrina thought it was a lame excuse, too, but she just rolled her eyes and shook her head.

"Just forget it," she grumbled as they made their way to the fellowship hall where the church's youth service was held. They had just passed through the doorway when Sabrina stopped and surveyed the large room in front of her.

As usual, anyone that was already there was either milling around the middle of the room or hanging out at the juice bar while the band tuned up their guitars. A few more were sitting at the circular tables lining the right edge of the room.

That's where Sabrina found Conrad. Like just about any other time that she had seen him before their service, he was sitting alone and doodling on the back of his bulletin. It was just the opportunity Sabrina had been hoping for.

But before she could try and get over there, Lance spotted

his friend and started walking over to him as well. Sabrina decided to try and use that to her advantage.

"Hey, I'm going to get some apple juice," she announced before Lance could get too far ahead of her. "Did you want me to get you anything?"

"Yeah. You think you could get me some orange juice?"

"Sure thing," Sabrina muttered slyly before making her way to the juice bar. Once she'd made their drinks and put the plastic lid on top of them, she stepped over to Lance and Conrad's table. Just as she hoped, Conrad was still doodling on the back of his bulletin.

"Okay, here's your orange juice," she told Lance once she was close enough to sit his drink down in front of him. Trying to sound as nonchalant as she could, she glanced at Conrad and added, "And what are you working on this morning?"

Conrad stopped hunching over his drawing just long enough for Sabrina to get a better look. It definitely wasn't finished yet, but she could tell it was of some kind of older sports car. She swore Conrad was obsessed with them.

"Hey, that's pretty nice," she said, halfway meaning it. "What kind of car is it, though?"

"It's a '73 Pontiac Trans Am," Conrad reported dryly. "It's my favorite car to race with in Super Soul-Time Speedway."

"That's the racing game that's set in the '70s we play a lot," Lance added with an enthusiastic smile.

"Yeah, I know," Sabrina grunted. "Anyway, that's still a pretty cool looking car. I've been kind of curious, though: do you draw this much in school, too?"

"Sometimes," Conrad said with a shrug right before he got back to working on his car drawing. "Only before class starts or when the teacher's not saying something, though. I've gotten in trouble a few times for that."

"Yeah, you definitely need to pay attention in class," Sabrina said awkwardly before taking a sip out of her apple juice. As usual, it tasted extremely watered down.

"I know," Conrad droned. "But the tests haven't been that hard yet, so I guess I don't feel like it matters that much sometimes."

Lance seemed to perk up a little. "So, middle school's not

really that hard?"

"Well, it's a lot different than elementary school, but I don't think it's that bad. At least, not yet," Conrad said without bothering to take his eyes off the drawing.

"I'm glad to hear that!" Lance exclaimed before nudging his head at Sabrina. "Based on the amount of homework she always seems to have, I figured I wouldn't have much to look forward to."

"Just wait until you get to eighth grade, buster," she warned them with a hint of sarcasm riding on her voice. Trying not to sound too harsh, she quickly added, "But you get used to it. Plus, River View's a magnet school, so maybe we get more homework than Meade does."

"Yeah, maybe," Lance hummed as he returned to absently watching Conrad work on his drawing.

"Speaking of middle school stuff, though," Sabrina began, "I heard it was pretty wild at Meade last week."

"What do you mean?" Conrad asked, still not looking up from his drawing.

"I've got a friend that goes there. He said someone pulled a prank on the superintendent during an assembly last week and that everyone kind of went nuts about it."

"He?" Lance chimed in with a raised eyebrow. "What friend is that?"

"Nolan," Sabrina answered bluntly.

Lance smirked and leaned in closer to Conrad. "She means her boyfriend," he whispered, making sure to say it loud enough for his sister to hear. He nearly burst out laughing when he saw the embarrassed look in her eyes.

"Um, yeah, Nolan's not my boyfriend," Sabrina snapped, realizing it sounded more defensive than she would have liked. She could feel her face starting to warm up when she saw the sly grin snaking across Lance's lips.

"Okay. Sure he isn't, Sabrina," he snickered, casting a knowing look back at Conrad.

"Anyway," Sabrina began firmly, "Nolan told me about it the other day. He said someone pulled a prank on Superintendent Richter and stole a USB drive out of the office, or something like that. He said your principal made a really big deal about it, too."

Conrad shook his head. "Actually, I don't think Principal Espinoza made that big of a deal out of it. He just thought it was some prank. Superintendent Richter definitely didn't, though. That guy was mad as all-get-out."

Lance shot him a perplexed look. "How do you know all that?"

A sheepish look fell over Conrad's face and he dipped his eyes back down to the drawing. "You know how Sabrina was saying that someone took a USB drive out of the office?"

"Yeah."

"Well, I'm the one that found it after they dropped it in the gym. When I took it back to the office, Superintendent Richter was still there and he was giving Principal Espinoza all sorts of grief about it, too."

"Just because someone took a USB drive out of the office?" Lance thought aloud.

"And messed up his speech," Conrad pointed out. Lowering his voice to a whisper, he added, "Whoever did it played the big butts song over the PA system."

Lance looked even more confused. "The what?"

Sabrina quickly jumped in before Conrad could elaborate. "Honestly, I don't think that matters so much. What does matter is that Nolan heard someone say the USB drive had a link to the syllabus on it. Apparently, someone took something off it and that's why Superintendent Richter thinks your principal and the eighth grade history teacher were messing with the tests," she explained after taking another sip of her apple juice.

When she noticed the curious looks in both Lance's and Conrad's eyes, she quickly added, "So, you know, that's probably why Superintendent Richter was going so ballistic about it. That and the prank."

A nervous twinge started to build in the back of Sabrina's mind. Even though Lance seemed satisfied with her explanation, Conrad looked more perplexed by it and she could tell it wasn't because he didn't understand what she was talking about either.

"Who'd he hear that from?" Conrad asked flatly, making Sabrina's mind race a little faster. She could feel both of the boys' eyes on her now, waiting for an answer.

"His assistant principal or something, I think. Why?"

Conrad let out a confused hum and shook his head. "Eh, it just doesn't match up with what Superintendent Richter said the other day when I was in the office. I think *he* told Principal Espinoza that the USB drive was supposed to cut down on cellular interference on the PA system."

Lance's face scrunched in a little. "How's a USB drive supposed to do that?"

"Beats me," Conrad said with a shrug. "It was plugged into the PA system, though, so I guess that kind of makes sense. Considering what was on that drive and all."

Sabrina cut her next sip of apple juice short. "What do you mean?" she pried, suddenly not caring about playing it safe anymore. "You actually saw what was on that drive?"

Conrad's face started to turn red and his eyes dipped back down to the unfinished car drawing again. Unfortunately, it wasn't as good of an escape route as he'd hoped and he still sensed Sabrina's eyes burrowing into the top of his head.

After taking a deep breath, Conrad looked up at Lance first and then back at Sabrina. "Look," he began in a hushed voice, "can you guys keep a secret?"

Lance and Sabrina exchanged confused glances before they both nodded. Conrad still seemed hesitant to say anything, though.

"Alright. I kind of tried to find out if the drive belonged to anyone I knew before I took it to the office. I didn't see anyone's initials on it, so I plugged it into one of the computers in the library first."

"Yeah?" Sabrina said, her voice urging him on.

"It was full of audio files," Conrad said shakily.

"Not a syllabus?" Sabrina cut in. Conrad shook his head.

"No, all I saw on there was audio files."

Lance's lips pulled back a little. "What, like, with music or something?"

"No, not that either. And that's what was so weird about it," Conrad said. "Every one of the files I tried to listen to had fifty minutes of nothing on them. There wasn't any sound at all! I mean, maybe it really is used to cut down on interference or something, but I couldn't figure it out."

"Was the sound on the computer turned up enough?"

Sabrina asked. Conrad nodded back at her.

"Yeah. I checked that, too. Still, there were about thirty files on that drive and none of them played any sound. Or, at least, I'm guessing they didn't. I only tried to listen to a few of them.

"Either way, Superintendent Richter was so mad about someone taking the drive when I was in the office last week that I kind of decided not to say anything about it. But maybe that's it, you know? Maybe those audio files are there to block out cell signals or whatever."

Sabrina took another sip out of her apple juice. Even though part of her wanted to accept that theory, something about it still didn't sound right.

"And you're sure that's what you heard?" she asked. "About the drive being used to stop cellular interference?"

Conrad quickly nodded. "Oh, yeah. Positive. It was after Principal Espinoza asked Superintendent Richter about it. I swear, it was almost like Superintendent Richter and the other guy he was with were the only ones that even knew the USB drive was there, too."

"Hang on. There was another guy there?" Sabrina blurted out.

Conrad nodded again. "Yeah. I'm not sure who it was, though. I think he was some computer guy from Central Office or something. He didn't say much, but I think his name was Trey or Troy or something like that. I'm pretty sure it started with a T, anyway. He had long black hair, too."

"Long black hair," Sabrina echoed distantly, trying to think if she'd ever seen a guy around her school that looked like that. No one was coming to mind, though.

"In any case, the whole thing was pretty weird," Conrad continued. "I'm just glad they don't think I'm the guy that did it anymore."

A shrill snort blasted out of Lance's nose. "Wait a second. So, you took it back to the office and they thought you did it?"

Conrad tossed his head to the side a little. "Yeah. I guess because I waited until after my orthodontist appointment on Monday to turn it in. They figured out I wasn't the prankster pretty quick, though."

"Well, if I see any USB drives lying on the floor when I'm

in middle school next year, I guess I'll know better than to pick it up and take it back to the office," Lance announced in a tone that almost made Sabrina roll her eyes. Next to him, Conrad shrugged and tried to return to his drawing.

"Yeah, that's probably a good idea. Or at least not the ones with the red logos on them. That's the one I found the other day."

Sabrina suddenly stopped trying to scour her mind for anyone she'd seen that fit the other guy's description and turned her attention back to Conrad. "Yeah? What'd it look like? Do you remember that?"

She felt a pulse of anxiety as soon as the words left her mouth, realizing she might have sounded too curious. Thankfully, Lance took some of the edge off it for her.

"Why? Did you find a drive out in the street or something?"

Sabrina felt her cheeks constrict and hoped Lance didn't notice the panicked look in her eyes. "No. I'm just curious is all," she said as flatly as she could. Lance still didn't look too convinced, though.

"Jeez, you can be so weird sometimes," he groaned before looking back at Conrad. Sabrina followed his gaze, hoping she wouldn't find the same puzzled look plastered across Conrad's face. Unfortunately, she couldn't tell. Conrad's head remained down as he drew on the bulletin. This time, though, she realized he wasn't continuing his work on the car drawing.

A second later, he stopped drawing and handed the insert about the fall retreat up to her. "The logo sort of looked like this," he reported.

After taking a second to look back at Conrad, Sabrina turned her attention to the slip of paper he'd given her. She could have sworn everything going on in the assembly hall stopped cold an instant later.

Conrad had drawn an N and a 2 inside of a pair of brackets. The degree symbol was missing, but, otherwise, the logo was unmistakable.

The USB drive belonged to Intuitive Degrees.

21

Behind The Action

As far as movies go, Nolan didn't really care to see Backwoods Zombie Killers 2. Eli had dragged him into seeing the first one a few years ago and, even though Eli thought it was awesome, Nolan didn't think too much of it. The special effects were bad, the acting was somehow worse, and the story didn't even make much sense.

He seriously doubted the second one would be much better.

Still, it was the only movie showing at the Action Theater that Eli had any interest in, so Nolan didn't have much of a choice. All the same, they weren't exactly trying to beat the crowd when Nolan had his dad drop them off thirty minutes early.

Unfortunately, Eli talked him into stopping at the theater's arcade first. He'd made a good point about doing it to convince Nolan's dad that they actually had gone into the theater and not stepped right back out again after buying their tickets, but, after Nolan checked his phone and noticed they'd spent ten minutes in there already, he was starting to get the idea Eli had other reasons for going to the arcade first.

"Hey, wrap it up, okay?" he told Eli. "My dad's probably out of the area by now, so we'd better head over to the Intuitive Degrees building while we still can."

Eli rolled his eyes and kept using the plastic gun wired to the gaming station to blow apart a few more robots that were coming at him. "Can't we do that after the movie?"

Nolan shook his head. "No, because that's when my dad's going to be picking us up, remember? He looked up how long this movie's going to last and said he'd be back around then. We have to do this now."

Eli just shook his head as he continued to mess with the game. "Then why don't you go check it out and meet me back here?"

"Because we told Sabrina that *we* would do it," Nolan insisted, too afraid to admit he didn't want to walk through a rough neighborhood by himself. "I mean, did you want to help out or not?"

"I do, but I just don't see how going over to this old school's going to help. We don't even know what we're looking for."

"Well, maybe we'll see something when we get there."

Eli glanced over his shoulder and glared at Nolan. "Like wh —"

Before he could finish his sentence, a swarm of robots suddenly materialized after the game hung up and were already in the process of blasting away at Eli's character. His health dropped down to 32% on the heads up display in no time at all.

Cursing under his breath, Eli tried to return fire as best as he could but it was too late. Within seconds an explosion rattled over the busted subwoofer and the screen turned red. An instant later, the word, 'CONTINUE?' appeared along with a countdown from 20.

"Piece of crap game," Eli snarled before tossing the plastic gun back on the console. Nolan was less than sympathetic.

"So, you want to go ahead and check out the office building real quick?" he suggested with a jerk of his thumb.

"Yeah, yeah. Let's go," Eli groaned before taking up step behind Nolan as they exited the arcade and passed into the lobby. They were stepping out of the theater and into the bright midday sun a few seconds later.

"I still don't see what the point is, though," Eli griped. "Even if you do get some pictures of this place, how's that going to help us?"

"You never know. It might. I guess we won't know for sure until we meet up with Sabrina after the movie."

"You really think she found out anything about the drive this morning?"

Nolan shrugged and habitually checked his phone for another text message. Nothing was waiting for him, though.

"I'm guessing so. She hasn't texted me about anything else, but I don't think she would have wanted to meet up in the park again if she hadn't."

"I just hope she didn't blab that I was the guy that pulled the prank last Monday," Eli grumbled as they rounded the corner of the theater. Nolan shot a frustrated look back at him.

"I seriously doubt Sabrina did anything like that, man."

"And you're sure of this, because…"

Nolan shook his head and glanced ahead. He was already zeroing in on the sidewalk leading into the residential area behind the theater.

"I don't know. I'm just sure. That's all," he said. A second later he pointed at the sidewalk ahead of them. "Anyway, there's the first street we'll be heading down."

"The first street?" Eli sneered. "How far off is this place, anyway?"

"Not that far. I looked it up before my dad drove us over here," Nolan said. "All we have to do is follow this sidewalk over to the next block, then take a right at the T-intersection there. The Intuitive Degrees building should be halfway down that street and on the left. With any luck, we can get over there, get some pictures, and get back to the theater before the previews start."

"If we don't get mugged on the way," Eli quipped as they crossed the street and started walking into the residential neighborhood.

Nolan wanted to disagree with his friend, but a hesitant, "Yeah," still slipped out of his lips. This had never been known as a great part of town, and things had only gotten worse after Dayton Elementary got shut down a few years ago in the wake of the cash for grades scandal.

He just hoped going through this neighborhood in the middle of the day would protect them enough.

The two walked most of the way down the first block in silence until the sharp barking from a dog across the street made them jump with a start. Neither seemed to relax until they realized the dog wasn't going to burst through the dilapidated fence it was being held behind.

"So, why do you think this N-2 place set up shop out

here?" Eli asked randomly, trying to settle his nerves a little. Nolan shrugged as they neared the T-intersection.

"I don't know. I guess they figured it would be easier to use an old school building than to build a new office or something."

Nolan suddenly took note of some of the houses around them. A lot of the windows had iron bars welded over them and heavy grates in front of the doors instead of the glass storm doors he was used to in his neighborhood.

"Or, as much as Sabrina thinks they're up to something, maybe this area gives them an excuse to beef up their security without getting a lot of attention for it."

"You really think they'd go through all that trouble, though? I mean, all they do is make our tests," Eli said just as they rounded the corner and started heading right. He was a bit surprised when he looked back and found a knowing grin sliding across Nolan's lips.

"Actually, it looks like they do a lot more than just that," he said.

A bewildered, "What?" had barely escaped Eli's lips before he looked ahead of them and spotted the large, blockish building halfway down the street and to the left. The campus was enclosed by a ten-foot cinderblock wall and white security cameras dotted the corners. The only break in it was a sliding, steel-barred gate that was nearly flush with the wall and topped with spikes.

Except for a couple of satellite dishes on the roof of the building, it was impossible to see much else from the street.

"You really think that's the place?" Eli scoffed. "It looks more like a prison."

Nolan cocked his eyebrows and started to pull his phone out of his pocket. "Yeah, I'm sure. It's definitely where Dayton Elementary was when I looked online," he said as he brought up the camera app on his phone. Even though he figured they were far enough away from the facility's security cameras to be noticed, he still stepped behind a van parked on the curb before taking a picture.

"Well, I guess there's no point in going any further, then," Eli mused lightheartedly as soon as he heard the shutter clicking noise come from Nolan's phone. He was already jerking his thumb behind him when he added, "You ready to head back to the theater?"

Nolan just shook his head and took another picture or two from behind the van. "No, not yet. I think we should still walk to the other side of the building in case we see anything over there."

"Why?" Eli demanded. Whisking a hand towards the building, he added, "There's a massive wall in the way, man. It's not like we *can* see anything else."

Nolan only shrugged in response. "Doesn't matter. We still need to be sure. Come on, we've still got about ten minutes before the movie starts, anyway," he said right before he stepped across the street. Eli cursed under his breath but still followed Nolan.

"You know, I'm starting to wish I would have worn my baseball cap now," Eli grumbled as he took up step next to him.

"Why? Because of the cameras?"

"Well, yeah," Eli snipped. "It'll be my luck that they'll have my face plastered all over the news sites by the end of the day. And it won't be like with all those stupid flyers they've got at school either. This time I won't be lucky enough to be wearing my hoodie."

Nolan couldn't help but scoff out lout at that.

"Dude, don't worry about it! We'll just walk by the wall up here, maybe glance inside the gate as we go by, and move on. I'm sure people walk by here all the time. No one's going to think twice about it."

"They'd better not," Eli snorted.

"They won't," Nolan assured him.

As they got closer to the walled-in campus, though, he noticed Eli was doing his best to keep his head dipped down a little. In the back of his mind, Nolan wondered if it wasn't such a bad idea to avoid getting ID'ed by the security cameras.

Before long, they were closing in on the steel gate and Nolan made one last check of their surroundings before they passed by. The sidewalk ahead of them was open, and no one seemed to be hanging around outside their houses across the street.

They were clear.

Nolan tilted his head a little to the left once he got to the gate to get a better look inside. He wasn't surprised when he found a parking lot on the other side of the gate, but seeing about ten cars and an unmarked delivery van parked inside did catch him a little off guard.

"What in the world are they doing up here on a Sunday?" Nolan thought aloud.

"Maybe they're watching a football game and grilling some BBQ," Eli joked.

A faint grin crossed Nolan's lips. "Good idea, but I doubt it. They're probably just printing tests for tomorrow or something. It's still kind of weird that they'd be doing it today, though."

"Unless there's just that many to print out."

"Yeah, but it still seems like kind of a stretch," Nolan hummed. He managed to get one last peek inside the gate before everything got hidden behind the wall again. Outside of the cars in the parking lot, the rest of the building still looked like the elementary school it used to be.

Biting his lip, Nolan turned his attention back to the area ahead of them. The sidewalk was still clear, but his eyes quickly fell onto an older pickup truck with faded red paint parked on the other side of the street. Even though he'd seen it when they first got onto this block earlier, he hadn't noticed the darkened profile of someone sitting inside until a plume of cigarette smoke wisped out the open window. His gut sank when he realized he could see the driver's face in the side mirror.

"Keep walking," Nolan whispered tersely under his breath. Even though he didn't glance back at Eli, he caught the panicked look on his friend's face out of the corner of his eye.

"Why? What's up?"

Nolan gave a subtle nod ahead of them and to the right. "There's someone in that red pickup over there," he whispered. "I think they're watching us."

"Crap!" Eli hissed. "I told you we should have gone back to the theater. You think we should go back now?"

"No, just keep walking," Nolan insisted. "Going back now would look weird. Maybe we can make a full lap around the building or cut through the neighborhood on the other side."

Eli glared back at Nolan. "Oh, that's just great! Then we'll have even more chances of getting mugged or something."

"Just shut up and keep walking," Nolan growled. He was thankful when Eli didn't argue back.

As they kept walking down the sidewalk, Nolan could just about feel the pickup driver's eyes pressing down on him like someone was poking two fingers against his temple. He was tempted to look back and he could already feel his neck muscles constricting, urging him to do so.

Nolan only lasted a second or two more before he glanced towards the pickup. It was parked under a couple of trees, so it was hard to see the occupant very well in the shade, but Nolan could tell it was a bigger guy with a pudgy face wearing a baseball cap and wrap-around sunglasses. He'd seen that getup on someone else before and a sharp chill ran down his neck an instant later.

The guy in the pickup looked just like Coach Grayson did during football practices last year.

"Are they still watching us?" Eli asked as soon as Nolan's eyes darted back to the sidewalk in front of them. Unlike Nolan, he hadn't dared to look up.

"Yeah, I think so," Nolan said, unable to hide the shiver in his voice. Every bit of him wanted to believe that was Coach Grayson, but he wasn't positive. He needed to take one more look just to be sure.

An instant later, Nolan glanced up and looked to the right and slightly behind him again. This time, he knew it was Coach Grayson as soon as he locked eyes with the pickup driver. Unfortunately, he could tell Coach Grayson recognized them too, and the look on his face made Nolan's stomach turn over.

He didn't like being seen here any more than Nolan did.

Nolan jumped with a start when a strained grinding filled the air before it turned into a low, steady grumble as the pickup's diesel engine lurched to life. The second Nolan heard the gear shifter getting shoved into Drive with a noticeable clack, he knew Coach Grayson was coming after them.

Nolan's legs tensed up and he was just about to tell Eli to make a break for it when the pickup's back tires made a shrill screeching sound and the pickup sped past them, roaring down the rest of the block.

"What the freakin' hell was that about?" Eli demanded. Nolan's heart was pounding hard enough that he barely had time to catch his breath.

"Didn't you see who that was?" he asked, turning to look back at Eli. His friend was just about to answer when they heard the tires squealing further down the block and looked up to the see the pickup careening around the corner on the left before disappearing behind a house.

Eli shook his head and looked back at Nolan. "No. Who was it?"

"I think that was Coach Grayson."

Eli shot a bewildered look back at Nolan, who was already nervously clutching the bright yellow cast around his left hand.

"Coach Grayson? Here? What in the world would he even be doing here?"

Even though he was clearly rattled, Nolan didn't look like he was about to second-guess himself. "Yeah. Look, I know it sounds crazy, but I'm sure it was him." He paused for a second before he added in an anxious voice, "I think he recognized us, too, man."

"Oh, for God's sake! Are you freakin' serious?" Eli snarled, glaring back at Nolan. His friend seemed to shrivel up in front of him but still nodded.

"Yeah. Or, I don't know, maybe he didn't. But I kind of get the feeling that he didn't like how I recognized him either. Maybe if we keep our mouths shut, he'll do the same."

"Yeah, because Coach Grayson's totally someone we can trust," Eli spat. "Come on, Nolan! That guy is going to rat us out the first chance he gets."

"Then why'd he leave like that?"

Eli's glare intensified. "I don't know! Probably to go tell the police or something."

"Instead of just calling them?" Nolan argued. He could tell Eli wanted to say something back, but all he managed was a frustrated groan.

"Look, I don't know, alright? I just don't want to be here when he gets back and I definitely don't want to keep walking around this stupid place. You think we can just say we're good here and head back to the theater?"

Nolan looked back along the wall. He got the feeling Sabrina would have wanted them to see more of the campus, but, at the same time, he had to agree with Eli. The wall made it almost impossible for them to see much else and if they stayed there much longer they were just pushing their luck, especially now.

"Alright. Yeah, let's go," Nolan conceded.

Eli didn't need any more of an invitation and started heading back the way they came. "Well, at least you're not completely nuts. I just hope we can get back in time."

Scowling a little, Nolan pulled his phone out and checked the time. "Don't worry. We've still got five minutes, and I'm sure there'll be plenty of previews and commercials before the movie starts."

Nolan was just pocketing his phone when he realized they were passing by the gate again. He impulsively glanced inside and saw a tall, lanky man with shoulder-length jet black hair standing just outside of the front doors of the building. He was staring them down.

Eli noticed him, too.

"What do you think he's looking at?" he whispered. The guy continued to stare at them, so Eli cocked his head back a little in acknowledgment. The man with the long hair didn't say anything or even gesture back, though.

An instant later, the two had moved passed the steel bars of the gate and the wall blocked out their view of the building and the man again.

"Maybe he heard Coach Grayson peeling out and came to see what's up," Nolan suggested, secretly hoping that's all it was.

"Yeah, maybe," Eli seconded uneasily.

Neither said anything more on their way back to the theater, but they kept glancing over their shoulders to be sure no one was following them. There wasn't a soul in sight the whole way back, though.

In the back of his mind, Nolan hoped he'd settle down once they got into the theater and started watching the movie, but the paranoia still lingered long after they'd taken their seats. He even jumped a little when the theater's stock footage montage of directors yelling, "Action!" started playing ahead of the previews to commemorate the theater's namesake.

"Dude, you okay?" Eli asked nervously.

Nolan took a deep breath and did his best to shrug off the anxiety.

"Yeah, I'm cool," he whispered, trying to hide the tension in his voice the best he could. The screening room barely had anyone in it, but he couldn't shake the feeling that someone was watching them.

It was still there when his dad picked them up nearly two hours later.

22

Hidden In Silence

The area around the playground looked a lot busier than it had yesterday, and, for a second, Sabrina wondered if she should have set up the meeting somewhere else. Unfortunately, Nolan had already texted her about thirty minutes ago saying he and Eli would be heading to the park as soon as his dad dropped them off at Eli's house, so she figured they were probably on their way by now.

She hoped the meeting would happen sooner rather than later, though. Sabrina still needed to get about twenty algebra questions and her reading assignment for English done before the day was through, and, as she closed in on the covered picnic bench they'd be using for their meeting, she caught herself wondering if she should have brought her English book with her. It looked like she was going to be the first one there again.

Sabrina was still mulling over it when a familiar voice snapped her out of her thoughts the second she made it to the picnic bench.

"So, did you find out anything at church this morning?"

Sabrina jerked her head around and found Nolan and Eli sitting against the brick pillars on the back side of the covered picnic area. Somehow she'd walked right past them.

"What? Yeah. Well, sort of," she gasped as she tried to compose herself. "What in the world are you guys doing down there?"

"Just waiting for you to get here," Nolan said flatly, though he still gave Eli a look like there was more to that answer than he was letting on. "So, what'd you find out?"

A nervous sigh trickled out of Sabrina's lips as she took a seat on the picnic bench across from them. "Well, for one, I'm pretty sure Superintendent Richter's lying about pretty much everything now."

"I guess that means you found out what was on the drive, then?" Nolan concluded as he pocketed his phone. Sabrina slowly nodded.

"I did, but I haven't been able to make much sense out of it."

"What do you mean?" Eli blurted out. Sabrina let out another sigh before continuing.

"Basically, Conrad told me the drive had about thirty audio files on it, and that each one of them was fifty minutes long."

Nolan's face scrunched in. "Seriously? Audio files?"

Sabrina slowly nodded back. "Yeah, and it actually gets weirder after that. Conrad said he plugged the drive into a computer in the library to see if he could figure out who it belonged to or whatever, but every time he tried to listen to one of the files he couldn't hear anything. They were completely silent."

"So what's the point of even having them on there?" Eli asked. Looking back at Nolan, he added, "Hell, why are they there at all? I thought the drive was supposed to have a link to the syllabus on it."

Sabrina quickly shook her head. "Maybe that's what they said, but I don't think it's true. They probably just made that up so people would think your history teacher and your principal messed with the syllabus."

"And that I also had something to do with it," Eli reminded her.

"Yeah," Nolan agreed dryly. He turned his gaze back at Sabrina a second later. "Still, if it's not that, I wonder what that USB drive's really there for."

A short scoff blurted out of Sabrina's lips.

"Based on what Conrad told me, your principal asked Superintendent Richter the same thing the other day. Apparently, Superintendent Richter told him they were using the drive to cut down on cellular interference over the PA system."

Eli cocked his eyebrows and he glared back at Sabrina through the tops of his eyes. "Cellular interference? Really?"

"Hey, I don't think that's what it's being used for either, but it still kind of makes sense," Sabrina argued. "I mean, if the drive's got about thirty files on it that are fifty minutes long, that's about how many classes our middle schools have and how long each one of those classes is."

"So?" Eli grunted.

"So, maybe the silent audio files could be used as a dampener or something," Sabrina said with a shrug. "Look, I'm not saying that's what's going on, but *it is* plugged into the PA system so it still makes more sense than saying the drive contained a link to the syllabus. At least at this point."

"Not by much, though," Nolan grumbled.

"And if that's all it is, then why'd they go completely nuts after I unplugged it?" Eli pointed out. "It's like what I heard Conrad say the other day. They were acting like I hacked into the system or something."

A thoughtful grin started to slide across Sabrina's lips. "Actually, I think that has more to do with what was on the outside of the drive than what was on the inside of it," she said, causing Nolan and Eli to exchange bewildered looks.

"You remember how I found the Intuitive Degrees logo on our tests yesterday?" Sabrina asked.

Eli rolled his eyes. "Well, yeah. You only made a pretty big deal about it."

"Yeah, I guess I did," Sabrina admitted somewhat shamefully. "Anyway, Conrad found the same logo engraved on the USB drive the other day. The freakin' thing belongs to them, too!"

As much as she expected them to realize how serious that was, both Nolan and Eli still had vacant looks in their eyes.

"So, what's that got to do with anything?" Nolan asked hesitantly.

"What's that got to— Guys, it means that Intuitive Degrees is making our tests *and* these USB drives!" Sabrina stressed. "That's probably why Superintendent Richter's making such a big deal about all this. Whatever they're really using the drive for has to have something to do with our tests and they don't want anyone to know that."

"Yeah, but how's it actually connected to our tests?" Nolan

pointed out. "Except for the logo, they're just playing a bunch of nothing through the PA system. It's not like anyone would notice if they weren't."

"Maybe so, but it's got to be doing something," Sabrina argued. "I mean, whatever it's doing got interrupted when Eli unplugged the drive for just a few hours the other day and right after that no one at your school knew anything about the Intolerable Acts."

"Unless that was just a coincidence," Nolan suggested. "It's not like they were telling us about the Intolerable Acts over the PA system or anything. And even if they were, no one would have been able to hear it.

"Honestly, I think the whole thing about blocking cellular interference is starting to make more sense."

"Not that that's really saying anything," Eli cut in. "That idea sounds pretty out there, too. Maybe they're using the drive for something else entirely and we just haven't figured it out yet."

Eli smirked and glanced back at Sabrina. "Maybe we never will."

She glared at him for a second before her gaze dipped away. "Yeah, maybe not," Sabrina said sadly before taking off her glasses and massaging the bridge of her nose.

When she put her glasses back on, her focus fell on a woman on the other side of the park's lake trying to get her dog to run through an obstacle course she'd set up. The dog ran through a small tunnel before zig-zagging through a series of poles.

Halfway through, it stopped and looked back at its owner with its ears perked up. Sabrina glanced back at the woman in time to see a shiny object drop from her lips and fall against her chest from the chain it was on. Considering how she never heard anything, Sabrina guessed the woman had been using a dog whistle.

Just then, her eyes glazed over.

"But what if they were playing stuff about the Intolerable Acts over the PA system and we just didn't realize it?"

The statement caught Nolan and Eli off guard.

"What are you talking about?" Nolan asked after glancing at Eli for a second.

A nervous breath trembled through Sabrina's lips before

she nudged her head directly ahead of her. "You guys see that woman with the dog across the lake?"

Nolan and Eli glanced behind them simultaneously. It didn't take them long to find the pair Sabrina was talking about.

"Yeah. What about them?" Nolan asked.

"The woman's training her dog with a dog whistle," Sabrina said. "We could be standing right next to her and never hear a thing, but that doesn't mean the whistle's not making any noise."

Nolan gave Eli a confused look before he turned his attention back to Sabrina. "So, what, the audio files are for dogs now?"

Sabrina quickly shook her head. "No, I'm just saying that maybe it's playing something that's below our range of hearing."

Nolan grimaced in confusion. "But what good would that do?"

"Maybe more than you'd think," Sabrina insisted. She paused unsteadily before she added, "There's still a chance we could be picking it up."

"How, though?" Nolan demanded. He could tell Sabrina already had an idea in mind but didn't want to admit to it. Eventually, though, she managed to spit it out.

"What if they're using subliminal messages on us?"

"Subliminal-what?" Eli blurted out.

"Subliminal messages," Sabrina repeated, still looking a little unsure of herself. "I actually heard about this from one of the Secret Agent Samurai books my little brother, Lance, was telling me about a few months ago. They're sub-audible messages that our minds aren't totally catching through our sense of hearing but we still process them on a subconscious level. That's why we can't exactly hear the audio files when they're playing over the PA system or why Conrad couldn't hear them when he plugged the drive into the computer. Or even why Chelsea didn't get some of her algebra questions right when she didn't get enough sleep! We must be processing the information overnight or something."

"Oh, yeah. Of course," Eli quipped with a roll of his eyes. "Using kids' books to come up with ideas for what's happening is a great plan."

"Hey, I'm serious!" Sabrina shot back. "I mean, I know it sounds crazy, but I think that's what might actually be going on since those files on the drive are, like, a perfect match for how many classes we have and how long they are. They could be sending test answers into our sub-conscious. That's how we just sort of magically knew some of the questions on our tests without having any notes on them, and why Nolan's class didn't know about the Intolerable Acts after you unplugged the drive."

"Yeah, and our science teacher is probably building a portal to another dimension full of... I don't know, unicorns or something," Eli sneered while glaring at Nolan to see if he shared his skepticism.

Much to Sabrina's relief, though, Nolan didn't seem to be ready to jump on the 'Sabrina's crazy' bandwagon yet.

"Well, it would explain a lot," Nolan said hesitantly. "Not just with our tests, but also why Superintendent Richter came up with two different explanations about what the drive's used for."

Sabrina eagerly pointed back at Nolan, though her gaze quickly shifted to Eli. "Yeah, and why he accused your history teacher and your principal of taking something off the syllabus. He's trying to keep people from finding out what's actually going on."

Eli quickly shook his head. "Why would he try to hide something like that, though? If all he's doing is making it easier to take tests, then I'm all for it."

"Yeah, I'm sure you would be," Sabrina griped under her breath. It was still loud enough for Eli and Nolan to hear, though.

"Say, what?" Eli huffed, already starting to sit up from his spot behind the pillar. Nolan jumped up and got between them before anything more could happen.

"Look, maybe Superintendent Richter's just trying to keep it under wraps because he knows it's something that would turn a lot of heads," he pointed out. "Some parents probably wouldn't be too cool with letting someone use subliminal messages on their kids, even if it was just a teaching tool."

"Yeah, an illegal teaching tool," Sabrina snipped.

Eli glared back at Nolan. "So, basically, you guys think he made up all the stuff about people taking things off the syllabus just to keep anyone from finding out he's using these subliminawhatevers on us?"

"Subliminal messages," Sabrina reminded him bluntly. Eli only whisked a hand at her before glancing back at Nolan for an answer. His friend shrugged in response.

"Yeah. Basically," Nolan admitted. He was a bit surprised when Eli only looked more disgusted by the answer.

"So, how's that going to help me clear my name?" he demanded. "I mean, what, am I just supposed to go up to Superintendent Richter and say, 'Hey, we figured out that you're using subliminal messages on us and tried to cover it up, so it looks like I'm off the hook now?'"

Across from him, Nolan tried to come up with an answer but was still stumbling over his words.

"Face it, guys," Eli growled, "telling someone that's what Superintendent Richter's doing isn't going to do jack squat for me–hell, for any of us–because no one's going to believe this crap. And even if it was true, who're you going to tell this to?"

"Well, maybe we could tell one of our teachers. Or maybe Sabrina could tell her mom about it," Nolan suggested optimistically.

Sabrina's head jerked up and she looked back at him with a panicked glint in her eyes. Eli already knew what she was worried about.

"Yeah? And how do we know that the teachers aren't in on this, too?" he said. "Actually, considering what we saw at the N-2 building earlier, I'd say they definitely are."

Sabrina felt an intense sinking feeling in her stomach.

"What do you mean? What did you see?"

Nolan glared at Eli for a second before speaking up. "I'm pretty sure I saw Coach Grayson there," he reported shamefully.

"Your history teacher?"

"Yeah," Nolan conceded through a slow nod. "And I'm pretty sure he recognized us, too. That's sort of why we've been sitting on the ground. You know, in case someone's looking for us."

"And why he keeps checking the news on his phone," Eli added.

"Just to be sure no one's posted anything about it on the local news sites," Nolan explained hesitantly.

"You really think they'd be doing that, though? Looking for you, I mean," Sabrina said with a skeptical tone in her voice. Across from her, Eli scoffed.

"Well, if Coach Grayson isn't, someone at N-2 probably is. They had security cameras all over the place and someone that worked there saw us, too."

Sabrina could hardly believe what she was hearing. "Security cameras? Really?"

"Yeah, and a massive cinderblock wall," Nolan grumbled as he started to fish his phone out of his pocket. He quickly brought up one of the pictures he'd taken of the building and handed the phone over to Sabrina. Her eyes went wide the second she saw it.

"Oh, my gosh! This place looks way different than it did a few years ago."

"Yeah. It looks like a freakin' prison, if you ask me," Eli grunted. "Still, kind of makes you wonder what Coach Grayson was doing there if he didn't know about the subliminal messages thing."

Nolan shot a frustrated look back at Eli. "Hang on, so do you think they're playing subliminal messages over the PA system or not? A few seconds ago you were acting like it was the stupidest thing you'd ever heard."

"And I still do," Eli sneered. "But the fact that you saw Coach Grayson at the N-2 building has to mean that the teachers are tied up with them somehow. And since N-2 apparently owns that stupid USB drive, I just want to be sure we know what we're dealing with before we start telling people about any of this. Does that make enough sense for you?"

Across from them, a nervous grimace crossed Sabrina's lips as she handed the phone back to Nolan. She tried to ignore how he started checking something on it as soon as he sat back against the pillar.

"I don't know. If Nolan just saw him there, that doesn't necessarily mean he knows about any of this," she mused, mostly to herself.

"Actually, it looks like it kind of might now," Nolan cut in morosely.

"Why? What's up?" Eli asked. He felt a chill run down his back when Nolan looked up from the phone.

"Coach Grayson just got arrested."

"Whoa! Are you serious?" Eli blurted out as he sprang to his feet and walked over to look at Nolan's phone. He let out a shrill, "No way!" as soon as he saw a picture of Coach Grayson being led to a squad car in handcuffs.

Across from them, Sabrina only leaned forward from the bench a little as if it would give her a better view of what they were looking at.

"So, what'd he get arrested for?" she asked.

Nolan briefly glanced up at her before his eyes dipped back down to his phone. "Apparently, he got caught trying to break into the server room at Central Office," he said shakily.

"And he said that he was trying to prove he didn't take something off the syllabus? What a freakin' loser!" Eli sneered as he continued to read what he could see over Nolan's shoulder.

Sabrina nodded a little. "Well, I guess that explains what he was doing at the Intuitive Degrees office, then."

Eli shot a perplexed look back at her. "What are you talking about? I thought Central Office and this N-2 building were two different things–like on the other side of town from each other."

"And they are," Sabrina said in a knowing tone. "But it's just like how we've found the Intuitive Degrees logo on our tests and on this drive. It has to mean that Central Office and Superintendent Richter totally works for them."

"So why'd Coach Grayson break into Central Office if we saw him hanging out around the Intuitive Degrees building?" Nolan asked after looking up from his phone. "I mean, he kind of looked like he was about to beat someone up and he took off as soon as he recognized me. Sort of like he didn't want to be seen there."

Sabrina only had to think about it for a few seconds before she came up with an answer.

"Well, I guess that means Coach Grayson just blames Intuitive Degrees for at least part of what happened to him."

"And it probably means that he knows about the subliminal messages, too," Eli cut in. Sabrina quickly shook her head, though.

"Actually, I don't think any of this means he knows about that."

"What?" Eli shrieked.

"Intuitive Degrees writes and prints out the district's tests," Sabrina explained. "The teachers know that much, and, based on what I've heard my mom griping about, there are some teachers out there that aren't too crazy about it either.

"If your history teacher got in trouble for a test he thinks Intuitive Degrees screwed up on, he might have decided to take it up with them instead of Superintendent Richter–especially if he couldn't get ahold of the superintendent or something."

"And breaking into Central Office is somehow easier?" Eli snipped.

"Maybe it was easier than breaking into Intuitive Degrees would have been," Nolan suggested. Looking back at Sabrina, he added, "Who do you think *does* know about the subliminal messages, though? Superintendent Richter?"

"At least him," Sabrina said. "And probably the people working at Intuitive Degrees. Maybe even Central Office."

"And you don't think it's more than that?" Eli asked.

Again, Sabrina shook her head. "No. Not much more, anyway. When Conrad was telling me about what happened in the principal's office the other day, he talked like your principal didn't know about the USB drive either. That's why he asked Superintendent Richter what it was doing there."

"So, what, the only person we can trust for sure right now is a middle school principal that got fired for messing with the syllabus?" Eli grumbled.

Sabrina reluctantly nodded her head. "Pretty much. At least for now."

"Well, that doesn't help much, does it?" Eli snarled.

"What do you mean?" Nolan asked. Eli glared back at him.

"Dude, we can't tell Principal Espinoza about this! It's just like me: everyone thinks he took something off the syllabus. No one's going to believe him if he starts going off about subliminal messages and that kind of crap. Didn't they even say that he faked a letter from Central Office or something?"

"Yeah, they did," Nolan said sullenly. Looking back at Sabrina, he added, "It's like I was telling you the other day; back when they were acting like the Intolerable Acts weren't supposed to be on our test to begin with. He said he got a note from Superintendent Richter saying it was okay to omit those questions since they weren't on the syllabus, but our assistant principal told us a few days later that he faked that letter."

Sabrina glanced down at the cement floor of the picnic area and nodded a little. "Then maybe that's our key to proving this," she announced.

"Wait, what is?" Nolan asked.

"Well, if Superintendent Richter, your principal, and your history teacher all agreed that the Intolerable Acts weren't on the syllabus at one point, maybe they never were. *Maybe* Superintendent Richter only made up the excuse that they were taken off when that cover story didn't work anymore," Sabrina suggested.

"Yeah? So?" Eli said impatiently.

"So," Sabrina began, "if we can get our hands on an eighth grade syllabus, we might be able to cross-reference it with the undocumented questions Nolan and I found on our tests. If we can prove that other undocumented questions aren't on there—"

"Then we can prove that Superintendent Richter lied about the Intolerable Acts ever being taken off it!" Nolan said with a grin. He cocked his head back at Eli and added, "That'd get you off the hook for sure, man."

Eli didn't seem to share their enthusiasm, though.

"Well, that's great," he grunted. "But how are we going to get a syllabus? Just ask a teacher for one and hope they don't wonder why?"

Nolan turned his attention back to Sabrina. He was a bit surprised when he saw a thin smile sliding across her lips.

"Actually," she began confidently, "I think I already know how to do that."

23

No Escape

Eli genuinely didn't want to go to school by the time Monday morning rolled around. He'd barely gotten any sleep, and, on top of that, part of him still wondered if he'd be better off staying at home while Sabrina tried to get the syllabus anyway.

Unfortunately, no matter how many times he tried to talk Nolan and Sabrina out of it, they still wouldn't listen to him. He'd even tried calling Nolan last night to talk to him when he knew Sabrina wouldn't be around, but his friend never called back. All Eli got from him was a single text message saying, 'Chill out.'

Of course, with Coach Grayson's arrest practically blowing up the news and social media last night, Eli didn't see how any of them could chill out right now. If Sabrina got caught, they'd probably get sent to jail just like Coach Grayson had and then it would be almost impossible for him to clear his name.

And if he couldn't do that, Eli didn't know what the point of any of this was.

The thoughts were nearly consuming him as he strode down the empty hallways during first period. And as Eli stepped past one of the bright red flyers posted above a water fountain, he couldn't help but wonder if Nolan and Sabrina would be so gung-ho about this if *their* pictures had been posted all over school for the last week.

They hadn't, obviously, but seeing the flyer made Eli realize how lucky he'd been so far. After all, no one had recognized him as the guy on the flyers. At least, he guessed that was the case since nothing ever seemed to come out of the thing with Jonathan Reed that Nolan told him about last week.

Biting his lip, Eli gripped the door handle of Room 157 and tried to open it as quietly as he could. It still made a noticeable pop when it unlatched, though, and he felt his stomach sink as soon as his entire algebra class stopped taking notes and turned to look back at him. Worst of all, Mrs. Fulton was glaring at him, too.

"Well, Eli, it's so nice of you to finally show up. And only thirty minutes late, too," she announced bitterly from behind the overhead projector. "I'm sure you know what this means?"

"Yes, Mrs. Fulton, and I already got a notice from the office," Eli grumbled as he made his way to his desk, referring to the detention slip that was crumpled up in his pocket. Even with that information, Mrs. Fulton was still glaring at him expectantly after he took his seat.

"Did you at least bring your homework with you?"

Eli only shrugged shamefully in response, causing a frustrated snort to whistle out of Mrs. Fulton's nose.

"Well, you can mark yourself down for a zero on that, then," she huffed. Eli's skin crawled a little when a chorus of hushed snickers rose over the class.

Thankfully, Mrs. Fulton returned to her algebra lesson a few seconds later and continued showing the class how to work whatever equation was on the overhead projector. Eli hardly cared anymore, though. He was just glad he only had about twenty minutes left in this class before he'd be moving on to second period.

Realizing he still needed to look like he was paying attention, Eli went ahead and pulled one of the spiral notebooks out of his backpack. Even though he had four of them, they weren't exactly organized very well. Sometimes his history notes ended up in his algebra spiral, and other times his English notes ended up in his science spiral.

They were all over the place.

Of course, if there was any truth to what Sabrina said yesterday, Eli wondered if it even mattered that much anymore. After all, if he wanted to, he could completely zone out in class and let the subliminal messages do the work for him. He'd probably still get A's and B's on his tests–maybe even more than he already was.

Unfortunately, that was one of the biggest reasons he'd been late this morning. No matter how much he tried to wrap his mind around it, he couldn't figure out if the school really was playing subliminal messages over the PA system.

It had made it nearly impossible to sleep last night, and, even though he knew he should be paying attention to Mrs. Fulton's lecture right now, his eyes still drifted up to the small plastic plate poking out of the ceiling tile directly ahead of him.

The PA speaker cover didn't look any different than all the others he'd seen since elementary school, but he still found himself gazing at it in the hopes that he'd see some subliminal messages billowing out of all the tiny holes in it–if only to prove that it was real.

Just as he expected, though, he couldn't see anything.

Eli frowned a little and casually glanced at the class around him. Everyone had gone back to listening to Mrs. Fulton's lecture after his interruption, but, as attuned as they were, Eli couldn't help but wonder if any of them were doing better on their tests than normal like he was.

It was about the only thing he'd been able to think of last night that might help him figure out if Sabrina was right or not. If someone else he'd known from Batts thought their tests were easier than they were in fifth grade, all this mumbo-jumbo about subliminal messages could actually be true.

But if they thought the tests were about the same, like Eli did, then he was sure it would mean Sabrina was just as nuts as he'd always thought she was.

Unfortunately, there was only one person in his algebra class that had gone to Batts with him, and, from what Eli could remember, Brad Wentworth had generally been a middle-of-the-road kind of student. He hadn't made the honor roll that much, but he still made it every now and then.

Either way, Brad was about the only person Eli could think of to talk to before lunch rolled around, and Eli made sure he was right behind him when they were walking out of algebra class about twenty minutes later.

"Hey, Brad. Where you headed?" Eli asked a little too cheerfully when he stepped up next to him in the crowded hallway. The look Brad gave him was more than enough to let Eli know he wasn't thrilled to see him.

"Latin," Brad answered bluntly. "And I'm not letting you borrow my algebra notes, so don't even ask."

"Hey, don't worry about it. I was going to be using the streaming service to catch up, anyway," Eli explained with a lot less zeal in his voice. It didn't change Brad's mood, though.

"So, what do you want?" he demanded as he stepped around a slower moving student.

"I was just going to ask you something."

"Yeah? Like what?"

"Do you think the tests you've been taking this year, and maybe even last year, are harder or easier than the ones we took back at Batts?"

Brad scoffed and glared at Eli out of the corner of his eye. "Seriously? What sort of messed up question is that?"

"I'm just curious," Eli said. Brad still didn't look convinced, though, and rolled his eyes.

"I don't know," he grumbled. "Maybe they're kind of easier."

Eli frowned a little. "So, you've been getting better grades?"

Brad shrugged and made a right at the first intersection they came to. "I don't know. I think they're about the same. Why?"

"No reason," Eli said while shaking his head. He tried not to sound too disappointed, but he was sure the tone was still there. After all, Brad might have been answering his questions but he wasn't giving Eli much to work with.

There was still one more thing he could ask, though.

"So, do you still study for them that much?"

"Yeah, I still study," Brad grunted with plenty of annoyance dripping off his voice.

"Like, a lot, though?"

Brad stopped and glared back at Eli in the middle of the hallway. "Look, I don't know, alright! I guess I study about as much as I usually do."

"You sure?" Eli choked out. He could almost feel his skin burning from the fiery look in Brad's eyes.

"Yes, I'm sure," he snarled. "So, what, is there anything else you wanted to know, man?"

Eli's inquisitiveness flat-lined. "No, I guess that's it," he sputtered. Brad didn't waste a second to start heading in the other direction.

"Good. Then leave me the freakin' hell alone," he called over his shoulder before disappearing into the crowd.

Eli stood in the middle of the hall for a few seconds before he started threading his way towards his keyboarding class. In the back of his mind, he found himself hoping Sabrina would be able to get the syllabus without getting caught. As sure as she and Nolan were that it would solve all their problems, he was starting to wonder if it would even solve his.

24

The Hard Copy

Mrs. Faridae wasn't exactly one of Sabrina's favorite teachers. It wasn't because she was the worst teacher, or the meanest, or even the most boring. Instead, it was because she refused to believe in technology.

While not using the interactive smart boards wasn't that big of a deal, the thing that drove Sabrina up the wall was that Mrs. Faridae actually made her students handwrite their reports instead of typing them up on the computer. Apparently, this was so she could be sure they weren't cheating by using modern conveniences like spelling and grammar checks.

But as much as that annoyed Sabrina, if there was anything her English teacher had going for her today it was that she didn't believe in looking at the syllabus over the district's intranet site either. She kept a hard copy on her desk, and Sabrina had seen it plenty of times since school started in August.

Unfortunately, knowing it was there and grabbing it without anyone noticing were two very different things, and Sabrina had spent most of her first period Spanish class trying to figure out a way to pull it off. It was turning out to be a lot harder than she expected.

Mrs. Faridae almost never left her desk except to go over notes on the whiteboard, and, when that was going on, no one was allowed to leave their seats–not even to go to the restroom.

But as Sabrina's Spanish class was coming to a close, she realized she might have a small window of opportunity right before her English class started. Whether or not it would even work was a bigger question, though.

Sabrina was still running through the plan in her head

when the usual blast of warm air greeted her as soon as she stepped into Mrs. Faridae's classroom. She swore her English teacher kept her room a lot hotter than anyone else at River View did, but, in spite of that, Mrs. Faridae was still hunkered down behind her desk with a quilt draped over her wiry shoulders.

Doing her best to ignore the heat and the anxiety running through her veins, Sabrina casually walked over to her assigned seat in the second row and sat her backpack down in the chair. She looked out at the classroom around her as she started flipping through the pages in her English textbook.

Six of her classmates were already there, but none of them seemed to be paying much attention to anything beyond their desks. More importantly, none of the seats closest to Mrs. Faridae's desk had been filled yet.

Biting her lip, Sabrina started heading for Mrs. Faridae's desk just as she settled on a sentence or two in her textbook that she could ask her teacher about. They hadn't been assigned any sentence diagramming homework over the weekend, so Sabrina hoped that'd come in handy.

"Um, Mrs. Faridae?" she asked shakily once she was close enough to her teacher's desk. Her English teacher glanced up from the paperback book she'd been reading and a feigned smile formed between her sagging cheeks.

"Yes, Sabrina. What is it?" she asked pleasantly, though Sabrina could tell she hated being pulled away from the romance novel she'd been working on.

"Hey," she began, still sounding uneasy. After making a gesture with the book in her hands, she said, "I, um, had a question about one of the sentences we went over last week. Right before the weekend."

Mrs. Faridae just glared back at her, causing Sabrina to divert her eyes to her teacher's desktop. Her heart raced when she didn't spot the syllabus right off the bat.

"Well, I didn't assign any homework on it and we probably won't be doing anything with those sentence modules until our test next week," Mrs. Faridae grumbled. "Are you sure you need to ask a question about it now?"

"Hmm? Oh, yeah. Actually, I think I do," Sabrina said a little too quickly. She'd been so busy looking over the desk that she'd barely even caught what Mrs. Faridae had asked her. Her teacher was looking at her expectantly, so she tried to buy a little more time.

"I mean, it's one of those things where I'm not sure if it should be one thing or another, you know?" she explained while she continued to broadly glance over Mrs. Faridae's desk. "It's sort of like it..." she trailed off when she spotted a formal looking piece of paper on top of some quizzes, but quickly realized it was only a holiday schedule for the teachers. "Well, it's like this thing could go either way."

"And we went over it in class?" Mrs. Faridae grunted.

"Yeah-yes. Yes, I think so," Sabrina stammered, quickly pulling her eyes back to Mrs. Faridae. She tried to ignore how tingly her face was starting to feel.

Mrs. Faridae's cracked lips dipped into a scowl. "So, didn't you put it in your notes?"

The tingling sensation raging across Sabrina's face intensified and, partly out of evasiveness this time, her gaze shot back down to the desktop right below her. Her eyes went wide when she saw a slip of paper with 'English Pre-AP (8th Grade)' in bold poking out from underneath an open spiral notebook containing Mrs. Faridae's lesson plan.

"Sabrina?" Mrs. Faridae coughed, making Sabrina jump a little. Her eyes were slow to pull away from the suspected syllabus while she tried to remember what they'd been talking about.

"What? Oh, um, no. I guess I didn't put in my notes. No."

A frustrated sigh shuddered out of Mrs. Faridae's lips as she slid a bookmark into her paperback book and sat it on her desk. Sabrina was glad when she didn't sit it down next to the syllabus.

"Alright. Which question is it?" Mrs. Faridae grunted.

Sabrina quickly slid in next to her teacher and sat the textbook down in front of her. She took care to try and place the book's left cover over the syllabus and hoped Mrs. Faridae wouldn't notice how deliberate the act was. With a trembling breath, Sabrina reached down and pointed to one of the sentences on the right.

"This one," she reported bluntly.

Mrs. Faridae tilted her head so she could read the sentence

in question with her trifocals. As she did so, Sabrina started to slip her left hand under the corresponding cover of the book.

"Roger Madison, Jessica Lee, and Henry Smith are celebrating Jessica's birthday in a house on Gregory Avenue, five blocks from the stadium," her teacher read aloud. She continued to stare at the sentence for a moment or two before she turned her attention back to Sabrina. "So what's your question?"

Sabrina smiled a little and tried to quickly read over the sentence she'd pretty much chosen at random. As nervous as she was, she could barely think straight anymore, let alone come up with an actual question.

"So, um… if I was diagramming this, and I was working with the preposition for 'on Gregory Avenue,' would I list 'on' as the preposition and 'Gregory Avenue' as the subject, or is 'Avenue' the subject of that preposition and 'Gregory' is just an adjective?"

Mrs. Faridae glared back at Sabrina like she'd lost her mind. "Why would you think that?" she huffed. "'Gregory Avenue' is a proper noun in this case, so the whole thing would be the subject of the preposition. As good as your grades have been, I figured you'd know that."

Sabrina bit her lip but didn't step away from the desk. Instead, she leaned back over and pointed down at the preposition in question. Once she was sure Mrs. Faridae was focused on where her right finger was, she carefully started trying to find the top of the syllabus under the book's cover with her left hand.

"Yeah, I know, but here's what I was thinking," Sabrina began just as her left hand located Mrs. Faridae's notebook and she started sliding it upwards from there.

"There could be all sorts of different avenues in this place," she continued, tapping her right index finger over the word to keep Mrs. Faridae's eyes on it. "So, if that's the case, I figured 'Gregory' would be like an adjective because it's just describing what avenue these people are having the birthday party at."

Sabrina's left hand slipped over the edge of the notebook, and, before long, it found what she could only guess was the top edge of the syllabus. She had just pinched her fingers around it when Mrs. Faridae shook her head and looked back at Sabrina, locking eyes with her. She was about to say something.

"I mean, isn't that the case here? Since it's a proper name?" Sabrina quickly asked, nudging her head back at the sentence. She nearly let out a sigh of relief when Mrs. Faridae followed her gaze.

"Exactly," her teacher grunted. She sounded aggravated but still had her eyes on the question. Sabrina took the opportunity to get a better grip on the edge of the paper with her index and middle finger while she moved her thumb to the top side of the book cover to make her grip on it look more natural.

"The only way what you're thinking of would have worked is if they'd used something else to describe the avenue. Like 'long' or even an adverb like 'winding,'" Mrs. Faridae explained.

The tardy bell rang, making Sabrina jump a little. Mrs. Faridae was still looking at her expectantly, though.

"Now, does that make sense, Ms. Chambers?"

Sabrina forced a smile and hoped it looked genuine enough. Even though she had a two-fingered grip on the syllabus, most of it was still stuck underneath her teacher's notebook so much it would be almost impossible to slide it out without causing the paper to rip or start pulling Mrs. Faridae's notebook up along with it.

She needed another distraction.

"Yeah, I think that makes sense," Sabrina said, realizing she probably sounded preoccupied. Her thoughts got even more muddled when the two-toned chime played over the PA system to usher in the start of the morning announcements. Ultimately, Sabrina threw out the first thing that popped into her head.

"And the test is next Wednesday, right?" she asked reluctantly, her voice barely rising over Assistant Principal Greenwood's as it mumbled over the PA speaker.

Mrs. Faridae gave Sabrina an impatient look and whisked the quilt she had on her shoulders over the top of the chair as she stood up. "Yes, it's next Wednesday," she huffed as she started moving around Sabrina to head to the whiteboard. "Now, please get back to your seat so we can start class."

Sabrina heard a couple of people in the class snicker at their teacher's remark and her face started to get hot and tingly again.

"Yes, Mrs. Faridae," Sabrina said shamefully. However, once

she was sure that Mrs. Faridae had her back turned to her, she pulled the textbook up off the desk and carefully slid the syllabus out from underneath the notebook.

Praying no one would notice, Sabrina clasped her left hand over the piece of paper to keep it firmly pressed against the book's cover and then cradled it against her chest before she turned to take her seat. She nearly jumped out of her skin when everyone suddenly rose out of their seats, but quickly realized they were just getting ready to say the Pledge of Allegiance along with Assistant Principal Greenwood.

Sabrina would have continued to her desk if it hadn't been for the sharp look in Mrs. Faridae's eyes that told her to stop and say the pledge along with everyone else. As much as she hated it, and as sure as she was that her face was probably bright pink right then, Sabrina stopped at the front of the class and went through the routine like she had every morning since kindergarten. She retreated to her desk as soon as it was over.

"Losing your cool?" someone whispered next to her once she made it back to her desk and carefully sat the textbook and the hidden syllabus down on top of it. She moved her backpack out of the way and took her seat a second later.

"No," Sabrina hissed back blindly before turning to look at Carlitta. "Just making sure I have a few things right before next week's test."

"Well, we'd hate for you not to get the best grade in the class again," Carlitta snipped playfully.

"Whoever's talking better stop!" Mrs. Faridae growled from the whiteboard without looking back. With an annoyed roll of her eyes, Carlitta quickly turned her attention back to the front of the classroom and did as she was told. Sabrina nearly did the same, but hesitated.

While everyone else was busy jotting down the notes off the whiteboard or zoning out to the announcements, Sabrina tilted her textbook up just enough to look at the piece of paper she'd taken off her teacher's desk. A load of anxiety slipped off her shoulders as soon as she saw the word, 'Syllabus,' in bold at the top of the page.

She'd gotten what she needed, but she still wasn't sure what it would get her. Unfortunately, a quick glance at the clock at the front of the classroom reminded her she still had seven hours to go before she could even think about reviewing it.

Of course, she knew the temptation would be there the entire time.

Sabrina pulled her lips in tight as she slid the syllabus into her backpack. She got the feeling the rest of the school day was going to be a pain to get through.

25

Shortcomings

Nolan's nerves were nearly shot by the time he got home from school. Even though Sabrina sent him a text message of, 'Got it!' during lunch, which he guessed was about the syllabus, he hadn't heard from her since.

Granted, he didn't expect to get any more texts during school, but when five-thirty rolled around without an update he started to wonder if she'd been caught. The fact that Eli had gone on and on during lunch about how they'd probably end up in jail if something like that happened hadn't done much to ease his nerves either.

But as much as Nolan tried to brush off Eli's ravings, they were still rattling around in the back of his mind. And after what Coach Grayson did yesterday, it seemed like just about anything was possible now.

Anything.

Biting his lip, Nolan tried to push it all to the back of his mind as he started re-reading the section on metamorphic rocks in his science book again. He'd been working on it for the last twenty minutes, mostly to try and keep his mind off everything else that was going on, but he'd spaced out so much he wasn't even sure how many times he'd started the section over.

It was more than five. He was sure of that.

Nolan had barely made it past the fourth paragraph for the sixth or seventh time when his cell phone started going off. It was Sabrina's ring.

In an instant, Nolan jolted out of his seat and grabbed the cell phone off his bed. He hated how out of breath he sounded when he answered it.

"Hey, there, Sabrina."

"Hey, Nolan," Sabrina said softly. "Are you good to talk right now?"

Even though Nolan knew he'd shut his bedroom door earlier, he still glanced over his shoulder to be sure. "Yeah. Yeah, I'm good. So what'd you find out? Or, I mean, *did* you find anything out?"

"I did," she reported flatly. "And it's just like I thought. None of the undocumented questions I found on my last English test are on the syllabus."

"Really?" Nolan gasped.

"Oh, yeah. Really," Sabrina said. "I even went over the syllabus twice just to be sure. The undocumented questions definitely aren't on there."

A short scoff slipped out of Nolan's lips and he slumped back into his desk chair. "So, I guess that means Eli's off the hook, then."

"Yeah, and my mom, too," Sabrina reminded him. "This proves the teachers probably don't know anything about it either."

"Well, yeah, obviously," Nolan added sheepishly. He hesitated for a second before he managed to choke out, "So, I guess that means you'll be telling your mom about this, right? Or have you already done that?"

A brief silence fell over the phone line before Sabrina said anything.

"Actually, I haven't told her yet."

Nolan sat up in his chair. "Seriously?"

"Hey, I'm just not so sure that I should, alright?" Sabrina argued back.

"Why not, though?" Nolan demanded. "I thought that was the whole reason you were going to try and get a syllabus; so we could tell your mom about this and get her to do something about Superintendent Richter."

"It was," Sabrina conceded reluctantly. "But, you know, after what happened to your history teacher yesterday..."

Nolan slouched back in his chair. "Look, I don't think she'd be doing anything like trying to break into Central Office, Sabrina."

"Yeah, I know, but that's not the point. I'm just saying that we probably need to think this through a little bit more, you know? Before we do anything stupid."

"Well, we've still got to do something!" Nolan insisted. "I mean, now we know Superintendent Richter lied about Coach Grayson and Principal Espinoza taking the Intolerable Acts off the syllabus."

"Yeah, and when those guys told Superintendent Richter the Intolerable Acts weren't on there, he ruined their teaching careers just to keep anyone from finding out about it," Sabrina shot back. "I'm not going to let that happen to my mom, Nolan."

Nolan thought about pushing the argument some more but ended up nodding his head. "Okay. Fair enough. So, do you have any other ideas?"

"Sort of," Sabrina began tepidly. "Basically, I think the only reason Superintendent Richter was able to get away with saying your principal and your history teacher took something off the syllabus is because they couldn't prove that they *didn't* do that. If we're going to do anything about this, we need to have something to back ourselves up with."

"You mean besides the syllabus?"

"Definitely!" Sabrina stressed. "I've been thinking about this pretty much all day. All the syllabus does is show that the undocumented questions–or, I guess, the concepts for them–aren't on there. I don't think it would be enough to get anyone that wasn't in one of our classes to believe us. We need to get something that's more real. More concrete."

Nolan cocked his head to the side a little. "Like what, though?"

"Well, I think figuring out a way to get one of those USB drives would be a good start," Sabrina said so casually it made Nolan wonder if she was joking about it.

"A USB drive? Seriously?"

"Well, yeah!" Sabrina exclaimed. "It has all the subliminal messages on it, doesn't it? All we'd have to do is show it to someone and they'd know what's happening. Then we could use the English syllabus I snagged today as Exhibit B to kind of drive the point home."

Nolan was aghast. "Yeah, well, I think there's going to be

a lot more to it than that, Sabrina."

"What do you mean?"

Nolan couldn't help but shake his head a little. "Well, for one, we'd actually have to get one of those USB drives and I don't know how we'd be able to do that."

"Hey, Eli got one, didn't he?"

"Yeah, and I'm still kind of surprised he was able to pull it off," Nolan shot back. "Then again, he did do it during an assembly when there was, like, no one in the main school building, so I'm sure that helped a lot."

"Well, why don't you talk to him and see if you can get him to tell you how he did it?" Sabrina suggested. "Getting a USB drive like that might be the only way we can prove what Richter's doing."

Nolan closed his eyes and moved his left hand up to reflexively massage his forehead before the cast stopped him from doing it. "I thought you said we needed to make sure we didn't do anything stupid."

"Yeah, I know, but I'm not saying that we're going to be doing this tomorrow or anything," Sabrina assured him. "I'm just trying to come up with ideas right now."

"Including really bad ones? I mean, what if there's another way to get this stuff without taking the USB drive and we just haven't thought of it yet?"

Sabrina's frustrated sigh rasped over the phone line.

"Look, you're welcome to try and think of something else, okay? And I'll try to do the same. But just so we're not wasting any more time, do you think you could just check with Eli about this?"

A sharp grimace formed on Nolan's lips. His mind was arguing with him the entire time, but he still ended up nodding his head. "Okay, I'll ask him," he grumbled.

"Great!" Sabrina beamed triumphantly. "Anyway, I guess I'd better get on my homework. Let me know what you find out, though, okay?"

"Sure. I'll do that," Nolan grunted.

Sabrina hardly seemed to care about his lack of enthusiasm, though, and only let out a hurried, "Okay. See ya," before the line went dead.

Nolan pulled his lips in tight as he set the phone down next to his science book. He already knew Eli wouldn't want to try to take the drive off the PA system again since there were still so many bright red reminders about what happened last week posted all over Meade, but he knew Sabrina wasn't going to let him get around this either.

He had to do it.

Still, Nolan couldn't help grumbling about it under his breath a little as he picked up the phone and started typing in part of Eli's number. He tapped the Call button as soon as his friend's name appeared on the screen.

If anything, Nolan was just glad Eli had texted him right after school asking to call him when he got a chance. It at least gave him an excuse for what he was about to do.

"Hey, Nolan," Eli answered flatly after the third ring.

"Hey. You got a second?" Nolan asked. He swore the uneasiness bearing down on him was dripping off his voice, but Eli didn't seem to notice.

"Yeah, hang on. Let me get back to my room," he grumbled. A second later, Nolan could hear him shuffling out of a creaky chair and walking away from wherever he had been. From the times he'd been over there, Nolan remembered the chairs around the Rezniks' dining room table creaked like that.

"You weren't eating supper or something, were you?" he blurted out, almost hoping it would give him an excuse to put this off until later. Unfortunately, the dismissive tone in Eli's response was all too easy to pick up.

"No, my mom hasn't even started making it yet. I'm just catching up on my first period algebra class with the sick day streaming service. I came in about thirty minutes late this morning."

Nolan grunted in acknowledgment. "Well, that sucks. Is the streaming service working any better than it did last time?"

"I guess," Eli said right as Nolan overheard the soft clack of him shutting his door. "I don't have as much to catch up on today, though, so maybe that helps. Either way, I'm in my room now. I guess you got my text earlier?"

"Yeah. Sorry for not calling back sooner, but I figured you were wanting to know if Sabrina managed to get the syllabus."

"Well, that's not exactly what I texted you for, but, now that you mention it, *did* she get the syllabus?"

"Yeah. She called me just a few minutes ago," Nolan said, sounding a little uneasy. It was mostly because he was already wondering what Eli had actually texted him about, but his tone caused Eli to get nervous, too.

"She didn't get caught, did she?"

"No, no. Everything's fine," Nolan grunted. "She actually compared it to her last English test this afternoon and she didn't find any of those undocumented questions on it either."

"So, that means we've got proof that I didn't take anything off the syllabus now, right?"

"Yeah. Basically," Nolan droned unenthusiastically. Eli noticed.

"Then why doesn't it sound like that's a good thing?"

A heavy sigh slipped out of Nolan's lips before he answered.

"Look, I'm just as glad about this as you are, alright? It's just that Sabrina still doesn't want to tell her mom about it."

"What? Why the hell not?" Eli demanded shortly.

"Well, after what happened to Coach Grayson and Principal Espinoza, she thinks we need to get some more, like, concrete evidence before we tell anyone."

Eli's reaction was swift.

"Concrete evidence? Are you freakin' kidding me? What's she need more evidence for? She found everything she needed on that syllabus, didn't she?"

"Mostly," Nolan conceded. "Either way, she still doesn't think it's enough to prove that they're playing subliminal messages over the PA system."

A derisive scoff shot over the phone line. "Yeah, of course not! So what does The Great and Powerful Sabrina think we should do now?"

Nolan felt his lips suck in tight and his voice got stuck in his throat for a second.

"She thinks we should try and take one of the USB drives off the PA terminal in the office," he reported flatly. "Like actually steal it and show it to someone."

Eli let out a series of bewildered chuckles. "Jeez, dude! This just keeps getting better and better."

"Look, I don't like it either, alright, but I don't think we have any better choice."

Eli scoffed again. "Dude, just about anything sounds better than that! I still don't get why the freakin' syllabus wasn't enough either. I mean, did you get to look at it, too? Did it match up to the undocumented questions you found on your test or whatever she's doing?"

A pang of embarrassment shot through Nolan's gut. "No, I just talked to her over the phone. I never actually saw the syllabus. And it was for her English class, too, so I haven't looked over that test yet to see if I could find any undocumented questions on it either."

Eli let out a frustrated groan before continuing. "Well, did she at least tell you which questions they were so you could look it up yourself?"

The embarrassment swirling around in Nolan's gut intensified. "No. She didn't tell me that either."

"So, how do you know that she even got a syllabus or if it had all the stuff on there that she said it did?" Eli snarled. "Seriously, what if the syllabus thing didn't work out like she was hoping it would? Maybe that's why she doesn't want to tell her mom about it."

"I don't think she's making it up, Eli. She just doesn't want Superintendent Richter to go after her mom like he did with Coach Grayson and Principal Espinoza."

"And so we're just supposed to believe her because of that?"

"Well, I do!" Nolan shot back. He hardly believed his own voice and Eli seemed to pick up on it.

"Oh, yeah? And does that include the stuff she came up with about subliminal messages?" he asked sharply. "*That's* what I was wanting to talk to you about earlier. I didn't say anything about it at lunch since there were too many people around, but I decided to ask Brad Wentworth from Batts if he thought his tests were any easier now than they were in fourth or fifth grade and he thinks they're about the same, man!"

"So?" Nolan grunted, sounding a little distracted. As familiar as the name sounded, part of him was trying to remember who Brad Wentworth even was.

"So, if someone was really playing subliminal messages

over the PA system, don't you think our tests would be, like, a lot easier now?"

"Well, apparently, they're a lot easier for you."

A guilty twinge shot down Nolan's back and he felt the hairs on the back of his neck stand up as soon as he heard Eli's shrill scoff on the other end of the line.

"And, what, that's a bad thing?"

Nolan struggled to think of the right response. Unfortunately, all he could come up with was, "No, it's just..."

"It's just that idiots like me don't deserve good grades, right?" Eli snapped. By now, Nolan could feel his face tingling.

"Look, man, I never said that, alright?"

"Well, it sure as hell sounded like you did," Eli snarled. "And that's the thing. That's what I think Sabrina thinks this is all about, alright? Her dad was one of the teachers that got caught a few years ago, and now that this new guy is making things better she doesn't like it–especially since *people like me* are getting better grades all of a sudden.

"I'm telling you, man. She's gotten in your head and now you're thinking the exact same way."

Nolan took in a deep breath and let it trickle out of his lips before he said anything. "Maybe. But whether it's with you, or me, or Sabrina, or even Brad, you've got to admit something weird's going on with our tests."

"Could be," Eli conceded curtly. "But at the same time, if there is something going on and we're all getting better grades from it, why should we try and stop it, you know? Like, how is this a bad thing?"

The argument cut into Nolan's mind. In a way, he knew this really wasn't such a bad thing and, worst of all, he could see how it might take some of the stress off him with his athletics schedule, too.

But in spite of it all, he reminded himself that their principal was on forced leave, his history teacher was in jail, and his best friend was being hunted down like an Old West outlaw because someone didn't want anyone else to know what was going on.

Deep down, he knew there was definitely something wrong about their tests.

"See, you can't even think of a reason!" Eli sneered. It quickly snapped Nolan back to reality.

"Actually, I can think of several reasons," he said plainly. "But it's not because I've got a problem with you getting better grades."

The short pause that followed told Nolan he'd at least gotten Eli's attention.

"You mean that?"

"Yeah," Nolan said with a nod of his head. "But even if whatever's going on is giving us better grades, someone's still trying to cover it up and they don't care who they're screwing over to do it. That's what we've got to put a stop to, and, like it or not, the best way to do that right now–probably–is to get a USB drive out of the office."

Eli still cursed under his breath but seemed to come around.

"Alright, I guess you've got a point," he said at length.

"So you'll help us?"

"Yeah, I'll help you do it," Eli grumbled. "Just one thing, though."

"What's that?"

"If we do this, I'd better not end up like Coach Grayson."

26

D.I.Y.

A familiar, two-toned chime played over the PA system about a minute into second period. As usual, everyone in Sabrina's English class rose out of their seats and waited for what was coming next.

"Good Tuesday morning, River View Kingfishers," Assistant Principal Greenwood greeted over the PA system with feigned enthusiasm. "Please join me in saying the Pledge of Allegiance."

Placing their right hands over their hearts, the class proceeded with robotically reciting the pledge and staring at the flag. Once it was done, everyone took their seats again and Assistant Principal Greenwood continued with the rest of the morning announcements.

"Today's lunch will be a choice of taco salad with a side of corn, or chicken tenders with a side of tater tots. Also, the cafeteria staff would appreciate it if everyone cleaned up their areas when they're through with their lunches."

"Seriously? They're actually reminding people to clean up after themselves? How old do they think we are?" Carlitta sneered. Sabrina just shrugged in response.

"Well, they wouldn't be saying it if it wasn't a problem. I'm betting it's something the sixth-graders are doing."

"Or some of those bozos on the football team," Carlitta added. "Have you s—"

"Quiet during announcements, please," Mrs. Faridae cut in from behind her desk. Sabrina and Carlitta quickly piped down, and, much to her annoyance, Sabrina started picking up on what their assistant principal was saying again.

"...seventh grade football team will be playing against Hawker Middle School here at five-thirty, and the seventh grade volleyball team will be playing Meade Middle School *at* Meade Middle School at six this afternoon. Everyone is encouraged to come out and support our Kingfishers and Lady Kingfishers at either of these games."

The news made Sabrina cringe a little. If the seventh grade volleyball team was playing tonight, that probably meant the eighth-graders would be playing tomorrow. She could almost bet Chelsea Waters would be asking her if she was going to go to the game again sometime soon. She'd done it so much, Sabrina was starting to wonder if it was going to become a weekly thing.

The announcements continued.

"We'd also like to wish Braxton Davis, Misty Foye, Leroy Little, Emma Perez, and Francesca Thompson a very happy birthday today," Assistant Principal Greenwood droned with a slight hint of cheer in his voice. He paused a little before saying, "And that wraps up today's River View Middle School announcements. Have a good rest of your Tuesday, Kingfishers!"

No sooner had the PA speaker made a noticeable pop from the intercom being turned off than Mrs. Faridae stood up from behind her desk and started threading the straps of her purse over her shoulder.

"Okay, if you'll gather up your things, we'll head to the library and get started on our research projects," she told the class amidst the onslaught of backpack shuffling that was already going on. "As I mentioned yesterday, I want you to get three sources for your paper and two of them *have* to come from a book instead of the anything-goes-internet. Do I make myself clear?"

"Yes, Mrs. Faridae," Sabrina grumbled along with the rest of the class. She rose out of her seat and started filing out of the classroom with everyone else a few seconds later. Carlitta quickly took up step next to her.

"So what are you doing your paper over?" she whispered as soon as they were out in the hallway.

"Athena," Sabrina answered back. "You?"

"King Midas," Carlitta reported. "I'm kind of glad I was able to put my name next to it on the sign-up sheet first. The whole story's about the evils of greed, so I'm hoping it won't be too hard to do a paper on that."

"Yeah, that's probably a good one," Sabrina reflected. "I'm kind of glad I got Athena, too. I've always thought she's a pretty awesome character."

"Is she? I don't know that much about her."

"Oh, yeah," Sabrina hummed. "I mean, she's only the goddess of wisdom, strategy, and the arts, among other things. The Greeks even named Athens after her."

Carlitta rolled her eyes. "Well, thanks for making my King Midas choice seem puny. But speaking of the arts, check this out," she said before reaching into her embroidered satchel. She pulled out a red eraser a second or two later and proudly exhibited it to her. Sabrina only looked at it for a moment before she glared back at Carlitta.

"So, it's an eraser," she droned, hardly impressed. Somehow her response seemed to make Carlitta that much more excited.

"Yeah, I know that's what it looks like, but it's not. Or, it is, but I'm not really using it as an eraser. See?" she said before pinching one end of the eraser and pulling the top quarter away, revealing a USB port underneath.

"Oh, so it's a USB drive," Sabrina observed. "That's pretty neat."

"Yeah, I saw a video for it on Make/Itz the other day–you know, that D.I.Y. crafts app everyone's talking about–and made it over the weekend."

"D.I.Y?" Sabrina echoed.

"Do-It-Yourself. Have you seriously not heard about this app?"

"Oh, right. D.I.Y. Duh," Sabrina said, remembering she'd seen the acronym before but rarely heard it said out loud. Carlitta quickly continued with her story.

"I've been anxious to plug it into one of the school's computers and see what everyone says," she said excitedly. "Hopefully I'll be able to get on one of the computers in the library before someone else does."

"Yeah, it'll be interesting to see what happens" Sabrina cooed. "What are you going to use it for, though? You know Mrs.

Faridae doesn't let us type up our reports."

"Yeah, I know. I was thinking about using it to save some notes and the links I pulled them from on it so I can take it back home and do more research for my online source later."

"You're not just going to print it out?" Sabrina asked. Carlitta quickly shook her head.

"Not if I can help it. Don't want to waste paper, you know?"

"Oh, right. Gotcha," Sabrina said just as their class made it to the library. Ahead of them, Sabrina could see the tall figure of Mrs. Cooper, the school's librarian, standing behind the checkout counter. A cart with about thirty books was sitting just in front of it.

"Okay, we've got about fifty minutes before the next bell rings, so please try and make the most of your time," Mrs. Faridae reminded them as soon as they were all inside. "You'll find the books that Mrs. Cooper was kind enough to pull by the checkout counter. If a book you're needing is being used, try using another book or get your online source printed out until the book's available."

"But what if our book's still not ready before the class is over?" one of Sabrina's classmates asked aloud. Mrs. Faridae sent a chilled look back at her.

"Then I guess you'll have to come back later and work on it on your own time. Remember, this is a college-level class. Now, get to work."

Carlitta snagged Sabrina by the forearm just as everyone started splitting off. "So, I'm going to grab a computer station before they all get taken. You coming?"

Sabrina thought about it for a second before shaking her head. There were about thirty people in her class and she doubted there'd be enough books to go around. "No, I think I'm going to go see what I can get from the books first."

"Okay. Well, I'll see you later, then," Carlitta said before striding off to the nearest computer station with her custom made USB drive in hand. Behind her, Sabrina made her way to the book cart.

She was hoping most of her classmates would be heading for the computer stations like Carlitta had, but there was already a small crowd gathered around the cart. Thankfully, after glancing over the remaining book selections, Sabrina quickly found one on gods and goddesses of ancient Greece. The focus of the book seemed a little broad, but it was thick enough that Sabrina figured she'd at least be able to get a few things out of it.

She would have liked to get another book, but the big yellow sign Mrs. Cooper had taped to the front of the cart saying, 'Please take only <u>ONE</u> book at a time,' was a little hard to ignore.

Snagging her book off the cart, Sabrina walked over to one of the few tables that didn't already have someone sitting at it and sat her backpack down on top as she retrieved her English spiral and a pen. An instant later, she took her seat and turned the book over to the table of contents to look for a chapter on Athena.

"Page 105," Sabrina muttered under her breath right as she started flipping through the pages. She'd made it to her chapter and was just about to start reading when an excited gasp broke her concentration.

"Oh, neat! You made one of those eraser drives, too?" Molly Perkins exclaimed near one of the computer stations. Just about everyone glanced up from what they were doing to see what she was talking about, including their teacher.

"Ms. Perkins!" Mrs. Faridae sneered. Sabrina swore her classmate's eyes actually sank into their sockets when she saw the way their teacher was glaring at her.

"Sorry, Mrs. Faridae. It's just..." she stammered while glancing down at Carlitta for a second. "Sorry. I won't do it again."

"See that you don't," Mrs. Faridae grumbled. When it seemed obvious that Mrs. Faridae was settling back into reading the romance novel she'd brought with her, Sabrina turned her attention back to Carlitta's computer station. Molly was still standing next to her.

"That really is adorable, though, Carlitta," Sabrina heard Molly whisper. "I think I came across a post about making one of those on Make/Itz a few days ago. Was it very hard to do?"

Carlitta shook her head, making her long, black hair sway a little. "No. It was a cinch. All you have to do is take the shell off of a USB drive, then take the actual memory stick out and put it into a hollowed-out eraser. There's plenty of videos about it online, but, just like you, I found the how-to on this one on Make/Itz."

"Sweet! I'll have to look that up later. And you can do it with any USB drive?"

"Yeah, pretty much," Carlitta said. "As long as you can pry the original case open without damaging the memory stick or its port. It's seriously easy to do with an X-Acto knife, though."

"Girls..." Mrs. Faridae growled from across the room. This time, Molly didn't look like she had any interest in lingering around Carlitta anymore.

"Okay. I guess I'll go get me a book. Catch you later, girl!" Molly said cheerfully.

"Yeah, see you later. And thanks!" Carlitta beamed before the two parted ways.

Rolling her eyes at it, Sabrina tried to get back to reading through the chapter on Athena. All the while, she couldn't shake the thought that Carlitta's special USB drive was a lot simpler to make than she thought it would be.

Knowing she could make one on her own wasn't the thing that caught her attention the most, though. Instead, Sabrina almost wondered if they could do the same thing with one of the USB drives in the office.

Of course, she still hadn't figured out how to get the drive, or even when to do it, but, if they did manage to get one, Sabrina wondered if they could sneak it out of school in a hollowed-out eraser like that. It would certainly make it harder to find, especially if they found out the USB drive was missing and started doing an extensive search to find it.

Sabrina tapped the end of her pen on top of her spiral a few times just thinking about it. Getting a USB drive out of the office would be nice, but getting it without anyone noticing would be even better. Unfortunately, Intuitive Degrees' drives were such an important part of what was going on that she didn't know if that was even possible.

Biting her lip to try and push the thoughts to the back of her mind, Sabrina forced herself to get back to reading the chapter on Athena. But no matter how hard she tried, the subject kept spilling into her mind for the rest of the class.

By the time 9:54 rolled around, she'd come to the realization they would need Eli there to show them where the PA terminal was, and, because of that, they'd probably have to take the drive out of Meade's office, too, since other schools could have a different layout. Unfortunately, she was still wrestling with how to steal the drive without anyone noticing.

Something Nolan and/or Conrad said had just started swirling around in the back of Sabrina's mind when a sharp ringing sound snapped her back to reality. Her gut sank as soon as she realized second period was over and she'd only made four bullet points in her notes. She felt even worse knowing they were from the same page in her book.

"Oh, that's great," Sabrina grumbled. It didn't help her mood any when Mrs. Faridae barked out her end-of-the-class overview a second later.

"Now, remember, your papers will need to be four pages long, and that does not include the bibliography page. And unlike your last paper, I'll be counting off a point for every spelling or grammatical error I find, so be sure to proofread at least twice before you turn it in.

"Also, if you've still got any of the library books at your table, please turn them back in to Mrs. Cooper's cart by the checkout counter so the next class can use them."

Suddenly, Mrs. Faridae snickered and turned to look back at the librarian. "Hmph! Mrs.-Cooper's-cart-by-the-checkout-counter. I bet you can't say that three times fast!"

The remark brought a polite smirk from Mrs. Cooper, but everyone else in the library largely ignored it as they got busy putting their things in their backpacks and heading for third period. Once Sabrina returned her book to the not-so-tongue-twisted-cart, she stepped through the library doors and headed on for algebra with a split mind.

While part of her was trying to figure out if she should go to lunch or skip it and do more research in the library, another part was thinking back to what Nolan and Conrad had both told her. Apparently, the administrators at Meade just about lost their minds after they realized Eli had taken the drive off the PA system last week.

But what if they never knew it was gone?

Finding out about Carlitta's eraser drive had given Sabrina another idea. Since they would have to remove the shell on the Intuitive Degrees drive before putting its memory stick into the hollowed-out eraser, they could probably put a blank USB drive in the eraser and swap out the memory sticks at the same time. Then maybe no one would ever know the real one had been taken.

At least, that's what Sabrina hoped would happen as she walked into Mrs. Sidney's algebra class and took her seat, practically running on autopilot. It would definitely be a tricky maneuver since they'd have to dismantle the Intuitive Degrees drive and put it back together inside the office, but Sabrina still felt like patting herself on the back for thinking about it.

Plus, even though convincing Nolan and Eli probably wouldn't be easy, she already had a good argument that wasn't just about ensuring their pictures wouldn't get posted all over school.

"Hey, Sabrina!"

Aside from the obvious, swapping out the drive with a fake would give them some extra time to show the evidence to someone that could actually do something about it *and* Superintendent Richter.

"Um, Sabrina?"

But, more than that, Sabrina hoped replacing the drive with a fake would also—

A soft poking sensation against her shoulder pulled Sabrina out of her thoughts. Slowly, she turned to look at the source and found Chelsea Waters' perplexed eyes staring back at her.

"Hey? Are you here today?"

An involuntary sigh whisked through Sabrina's lips. "Mostly," she grumbled. Unfortunately, it only spurred on Chelsea's concerns.

"Oh, no! Are you having another rough day?" her classmate whimpered. Sabrina was sure she felt her blood curdling over and tried to think of something to get Chelsea off the subject. Only one thing came to mind, though.

"No, I'm fine. So, your next volleyball game's tomorrow night, right?"

Chelsea's face lit up. "Yes, it is! And I'm so excited about it, too. Are you going to come to this one? It's at Meade this time and I think that's the district you live in, right?"

Sabrina's heart skipped a beat. After everything that had been on her mind during second period, she'd completely forgotten where the volleyball game was being played. But after all the distracted research she'd done in the library, the game's venue suddenly meant a lot more to her now.

Gradually, the words Sabrina never thought she'd say seeped out of her mouth.

"You know, I think I might just do that this time."

27

Chain Reactions

Eli had spelled it out very clearly for Nolan yesterday evening. He'd told him everything he did when he pulled the prank last week, about how long it took him to do it, and how he'd avoided getting noticed by almost anyone through the whole process.

But even though every bit of it was just as amazing to Nolan as it was when Eli first told him about it on Friday, one thing still bothered him.

"So, do you remember when you got the idea for the prank?" Nolan asked abruptly. Eli's eyes went wide across the cafeteria table from him and he stopped chewing on the curly fry he'd just popped into his mouth.

"Dude, you're seriously asking about that now?" he sneered just loud enough for Nolan to hear over the crowd noise. As always, they were surrounded by plenty of other students at the cafeteria table.

"Hey, it's just a general question," Nolan assured him. Eli was still slow to respond, though.

"I don't remember exactly," he said while keeping a watchful eye on his surroundings. "I'm pretty sure it was a few weeks ago, though."

"Was it around the time you got sick?" Nolan asked like he was already pretty sure that was the case. It sent chills racing down Eli's back.

"Yeah, it probably was around then. How'd you guess that?"

"You know how you told me that the streaming service was working fine for you last night?" Nolan asked as he took a sip of lemonade. By now, Eli had almost forgotten about the carton of curly fries in front of him.

"Yeah, what about it?"

"It kind of got me thinking after I got off the phone with you," Nolan began. Lowering his voice, he added, "What if they're playing the same thing over the streaming service that they are over the PA system? You know, so the people that are out sick will still know the test answers."

A slight scowl tugged at Eli's lips. "Okay, I guess they could be doing that," he agreed uneasily.

"So, if they're doing all that, and if your streaming service worked fine last night, it made me wonder what could have caused it to have so many problems when you used it a few weeks ago," Nolan said.

Eli shrugged. "Beats me. A bad connection, maybe?"

"Maybe," Nolan echoed skeptically. "But what if it was because of something else? Like, what if it was acting that way because someone hacked into it?"

Eli felt all the tension that had been building on his shoulders drift away. "A hacker? Really?" he grunted right as he reached down and pulled another curly fry out of the carton.

"Well, it could have been. I mean, how else can you explain that?"

"I'm sure there's plenty of other less Sabrina-ish reasons," Eli snipped with a roll of his eyes. Sensing Nolan's determined look still on him, he added, "Seriously, why would someone hack into the streaming service? It's just a bunch of slide shows and stuff from teachers about what they went over in class."

"Maybe. But, like I said, it might have a lot more on it than just that."

"Okay. Even then, though, why would someone hack into it?" Eli prodded.

This time, Nolan hesitated before he said anything. He made sure to lean over the table when he said it, too.

"Because if they did and they transmitted, like, a special version of that thing we've been talking about, someone might have given you the idea for that prank you pulled."

Eli stopped chewing on the curly fry in his mouth. "Hang

on. What?"

"What if that's how you got the idea for the prank?" Nolan reiterated. "I mean, you just sort of knew how to do it like *we* just sort of knew what answers we needed to put on our tests."

Doing his best to shrug it off, Eli rolled his eyes and popped another curly fry into his mouth. "Okay. But even if that was the case, why would they do that? I don't think someone would go through all that trouble just to interrupt a freakin' assembly."

Nolan tossed his head side-to-side in a shrugging motion. "Yeah, probably not, but I think there's more to it than that. Just think about it, though. If you'd never done what you did last week, all the stuff with our tests and everything else probably wouldn't have happened either."

"So now you're blaming me?" Eli said frigidly. Nolan quickly shook his head.

"No. It's just... It's like what you did caused a chain reaction, you know? And if someone did give you the idea, maybe that was *their* idea. Maybe they're trying to put an end to this stuff just as much as we are."

Eli snagged a curly fry out of the carton and glared back at Nolan. "Yeah, and maybe Coach Grayson was trying to break into Central Office so he could drop off some love letters to Superintendent Richter."

"Dude, I'm serious here," Nolan insisted.

"And so am I!" Eli shot back before biting the curly fry he had in his hand in half. He pointed the other half back at Nolan. "I'm telling you, man, if you keep letting Sabrina get in your freakin' head like that you're going to end up just as crazy as she is."

"Well, it was just a thought," Nolan said.

"Yeah, a crazy one," Eli scoffed. "But, hey, what else can you expect from someone that hangs out with Sabrina Chambers all the time?"

As much as Eli expected Nolan to say something back defending Sabrina, it never came. Instead, Nolan just looked back at him morosely and took a bite out of one of the chicken tenders on his tray before he said anything.

"Do you really think she's crazy?"

If Nolan had asked any sooner, Eli probably would have

said, *I don't think, I know*, but he didn't feel right saying that now.

"She's definitely got a chip on her shoulders. You gotta admit that," Eli relented.

"And you don't?" Nolan said with a knowing grin. Eli couldn't help but laugh a little.

"Okay, maybe I do. But it's different with her, man. I mean, you told me what happened to her dad the other day. I don't know, sometimes I think that's messing with her mind."

"What do you mean?" Nolan asked flatly.

Eli bit his lip and absently dipped his hand into the carton he'd been pulling the curly fries out of. It was nearly empty.

"It's like this whole thing with what she wants us to try and do," Eli said cautiously. As vague as it was, he hoped Nolan could tell he was talking about Sabrina's plan to steal a USB drive. Nolan cleared any doubts about that a second later.

"Yeah, I know what you're saying. What about it?"

Eli stared straight back at him as he bit another curly fry in half. "Are you really sure it'll help us out? What if everything that she thinks is on there, isn't on there?"

Nolan shrugged and took another bite out the chicken tender he'd mostly been neglecting for the last five minutes. "I bet everything's on there," he assured Eli. "I'd say she's found pretty good proof that that's what they're using it for."

"Yeah, I know, but what if it isn't?" Eli suggested hesitantly. He got a confused look from Nolan for it.

"Well, what else could it be?"

"Maybe it's something a lot simpler than that," Eli said. Seeing the inquisitive look in Nolan's eyes, he brought up the thing that had been hounding him ever since he got off the phone with Nolan yesterday. "I mean, am I the only one that thinks it's kind of weird that Assistant Principal Horne's the principal now, even though I think she was, like, gone when all this stuff happened last week?"

Nolan didn't seem to be too phased by the accusation. "Maybe. But, come on, Horne's just the *acting* principal right now. She hasn't exactly taken over or anything."

"Either way," Eli began firmly, "what if she set all this up just to get rid of Coach Grayson and take Principal Espinoza's job? Maybe she even worked with the N-2 people to do that."

Nolan glared back at Eli. "Seriously, man, do you know how out there that sounds?"

"It can't be any worse than what you and Sabrina came up with," Eli said coldly.

"Actually, it kind of is," Nolan shot back. "Sabrina came up with her thing after she looked at a couple of different tests and compared it to what I've got. You just sort of came up with that all on your own–out of nowhere."

"Okay, maybe I did," Eli grunted. "Either way, I still don't know how much good this thing's going to do for us."

"If we can prove that other stuff's going on, we can clear our names," Nolan reminded Eli. "That's all there is to it."

"Yeah, I guess so," Eli hummed. Across from him, Nolan shrugged and pulled one of the tater tots off his tray.

"And, who knows, maybe Sabrina will think of some other way we can get this done."

A short scoff burst through Eli's lips. "Well, I sure hope she does. After what happened last week, I definitely don't want to go through *that* again," he said, nudging his head towards the main doors leading into and out of the cafeteria. Even from their table, it was easy to see the bright red flyers taped to them.

"I mean, seriously, I'm still dealing with that crap," Eli sneered.

Nolan nodded and looked back down at his tray. "Yeah, I know. But, hey, maybe all that will be over before long."

Eli pulled his lips in tight and stared straight back at Nolan for a second or two. He could have sworn he caught a bit of doubt in his friend's voice, but he couldn't see it in Nolan's eyes.

"Well, here's to hoping you're right," Eli said eventually as he took the last curly fry out of the carton and popped it into his mouth.

28

The Game Plan

Sabrina sent her text at exactly 3:27, just two minutes after the last bell rang. By 4:11 and 4:23 she'd gotten two responses from Nolan. One to say he could meet her in the park by five-thirty, and another saying that Eli would be there, too. Unfortunately, the two didn't make it until 5:45 and Eli hardly looked like he wanted to be there when they did.

"You do realize this picnic bench is, like, a mile from the last one we met at, don't you?" he griped as soon as he was within earshot. "Why couldn't we have just met at that one again?"

"Because if we did, someone might catch onto us," Sabrina snipped, doing her best to ignore the weird looks she got for it. "Besides, I bet it's only about an eighth of a mile from the other picnic bench. It's not *that* much harder to get to."

Eli was about to say something back when Nolan cut him off. "Either way, we're here now," he said firmly. "What'd you want to see us about?"

Sabrina gave Eli one last glare before reaching into the front pocket of her jacket. "This," she said right as she took something out and tossed it towards Nolan and Eli. Remembering the cast around his left wrist, Nolan's right hand shot out and snatched the red object out of the air before Eli even flinched. They both looked at it an instant later.

"Seriously? She called us out here to look at an eraser?" Eli snarled. He shot a perplexed look back at Sabrina, and, even though she could tell he was trying to hide it, Sabrina noticed Nolan was doing the same. A smug grin started to tug at her lips.

"It might look like just an eraser now, but it'll be a lot more than that when we go to the volleyball game at Meade tomorrow night."

Sabrina was already pulling out her phone and unlocking it when Nolan asked the obvious. "More than that? What are you talking about?"

"And why are we going to some stupid volleyball game?" Eli added.

Sabrina smiled and exhibited her open palm to the two of them. Nolan got the hint and tossed the eraser back to her. She wasn't as good at catching it as Nolan had been, though, and it plopped onto the ground after grazing against her right forearm.

"We're going to the game because I think it'll give us a good enough distraction to sneak into the office and get the drive without anyone noticing, especially if we do it between sets," she said as she crouched down to pick up the eraser.

"Between what?" Eli blurted out.

"Sets," Sabrina huffed. "Volleyball matches are split into sets. The first team to win two of them wins the match."

Once it looked like Eli finally understood how a volleyball game worked, Sabrina continued with her explanation. "Anyway, before we go to the game, I'm going to turn this," she said while exhibiting the eraser in one hand and turning her phone around to face them in the other, "into this."

Nolan and Eli turned their attention to the phone. A picture of a red eraser that had been converted into a USB drive shell was displayed on the screen. Unfortunately, neither looked that impressed.

"And what good's that going to do us?" Eli grunted.

Sabrina smirked a little before slipping the phone back into her jeans' pocket. "If we can get the drive, I figured we should be able to use this eraser thing to sneak the drive out of the school without anyone noticing. All we'd have to do is snap the shell off Intuitive Degrees' drive and put the memory stick into the eraser–after I make it into a USB shell, that is."

Eli stared back at Sabrina in disbelief for a second or two before his reaction slipped out of his mouth. "Seriously, are you nuts? I mean, what, you don't think anyone would think it's weird for you to be walking around with an eraser at a freakin' volleyball game?"

"Well, it'll be in my jacket pocket," Sabrina argued back

right as she slid the eraser into the same pocket she'd been keeping it in and tapped it as if to show Eli what she meant. He still didn't seem to be convinced, though.

"Okay, but what if they find out it's missing and make everyone, like, empty their pockets and stuff on the way out the door? Seriously, why can't we just grab the drive and get out of there?"

Biting his lip, Nolan partially looked back at Sabrina while he glanced at Eli. "Maybe because our parents are going to be driving us there?" he began hesitantly. Once Sabrina indicated that was the case, he continued like it was his own plan.

"So, you know, it's not like we can leave early or anything. And even if our parents were at the game or parked out front, they'd probably think it'd be weird if we decided to leave before the game's over."

"Well, maybe it'll be a blowout," Eli suggested. Sabrina wasn't budging, though.

"Look, as far as I can tell, this is the best chance we've got," she said matter-of-factly. "We can use the game as a distraction, and, since it looks like your school's gym is in the back-middle of the building from what I saw in a satellite photo online this afternoon, most of the crowd will probably be going through the front doors to get in."

"So?" Eli sneered.

"So, they probably won't have the hallway that goes past the office blocked off or locked up or anything," Sabrina said. "It should give us a chance to get in there between sets."

"Okay, but even if they don't have that hallway blocked off, how're we going to get into the office?" Eli asked her bitterly. "You think they're just going to leave the doors unlocked for us?"

"You got in during the assembly, didn't you?" Nolan pointed out.

Eli let out a shrill scoff. "Yeah, but that was in the morning while school was going on. This is going to be after school's been out for a few hours. I mean, maybe I'm crazy, but I bet they lock things up after a while."

Sabrina glanced back at Nolan. She could tell he didn't have any other suggestions, but then her eyes fell on the bright yellow cast around his left hand.

"Well, what if we had to go to the nurse's office for something? I guess that's attached to the office somehow, isn't it?"

Both Nolan and Eli shot confused looks back at her.

"What do you mean?" Nolan asked before Eli could.

Sabrina nudged her head at Nolan's cast. "Do you ever take pain killers for that?"

Nolan glanced down at his left hand. "Sometimes. Not as much as I was when I first broke it, though."

"But do they keep any of those pain killers in the nurse's office in case you need any during school?"

"Probably. Why?"

Sabrina took in a deep breath. "Well, maybe you can act like you had a flare-up or that you fell on it or something. Then we can try to find someone to let us into the nurse's office to take your pills, and, while you're doing that, one of us can sneak into the office."

"Yeah, and then whenever the drive goes missing they'll have a pretty good idea who took it, too," Eli said. Surprisingly, it caused another grin to form on Sabrina's lips.

"Actually, I'm kind of hoping they won't even notice it's gone," she said. "I was going to put one of my own USB drives in the eraser before we go to Meade tomorrow night and then swap out the memory sticks. That way, when they look at the PA terminal, it'll look like Intuitive Degrees' drive is still in there while we sneak the real one out in my eraser."

Sabrina's grin quickly spread to Nolan's lips. "Okay. That's pretty awesome," he said with an approving nod. Unfortunately, Eli still had a skeptical look smeared across his face.

"Yeah, unless we get caught," he hissed. "Then we'll end up in jail just like Coach Grayson, and, hey, since I'm involved, they'll probably figure out I was the prankster, too. Then they'll be able to pin all this other stuff on me and I'll really be screwed."

Sabrina let out an annoyed groan. Nolan looked pretty frustrated as well.

"Well, what else are we supposed to do, Eli?" he stressed. "The longer we wait around, the harder it's going to be to prove that you, or Principal Espinoza, or even Coach Grayson had nothing to do with all this stuff Superintendent Richter's been saying."

"Okay, then," Eli huffed. "Let's say we get the drive tomorrow night. Then what? Who are we going to tell about this? I mean, I figured we'd be able to put all this to an end the other day when Sabrina decided to get the syllabus, but then she decided that still wasn't good enough. I'm not going to put my neck out if that's going to happen again, man."

Nolan turned his attention back to Sabrina. She met his gaze, but the look in her eyes didn't hold any promises.

"I'm sure we'll be able to find someone to tell," she suggested optimistically. Unfortunately, it still wasn't enough to get Eli on board.

"Yeah? Who, though? That's what you said before you got the syllabus–*if* you even got the syllabus, that is."

"I got the syllabus, Eli!" Sabrina snapped.

"You mean the one you never showed us?" he shot back. "Or maybe you were too afraid to show us that your mom's just as much of a creep as your good-for-nothing dad was."

Nolan glanced back in time to see Sabrina's face getting drawn in tight as she sucked in a deep, quivering breath.

"I'm sorry," she growled. "Does the moron that had to go to summer school because he couldn't pass fourth grade social studies want to run that by me again?"

"You know, we might not have to tell anyone at all," Nolan blurted out as he moved between the two of them. He sent a stern look at both before he added, "I think taking the USB drive off the system for a while might be enough."

Sabrina was still glaring at what she could see of Eli behind Nolan's wiry frame when she croaked out, "Really? How would that be enough?"

"Oh, wow! You mean the super genius can't figure it out for herself?" Eli sneered. In an instant, Nolan turned to look back at Eli and pointed a finger right in his face.

"Hey! Stop it, alright? This isn't helping anyone." He turned to look back at Sabrina and pointed the same finger at her. "You, too. You got that?"

Sabrina looked like she could barely keep herself rooted to the picnic table she was sitting on top of, but she still managed to nod her head. Eli slowly nodded when Nolan looked back at him, too.

"Okay. So, like I was saying," Nolan continued, keeping an eye on both of them, "I really think just taking the drive off the PA system might be enough. I was talking to Eli about it earlier today. It's like unplugging it last week caused a chain reaction or something."

"How's that?" Sabrina grunted. She was still staring a hole through Eli from the picnic table.

"Well, the drive contains all the subliminal messages, right?" Nolan began, making Eli cringe a little. "If that gets unplugged, the subliminal messages don't go out to the classes, and, if the classes don't get the subliminal messages, then we start missing questions on our tests. If that happens enough and whole classes start missing sections or concepts on their tests like my history class did with the Intolerable Acts, maybe more teachers will start looking at the syllabus again."

The anger simmering across Sabrina's face started to fizzle. "And then they'll realize that the Intolerable Acts aren't the only thing missing," she mused aloud. "Oh, my gosh! That's awesome. And if a bunch of other teachers start noticing it, Superintendent Richter probably won't be able to cover it up again either."

"Exactly!" Nolan beamed. He was a bit disappointed when he looked back at Eli and found the same cold expression on his face.

"Don't you think doing it at Meade's going to be a problem, though?" Eli pointed out. When he saw the puzzled looks on Nolan and Sabrina's faces, he added, "I mean, if we're doing it there, wouldn't that just mean Superintendent Richter could say one of the teachers took something off the syllabus again or that it was a problem with just our school like he did last time?"

"Oh, yeah. Maybe so," Nolan conceded as the excited look on his face drifted away. Sabrina wasn't giving up yet, though.

"Unless he didn't realize that someone had unplugged the drive until it was too late," she reminded them. "If we really can swap out the drives like I want, and if we can pull it off without anyone noticing, then maybe Superintendent Richter won't know that we changed out the drive."

"Yeah, but I think you're still forgetting one thing," Eli snipped. "The office is crawling with security cameras. I mean, come on, all the lights were off when I went in there last Monday and they still got a pretty good picture of me. They'll know if someone messes with the drive."

A deflated sigh slipped out of both Sabrina and Nolan's lips.

"And just when I thought we were on to something, too," Nolan chuckled in resignation. He turned to look back at Sabrina a second later. "So, you got any more ideas?"

Sabrina didn't say anything but slowly shook her head as she continued to stare at the concrete beneath her. Nolan was just about to say they might as well head back home when she suddenly spoke up.

"Do you think someone's always watching the security cameras, though?"

"What do you mean?" Nolan asked.

Sabrina whisked one of her hands up. "Well, think about it. We're not talking about a Vegas casino or an art museum or something. Why would some security guard or whatever be constantly watching the live feed from a camera overlooking a middle school's network cabinet?"

"Well, they got pictures of me, didn't they?" Eli pointed out. Sabrina quickly shook her head.

"Yeah, but that was only after they knew someone messed with the PA system. As long as no one finds out about the swap, I don't think they're ever going to check the footage."

"And if they don't, then we might actually be able to get away with this?" Nolan thought aloud. Sabrina's eyebrows cocked above the rims of her glasses.

"In theory, yeah," she said, grinning. It wasn't long before a grin started to creep across Nolan's lips, too.

"Well, I guess it's worth a shot, then," he declared.

A sense of dread fell over Eli as soon as his friend's eager eyes fell on him. Even though he wanted to point out the cameras could be motion-activated just like the camera on Nolan's doorbell was, he knew he didn't have much of a choice anymore. They were doing this whether he liked it or not.

"Yeah," Eli said in resignation. "I guess so."

29

Terms

It only took Nolan and Sabrina ten minutes to finish ironing out their plan. There wasn't much to discuss, though.

The three of them would head for the office right after the first volleyball set was over so they could blend in with the rest of the people going out for snacks or bathroom breaks. Then, once they were in the office, Eli would help Sabrina find the drive while Nolan acted as the lookout. After the drives had been swapped out, they would head back to the gym with the spectators that were still in the halls and hopefully no one would give them a second glance.

For a while, Eli hoped they had forgotten about the possibility that the office might be locked or sealed off, but, much to his annoyance, Nolan asked Sabrina about that right before they went home. She quickly decided they should use her idea to get Nolan into the nurse's office right before the second set ended if that was the case. That way, they would have a chance to get the drive no matter what.

Nolan hadn't been too thrilled about Plan B but still agreed. More out of obligation, Eli had done the same.

He didn't really say much after that since he didn't think they cared to hear what he had to say, but the more he thought about it, the more Eli started to wonder if swapping out a drive would actually do him any good.

Trying to break into Central Office's server room definitely hadn't done Coach Grayson any favors, and, as much as Eli tried to ignore it, he couldn't shake the feeling that swapping out the drive wouldn't be much different than what his old coach had done. Both of them had been accused of taking something off the syllabus, and both of them were so desperate to clear their names they were willing to do just about anything for it.

But as much as Eli wanted to clear his name, he definitely didn't want to end up in jail like Coach Grayson already had. It was something he kept reminding himself of as he sat alone in Principal Horne's office the next morning.

Unfortunately, the guilt and the shame about turning himself in still lingered.

An anxious sigh slipped out of Eli's lips as he glanced up and checked the time on the clock to his left. It was coming up on nine-thirty.

Of course, he'd made sure to turn himself in halfway through first period so Nolan wouldn't see him, but, as time wore on, Eli was starting to wonder if that was going to backfire on him. He'd been stuck in the office for nearly an hour now, which meant he hadn't been able to get his backpack out of Mrs. Fulton's class after taking his fake bathroom break either.

If anyone noticed, rumors could start floating around school and then Nolan might hear something.

Eli lightly tapped a thumb on the edge of Principal Horne's desk. Even though she'd been busy grilling him about his prank ever since he turned himself in, Horne suddenly got up and left a few minutes ago after getting a phone call. She still hadn't come back.

After letting out another sigh, Eli glanced over his shoulder at the shut door again. Since this was taking a lot longer than he expected, he was tempted to see if someone in the office could at least go and get his backpack for him, but, before he could get out of the chair, he saw the door handle dip down with a distinctive clack. His breath nearly got stuck in his throat when a man with a recognizably gaunt face strode in.

"So, you must be the little punk that made a laughing stock out of me the other day," Superintendent Richter began crossly. He allowed another man to pass by him before he shut the door. Eli could hardly get the words to form in his mouth.

"Yeah, look, I—"

"Save it," Richter grunted. "Your principal gave me the full report when we got here. She says you've been adamant that you had nothing to do with taking anything off the syllabus and that this was all just some prank. Am I getting that right?"

Eli was already nodding before he said anything. "Yes, sir. Yes, it is," he stammered as Superintendent Richter took a seat in the chair across from him and pulled it closer to the desk.

"Any reason we should believe that?" the other person asked, pulling Eli's attention over to him for the first time. He nearly fell out of his seat when he noticed it was the same guy with long, jet-black hair he and Nolan had seen standing outside of the N-2 building the other day. He could have sworn the man recognized him, too, but, so far, he hadn't said anything about it.

"Oh, yes. This is Troy Hayashi," Superintendent Richter grumbled when he realized Eli was still staring at the guy standing next to him. "Troy works for a consulting firm Grafton ISD has partnered with. He's sort of a contact, I guess you'd call it, between the district and his firm.

"Anyway, getting back on track, I think what Troy means is that we think your claim that this was all just some stupid prank is a little hard to believe."

Eli looked back at Superintendent Richter like he'd just been punched in the gut. "Hard to believe? How's it hard to believe? All I did was plug an old MP3 player into the PA system."

"And take a USB drive containing highly sensitive information off the server rack in the process," Hayashi added dryly. "Let's not forget that."

"Okay. So, yeah, I did that, too. But I swear it was just an accident," Eli pleaded to both of them. "I didn't even know I had it in my jacket pocket until I got to the gym."

"So, why did you unplug it from the server rack in the first place?" Hayashi asked with a piercing glare. Eli had to divert his eyes to the front of the desk before he could answer.

"I'm pretty sure it was the only way I could plug the MP3 player into the PA system," he told them slowly. "The USB drive was just in the way."

"So, you unplugged it and put it in your jacket pocket?" Superintendent Richter sneered.

"Look, I must have been distracted or something, alright?" Eli cried. "I mean, I was just trying to get it out of the way, but then I was also trying to plug the MP3 player into the PA system, turn it on, and then get the hell out of there before anyone saw me. I don't even remember putting it in my jacket pocket!"

Eli looked back up at Superintendent Richter and Hayashi in time to see them exchange skeptical looks. Hayashi was the first to speak up.

"So, after you realized you had it in your pocket, was simply dropping it on the gym's floor the first thing that popped into your mind?"

The question sent an uneasy jolt running down Eli's back. It was almost like Hayashi knew he'd thought about dropping the drive in the trash can outside of the gym first.

Eli was just about to answer when Superintendent Richter broke in.

"Look, I know it was your firm's USB drive, but how this kid got rid of the thing isn't what's bothering me, Troy. It's how he executed his prank."

Eli's eyes shifted back to Superintendent Richter. "What do you mean?"

The superintendent shrugged mockingly. "Well, how about we run through how this looks to me?" he said right as he started counting off the reasons on his fingers.

"First off, some eighth-grader waltzes right into the office during my speech like it's no big deal, then makes a B-line straight for the secretary's desk to get the key for the network cabinet like there's a big neon sign saying exactly where it is, and, finally, as if all that wasn't bad enough, that same thirteen-year-old-eighth-grader does it all without leaving a shred of evidence behind that we can use against him. He wears a hoodie so we can't see his face, uses some outdated technology for the prank that we can't trace back to him, and he uses crowds to blend in.

"Now, you tell me, kid. What part of that doesn't sound like the work of someone that got some serious coaching? I mean, hey, maybe you tell me who told you how to do this and we'll call it even."

Eli looked a little dumbstruck as he shook his head.

"But nobody told me what to do," he said uneasily. When he saw the aggravated looks in Richter and Hayashi's eyes, he added, "I seriously just came up with this on my own, okay? I mean, I've pulled lots of pranks before. It's just something I do."

"So, how did you know where the key to the network

cabinet was?" Hayashi asked flatly. He sent a knowing glance back at Superintendent Richter before he added, "I think that's the thing that's bothering us the most here."

Again, Eli shook his head. "I don't know, I just kind of knew where it was. It's like, I don't know if you guys have heard or not, but I've been sent to the office more times than I can probably count–mostly for pranks and stuff," Eli explained, looking back up at the two in front of him.

"We know," Superintendent Richter said. "I looked up your record before I came over here and Principal Horne showed me what she has on you, too. What relevance do you think that has here, though?"

"What?" Eli stammered.

"How does that explain how you knew where the key was?" Hayashi clarified. Eli was still slow to answer.

"Oh. Well, maybe I saw the secretary use it or get it while I was waiting to get called into Horne's or Espinoza's office."

Superintendent Richter cast a skeptical look back up at Hayashi. The man's thin lips skewed and he cocked his head to the side a little. "It's possible," he suggested.

"Yeah, and so's the possibility that this kid's just messing with us," Superintendent Richter grumbled. Eli felt his nerves slip out from under him.

"Look, I turned myself in, didn't I? That's got to count for something, right?"

Based on the look in Superintendent Richter's eyes, Eli guessed he still hadn't convinced him yet.

"Maybe. But if this was just a prank like you say it was, why did you wait a week-and-a-half to turn yourself in?"

This time, Eli glared back at Superintendent Richter. "Why do you think? I didn't want to get in trouble."

"And that's it? That's your only reason?" Superintendent Richter grunted. Eli readily nodded his head.

"Well, yeah. Plus, I didn't think anyone would believe me when y'all said the drive had a link to the syllabus on it or whatever."

"So, why'd you turn yourself in now?" Hayashi asked. "Were the posters getting to you?"

Eli's eyes shifted away from the two. For a moment, the

angry look in Sabrina's eyes from yesterday's meeting flashed through his mind. But, then, so did the hopeful glint he'd seen in his mother's eyes the other day when she'd decided to order stuffed crust pizza.

"Yeah, they were," he finally said at length. "Honestly, I don't know how much longer I could have lasted."

"Well, I'm still kind of surprised you lasted this long," Superintendent Richter said in reflection. He leaned back in the chair and stared at Eli for a second or two before he added, "Did you have another reason, though?"

A shiver rattled down Eli's back. He swore the guy could see right through him.

"Yeah. Basically."

Richter pursed his lips and slowly nodded his head. "Okay? So, what is it?"

Eli kept his head bowed a little and he felt every bit of the trembling sigh that rustled through his lips. In the back of his mind, he reminded himself this was the whole reason he'd turned himself in.

"My friend's going to try to steal the USB drive out of the PA system during the volleyball game here tonight," he said bluntly.

Even though Eli still kept his head down, he could sense the shocked looks on the two's faces from the silence that enveloped the room. Superintendent Richter was the first to speak up.

"So, someone else did know about your little prank," he sneered. Eli's head jerked up.

"No! Well, yeah, sort of. Look, my friend didn't help me pull the prank or anything. I just kind of slipped up and told him what I did last week. I made him promise not to tell anyone."

"He must have been a pretty good friend not to say anything," Superintendent Richter mused with a malicious grin. "What's his name?"

"His name?" Eli echoed shakily. The cold look in Superintendent Richter's eyes didn't fade.

"Yeah. What's your friend's name?"

Eli still hesitated for a second before he managed to spit it out. "Nolan. Nolan Leere."

"And now *he* wants to steal the drive?" Hayashi asked

quizzically. "I thought you said you didn't mean to do that last week?"

"I didn't!" Eli insisted. He briefly scowled before he added, "But it's not exactly Nolan's idea to do this either."

A thoroughly confused look was plastered across Superintendent Richter's tight-skinned face. "Okay, so who's idea is it?"

"Sabrina Chambers," Eli said without hesitation. "She's a friend of Nolan's that goes to River View Middle School. She's nuts, man!"

Superintendent Richter started to glance up towards Hayashi, but most of his gaze remained on Eli. "Nuts? Nuts, how?"

"Because she actually thinks your USB drive's got subliminal messages on it, and that you've been trying to cover it up," Eli said, taking turns between looking directly at Hayashi and Superintendent Richter.

While Hayashi remained stone-faced, Superintendent Richter's eyebrows cocked up and a surprised snort blurted out of his nose.

"Subliminal messages and cover-ups? Well, that's a new one," he laughed while looking back up at Hayashi. The man only snickered through tightly clenched lips.

"Yeah. That it is," he agreed.

"Well, that's what Sabrina thinks is going on," Eli said somberly. "And she's going to try and swap out the drives tonight to prove it. That's why I decided to turn myself in. I wanted to warn someone about this before Sabrina gets us all caught since they're making me show them how I did it last week."

"And you don't want to get in any more trouble than you already have?" Superintendent Richter thought aloud. Eli nodded.

"Yeah. And I also wanted to make sure you knew that I didn't want anything to do with what she's got planned tonight either. I just got into this because Nolan told me I'd be able to clear my name if I did. You know, prove that I didn't take anything off the syllabus like Coach Grayson did. That was before they started coming up with all this stuff about subliminal messages, though."

"So, you don't really think we're using the USB drive for that?" Hayashi asked.

Eli hesitated but quickly shook his head. "No. I don't. But Sabrina sure does, and I think she's managed to talk Nolan into believing it, too. I mean, they actually think y'all are giving us test answers over the PA system that way."

As much as Eli expected the other two to be just as blown away about that as he was, and maybe even laugh about it again, neither said anything. Superintendent Richter just sat quietly and continued to stare him down.

"Have they told anyone else about this?" Superintendent Richter asked eventually. "That's kind of a dangerous rumor to be spreading around."

Again, Eli shook his head. "No. I don't think they have. I think Sabrina's worried about what'll happen if they do. Or maybe she knows how crazy it sounds.

"Either way, I just want to put a stop to all this before we end up going to jail like Coach Grayson did," Eli insisted. "I mean, I'm pretty sure Sabrina's crazy, and I don't want her to drag my friend down with her."

Superintendent Richter nodded his head. "Well, that's understandable. I'll talk with the campus police and see if we can't round them up before the day's over."

"Do you think you could do something for me, though?" Eli asked reluctantly.

Superintendent Richter and Hayashi exchanged puzzled glances before they turned their attention back to Eli.

"What's that, kid?"

"If my friend, Nolan, asks how he got caught, can someone tell him that Jonathan Reed ratted me out. Nolan told me last week that Jonathan thought he saw me in the locker room when I was going from the office to the gym and was thinking about saying something about it."

"Which was another thing that amazed me about your plan–cutting through the gym, I mean," Superintendent Richter blurted out, sounding more impressed than he would have liked to have let on. He quickly whisked a hand up as if to silence himself. "Anyway, were you going to say anything else?"

"So, yeah, if Nolan asks about this, could you try and tell

him that? I don't want him to find out I was the one that ratted him out."

"Well, we'll certainly see what we can do," Superintendent Richter grumbled. He was just about to say something else when Hayashi spoke up.

"Actually, I think I might have a better idea. You said your friend, Sabrina, was going to *swap out* the drive during the game tonight?"

Eli still looked rattled but shrugged nonchalantly. "I wouldn't say Sabrina's a friend or anything, but, yeah, she's going to try and swap out the drive with a fake one."

"Then why don't we let her?" Hayashi suggested, catching the other two by surprise.

"Wait, seriously?" Superintendent Richter spat. Hayashi smirked in response.

"Why not? That way we can catch his other two friends red-handed and it won't look like he told on them. All we have to do is watch the security feed from the office and move in once they're in there. It would probably attract a lot less attention than detaining them during the middle of the school day."

"And I presume your company would like to avoid the attention?" Superintendent Richter said as he glanced back at his associate.

"That would be preferable," Hayashi seconded. "And after everything that happened last week, I'm sure you'd like to avoid as much publicity as you can about this, too."

"That I would," Superintendent Richter grumbled. His lips clamped down and his eyes glazed over as he thought about it. "But what about the volleyball game? Seems like that'd mean there'd be a lot of people around that could notice."

Hayashi quickly shook his head.

"That shouldn't matter. The only ways in and out of the office are by going through the front door or by going through the teachers' lounge. We can just lock up the teachers' lounge so they can't use that door, and I'm sure it wouldn't be too hard to detain them in here until any crowds in the halls clear out. And if anyone asks, we could just say we caught them trying to break into the office. It'd be an open and shut case."

Superintendent Richter drew his lips in tight and nodded

as he mulled over it. Suddenly, his eyes shifted back to Eli. "Are you okay with that? Or, more importantly, do you think you can keep your mouth shut about it?"

Eli felt his breath flutter. He'd never been very good at keeping secrets, but if this meant Nolan wouldn't know he'd ratted him out he would definitely do his best.

"Yeah. I'm fine with that," he said resolutely. He was a bit surprised when Richter only gave him a subtle, understanding nod in return.

"Good. So, what can you tell me about this girl's plan?"

30

Pre-Game Jitters

Nolan knew it wasn't the right thing to do, but he found himself glancing at the time on Eric's dashboard anyway. He felt his stomach sink when he noticed it was 5:47. They were running seven minutes late.

Before Nolan could dwell on it, though, Eric careened around the corner at the next stoplight and they started heading down the residential street leading to Meade Middle School. Eli's older brother didn't seem too thrilled about having to drive them to the volleyball game, but, based on the vacant look in Eli's eyes, Nolan guessed his friend wasn't overly excited about it either.

Forcing a smile, Nolan reached over and batted Eli on the shoulder just as Meade's two-story structure came into view.

"Hey, don't worry," Nolan said. "We're not that late. I'm sure Sabrina won't blow that much of a gasket."

"And I'm still getting you guys here a whole ten minutes before the game starts," Eric reminded him gruffly from the driver's seat, even though he had to shout a little to get his voice over the hard rock music blaring over the radio.

Nolan shrugged in understanding, but Eli still had a distant look in his eyes when Nolan glanced back at him.

"Yeah, I know," Eli coughed, like he was having a hard time getting his voice out of his mouth. "I guess I've just got more on my mind than that."

Nolan thought about asking Eli what was bothering him but decided against it since they were still in the car with Eric. Instead, he turned his attention back to the school ahead of them.

Eli had been acting sort of strange all day. Even when

they were at lunch earlier, Nolan half-expected Eli to try and convince him that Sabrina was wrong or that they needed to do something different again, but he'd barely said anything. He almost never made eye contact with Nolan when he actually did say something, too.

It had been a little unnerving, but Nolan had just shrugged it off as Eli's nerves getting the best of him. As Eric pulled into an empty spot along the curb, though, Nolan started to wonder if there was more to it than that.

"Alright, all ashore that's going ashore," Eric droned as soon as he put the hand-me-down SUV into Park. It had been a saying his dad had used on he and Eli plenty of times when he'd dropped them off at school in the past.

Without a moment's hesitation, Nolan popped his door open and stepped out onto the sidewalk. Eli was still a little hesitant to unbuckle his seatbelt but forced himself to do it when he saw the impatient look in Nolan's eyes. He started shuffling towards the open door a second later.

"Hope one of you gets the TV the school's raffling off," Eric said in parting as Eli scooted past.

Eli stopped himself short of asking what he was talking about before he coughed up a dry, "Yeah, me too," on his way out.

He and Nolan didn't normally go to volleyball games, so the raffle drawing was the best excuse Nolan could think of to get them to the game without their parents thinking it was weird. Eli thought it was kind of a dumb idea at first, but both Nolan's parents and his own–including his brother–had pretty much fallen for it hands down, so he guessed it wasn't that bad.

Eli wasn't about to give Nolan a high five for it, though.

"And don't forget to text mom when the game's almost over," Eric reminded Eli once he'd stepped out.

"Yeah. I know. I'll see you later," Eli grumbled as he shut the door. An instant later, he and Nolan started threading their way through the loose crowds gathered around the front of the school while Eric drove off behind them. As expected, Sabrina was already waiting for them by the flagpole.

"You do remember how I wanted to meet up at five-forty, don't you?" she sneered, glaring straight at Eli. Nolan quickly tried to wave her off.

"Hey, chill out, Sabrina. We still got here, didn't we?"

"Yeah, and nearly ten minutes late," she said icily. "I wasn't trying to get here that early just to find a good seat or something, you know? I think there's something else we need to do before the game."

"Like what?" Nolan groaned. Even though he'd chided himself throughout the day for overthinking everything they'd be doing at the volleyball game, Sabrina had clearly taken it a step or two further.

"I think we need to find out if the office door's locked or not," she said bluntly. "If we knew that, we'd know if we should go with Plan A or Plan B right off the bat. Then we could try and swap out the drives whenever we wanted to."

"I thought we'd already decided to do it at the end of the first game," Eli quickly pointed out. Sabrina shrugged.

"Yeah, but that was also to try and see if the door was unlocked. If we already know that, we could try and make our move near the end of the second set instead of the first."

Eli shot her a quizzical look. "Why then, though? I mean, if we do it after the first game, can't we pretty much get this over with right then and there?"

"We could, but these volleyball matches are a best two-out-of-three sort of thing. Whoever wins two sets wins the match."

"So?" Eli grunted.

"So, we wouldn't have to hold on to the real drive as long if we do it around the end of the second set instead of the first," Sabrina explained grudgingly. "Plus, if we do it then, there's a chance the second set will be the end of the game, too."

"Then we could leave right after we swap it out," Nolan concluded. Sabrina quickly whisked a hand back at him in agreement. She felt her blood boiling over when she realized Eli still didn't want to agree with her.

"Do you think there'll be as many people in the halls then, though?" he asked, sounding like he was looking for excuses. "I mean, what if everyone gets up to take bathroom breaks or whatever at the end of the first game instead of the second?"

"I'm sure there'll still be plenty of people in the halls, Eli," Nolan grumbled.

"Especially if the match is over," Sabrina pointed out. "Seriously, I know I didn't think of any of this at the park yesterday, but checking the office door now and trying to get in after the second set's probably our best bet."

Eli's mouth hung open and he lightly shook his head. "Yeah, maybe, but—"

"She's right, man," Nolan cut in sternly. He bit his lip apologetically before nudging his head back at the school. "And, seriously, if we're going to do this, we'd better get moving anyway."

Even though Sabrina was already starting to head towards the main entrance, Nolan stayed behind and waited for Eli to grumble out an abrasive, "Whatever you say," before he started shuffling towards the school with them.

Once Nolan was satisfied that Eli was following along, he stepped up next to Sabrina and asked her about another thing that had been bothering him all day.

"So did you manage to get that eraser thing made?"

As much as he expected a beaming smile to slide across Sabrina's lips, she actually looked a little embarrassed.

"Sort of," she conceded before dipping her hand into one of her jacket pockets. "I don't think it looks nearly as good as the one Carlitta showed me yesterday, but I think it'll still work."

A second later she retrieved the eraser drive and handed it over to Nolan. Even in the dim evening light the cut she'd made across the top third of the eraser to make the casing's cap was extremely noticeable. Nolan thought he could even see the dark plastic surface of the exposed memory stick underneath.

"You sure?" he blurted out. He didn't mean to sound so shrewd about it, but he could still tell it came out that way.

"Well, what else are we going to do?" Sabrina said through a hissed whisper as she snatched the eraser away from him and slipped it back into her pocket before they made it to the main doors. Surprisingly, the only encouragement she got was from Eli.

"I think it'll be fine," he said halfheartedly. When Nolan glared at him, Eli whisked a hand back at Sabrina. "The only thing we have to worry about is if someone really looks at it, right? You think someone's going to be looking for trick erasers before the game?"

"Probably not, but it could still happen," Nolan grumbled as he reached for the door handle and held it open for Sabrina and Eli. He shot an unnerved look at Eli as he walked past.

Everything his friend had just said seemed to go against all the arguments he'd made about this mission at the park yesterday. Then again, if he kept having second thoughts about it Nolan realized he'd be contradicting himself before long, too.

He was still trying to push it all to the back of his mind by the time they stepped through the second set of doors and were immediately greeted by the sound of one of the schools' bands warming up the crowd with an off-key rendition of some pop song. The tune sounded a little familiar, but Nolan had a hard time placing it–mostly because the sound was getting trapped behind the closed set of doors directly in front of them.

"Well, that's just great," Nolan grunted right before his eyes fell on the bright yellow sign that had been taped to one of the doors. It had, 'Tickets,' and an arrow pointing to the right written on it. He started heading in that direction a second later and Sabrina and Eli quickly took up step behind him.

Even though Eli already knew what Nolan was so upset about, Sabrina gave him a puzzled look as she slid in next to him.

"What's up?" she asked, hoping her voice got over all the noise echoing off the lockers and the tiled floors.

Nolan nudged his head back towards the closed doors. "That *was* the hallway that goes past the office," he said shortly. "I thought it'd be open since it leads to one of the gym's doors, but I guess they've got it blocked off."

Sabrina briefly glanced over her shoulder at the closed doors as if she needed visual confirmation of what Nolan was talking about. She turned her attention back to him a second later.

"What about the other end of the hall?" she suggested. "Maybe that's not locked up."

In the back of his mind, Nolan knew it was a good possibility. The main hallway had one of the few restrooms on the gym-side of the building, so he doubted they would have blocked that off.

He was still mulling over it as they took a left at the

next intersection and started heading towards the gym. Before long, he noticed everyone seemed to be collecting at some point just ahead of them, near the opening to the hallway that ran lengthwise through the middle of the school. He could already tell those doors were closed, too, though.

All the same, if this was anything like the basketball games he'd been to, Nolan guessed the ticket table had been set up another fifty feet ahead, near the entrance to the gym. At first, he was disappointed about having to stand in line, but then it gave him an idea.

"Save my place," he suddenly commanded as the three got closer to the end of the ticket line. He was already veering off to the side when Eli spoke up.

"Why? Where are you going?"

"To check out the other end of the hallway," Nolan said matter-of-factly over his shoulder. "Don't worry. I'll be back in a bit."

Eli and Sabrina were still giving him puzzled looks when he pivoted around and continued down the hallway. He made it past the ticket table a short time later and started heading into the hall to the left that ran parallel to the gym. It was the same hallway where the concession stand had been set up, so he had to weave his way through all the lines and the pre-game masses clogging it. Eventually, though, he made it to the next intersection.

Oddly, the first thing he noticed once he reached the main hallway was that the doors leading into the gym from this side were sealed up just like the doors near the school's main entrance were. It made him wonder if the school was trying to limit just how and where people could get into this game since Nolan was almost positive they usually had ticket desks set up at both ends of the gym during all the basketball games he'd been to.

Shaking it off, Nolan turned his attention to the left and felt a strange mixture of relief and dread wash over him. The doors leading into the main hallway from this side of the building were wide open. And even though all the overhead lights were off, he could just barely make out the sheen of the office's glass door in the darkness, just past the second intersection.

Biting his lip, Nolan checked the entrance to the restrooms directly across from him and then looked over his shoulder to be sure no one was watching from the concessions area before he slid around the corner and started heading down the main hallway. His own shadow stretched out in front of him for a bit, but it quickly faded into the gloom with everything else.

After what felt like a mile, Nolan finally made it to the office door and carefully wrapped his fingers around the doorknob. He made one last check of his surroundings before twisting it.

The knob turned easily enough, and, even though he couldn't hear it from all the noise resonating over the hallway, Nolan still felt the soft click of the door unlatching through his fingers.

A quivering breath slipped through his lips. The office door was unlocked!

The sound of Meade's band starting to play the national anthem snapped Nolan back to his senses and he glanced towards the gym to be sure no had spotted him yet. As before, though, it was still clear.

Looking back down at the doorknob, Nolan quickly eased the latch back into place so the door wouldn't swing open on its own, then strode back down the hallway to return to the ticket line. Somehow it seemed a lot farther away than it had on the way in.

As he was passing by the restrooms at the end of the hall, Nolan did a double-take of the boys' room door. He was almost positive one of the bright red flyers had been posted on it all week, but now the flyer was nowhere to be seen.

It seemed a little weird, but Nolan tried to shrug it off as best as he could and continued towards the ticket line. He'd nearly convinced himself that the flyer had just fallen off until he realized all the flyers that had been posted in the hall parallel to the gym for the last week were gone, too.

Nolan's mind raced as he rounded the last intersection and slid back in line with Eli and Sabrina. As much as he knew he should be glad that the flyers were gone, their sudden disappearance just made him feel worse.

He was about to check the local news apps on his phone

to be sure something hadn't happened to Principal Espinoza or Coach Grayson when Sabrina's voice broke his concentration.

"So, I guess the door must be locked?"

Nolan jolted himself back to reality and shook his head. He'd barely even noticed there were just two people ahead of them in the ticket line now.

"Huh? Oh, um, no. Actually we're all clear on that," Nolan reported distantly. Sabrina's eyes lit up a second later and she wrapped both of her hands around Nolan's right arm.

"Oh, my gosh! This is great!" she squealed. Remembering where they were, she quickly re-composed herself and stepped away from Nolan to look back at both he and Eli.

"So, we're good about doing this when the second set's over, right?" she asked quietly after making sure they still had enough space between them and the teacher manning the ticket table.

Nolan still looked a little dazed and the lines under Eli's eyes seemed to be sagging even more than when they first got there, but she could tell it had more to do with their nerves than anything else.

"Yeah, I'm good with that," Nolan relented. He swore Eli seemed to wither up across from him when he turned his gaze on him.

"Okay," Eli choked out as they stepped up to the ticket table. Nolan and Sabrina held on for a second to see if he'd say anything else, but it never came.

With a roll of her eyes, Sabrina turned around and bought her ticket. Nolan and Eli quickly did the same, and the three entered the gym just as the announcer was calling off the starting roster for River View Middle School.

They all knew there was no backing out of this now.

31

Match Point

A loud thwap echoed over the gym as one of the girls on River View's team popped the volleyball high over the net. The girl in the back center position for Meade was easily able to get under it, though, and the ball sailed over the net again a second later.

Nolan watched on with mild interest. The current volley had been going on for about a minute and he guessed it was an important one based on how riled up the crowd was getting, but all he could think about was what they'd be doing when this set was over and whether or not they'd be able to pull it off without getting caught.

Based on the distant look in Eli and Sabrina's eyes, he guessed they weren't faring much better.

Nolan's attention was drawn back to the court when he heard Meade's coach yell something to a girl in front of the net just as the ball came down to her. With almost perfect timing, she popped the ball up right as her teammate jumped up and softly batted the ball over the net and to the left, catching the corresponding defender off guard.

The girl on River View's team made a desperate lunge for the ball, but it was too late. The ball smacked against the court in front of her and the bulk of the crowd erupted in cheers.

Meade had just won the second set.

"And with Maxine Tennyson's score, your Lady Mountaineers have evened the match by taking the second set with a score of eighteen to twenty-five!" the announcer proclaimed with an overabundance of enthusiasm. "What an exciting match we have here tonight!"

Even though Sabrina didn't really care about the game that much, she still felt bad. The girl on her school's team that missed the play was Chelsea Waters and her classmate was already getting an earful from the coach as the team jogged off the court. The announcer's explosive voice cut through the applause a second later.

"The third and final set will start in ten minutes," he said right as Meade's band started playing the school's fight song. As the applause died down, people started shimmying through the rows to exit the gym. Nolan didn't exactly feel anxious to do the same, but got up off the bleacher seat anyway.

"Well, I guess that means we've got ten minutes to do what we came here for," he hummed unenthusiastically. He could already see Sabrina grabbing her jacket as she got ready to leave but Eli stayed in his seat.

"Yeah, I guess it does," he grumbled. Even though he tried to hide the nervousness racing through his mind, a trembling sigh still slipped through Eli's lips as he finally rose out of his seat. "Might as well get it over with, though, right?"

"That's the idea," Sabrina piped in. "You guys ready?"

Nolan turned to glance back at Eli. He swore his friend looked even worse than he had when they first met up with Sabrina about an hour ago.

"So, you ready?" Sabrina repeated impatiently when Nolan didn't say anything back.

"About as much as we're going to be, I think," he said dryly. He looked behind him in time to see Sabrina whisk a hand towards the end of the row as she carefully slid her jacket on.

"Alright, then let's get moving," she suggested.

After giving her a quick thumbs up, Nolan pivoted around and nodded his head towards the end of the row to urge Eli on. He still didn't look too thrilled to be doing this.

"I think there's still going to be enough people out there to keep anyone from noticing us," Nolan suggested as he moved in closer behind Eli. His friend shot him a puzzled look over his shoulder.

"Dude, what are you talking about?"

Nolan nudged his head towards the exits just as they made it to the steps leading out of the stands. "Well, you know, we were kind of hoping there'd be enough people in the halls between games to keep anyone from seeing us. I don't think as many people left their seats as they did during the first break, but I think it'll still work."

"Oh, yeah. Maybe," Eli droned distantly. He briefly glanced behind him as he and Nolan started going up the steps leading to the walkway encircling the gym. Sabrina had gotten stuck in their row for the time being as she waited for another group to go past her.

"You didn't find anything out about the flyers, did you?" Eli asked a second later. He'd seen Nolan periodically glancing through news apps on his phone during both games trying to find something related to it. The way Nolan sucked in his lips and shook his head as soon as they reached the walkway was more than enough of an answer, though.

"Not yet," Nolan whispered. Realizing they were still waiting for Sabrina, he added, "There's still nothing on the local news sites about Grayson or Espinoza or anything like that. And you're sure you didn't hear anything before we got out of school today?"

An odd tingling sensation seared across Eli's body as he thought back to meeting with Superintendent Richter and Hayashi that morning. In spite of it, he tried to act as casual as he could.

"No, I haven't heard anything," he said with a slight hitch in his voice.

Eli could tell Nolan wasn't entirely satisfied with that answer, but Sabrina made it to the top of the steps before Nolan could ask him anything else.

"What are you guys waiting for? Come on. Get moving," she snarled through a whisper, flicking a hand toward the exit at the end of the walkway.

Nolan gave Eli a stern look before the two started threading their way through some of the loose crowds in the walkway. In the back of his mind, Nolan hoped there'd be more people in the hallways than he expected, but, by the time they made it out of the gym they were greeted by a relatively sparse crowd.

"I'm starting to think we should wait until after the

game," Nolan grumbled just loud enough for Eli and Sabrina to hear. When they looked back at him, he added, "There's not enough people out here. Someone's going to see us."

"Well, if anyone does, they'll probably just think we're leaving early," Sabrina assured him as they made their way towards the main hallway. "Plus, we need to be sure the door's still unlocked. If it isn't, at least this match has gone into a third set so we can try Plan B if we need to."

"Yeah," Nolan droned, suddenly hoping beyond reason that they wouldn't have to resort to that.

With barely a glance behind them to be sure no one was paying attention, the three slid around the next corner and started heading down the darkened hallway leading to the office. The gloom enveloped them just as they got to the middle hallway.

Even though she'd never been to Meade before, Sabrina still recognized the administrator's office as soon as she saw the glass door appearing out of the darkness ahead. Like most other schools she'd been to, including Batts, it was about the only room inside the building lined with plate glass windows.

A quivering breath slipped through her lips as she stepped up to the office. Just like with the hallway, all the lights were off inside, and, as best as she could tell through her own obscured reflection, the office looked like it was completely vacant, too.

Sabrina blindly wrapped her fingers around the doorknob a second later.

"Well, here goes nothing," she announced dryly. Nolan and Eli barely had time to react before she twisted the knob and felt the latch slide free. A jubilant grin slid across her lips as she pulled the door open a little.

"Okay, we're in business," she said as plainly as she could manage. Pointing at Eli and Nolan in turn, she added, "Now, you show me how to get to the PA system and you stand watch by the door."

"At least I'll only have to worry about watching one side of the hallway," Nolan quipped as the three passed into the office. Sabrina wasn't in a joking mood, though.

"Yeah, well still watch both ends," she warned him. "The other end of the hallway might be blocked off, but that doesn't mean someone could still pass through."

"How? The doors are probably locked," Nolan protested. Sabrina quickly shook her head and glared back at him the best she could in the gloom. There was just enough light filtering in from the hallway by the gym for her to see his silhouette in the open doorway.

"Yeah, but just watch it anyway in case they aren't, alright?"

Sabrina turned her attention to Eli an instant later.

"Alright, where do we need to go first?"

Eli quickly pointed to the darkened shape of the secretary's desk from behind the reception counter.

"Over there. That's where they keep the key to the network cabinet."

"If they haven't moved it already," Nolan grunted as the other two moved around the reception counter and headed deeper into the office.

"Well, let's hope they haven't," Sabrina called over her shoulder. "And shut the door! We don't want anyone passing by the end of the hall to think someone's in the office with the lights out. That's a dead giveaway."

With a stab of guilt, Nolan quickly stepped back from the open doorway and slid the door shut just enough to press against the doorframe. He still wanted to be able to pop it open in a hurry if they needed to.

The sudden appearance of a white light reflecting off the glass door caused him to jerk his head back behind him. The panic surging through his veins died down a little when he realized Sabrina had just pulled her phone out and was using the flashlight app to navigate through the dark office.

Nolan pulled his lips in tight and looked back down the hallway towards the gym. There still wasn't anyone around, but he hoped no one going to the restroom would notice the faint light streaming out of the office windows.

They'd made it too far to screw up now.

There was a soft grating sound behind him as Sabrina pulled the desk drawer open and pointed her phone's flashlight into it. Luckily, Eli chimed in before she had to ask.

"Look under those sticky pads," he directed her, pointing at the bright yellow pads on the right side of the drawer. Without wasting a second, Sabrina reached over and grabbed the stack of Post-it Notes. Just as it had been last week, a small, brass key was hiding underneath.

"So what now?" she asked as she retrieved the key and put the sticky pads back in their place. She didn't bother to shut the desk drawer since she knew she'd be returning the key later.

Eli quickly walked towards a door just ahead of the secretary's desk, at the corner of another hallway. "Over here," he said, lightly tapping a knuckle against the network cabinet's door. "After you open this up, the drive will be on a terminal near the top. There's a stepstool inside, too."

"Well, that's convenient," Sabrina blurted out as she slid the key into the knob and twisted it. The doorknob turned with the same motion and the two were met with an electric hum and a myriad of flashing yellow, green, and red lights.

"Voila," Eli hummed distantly.

"Yeah, voila," Sabrina echoed as she pointed the light from her phone down at the base of the network cabinet and spotted the plastic stepstool. She quickly crouched down to grab it.

"And you said the drive's up near the top?" Sabrina asked as she placed the stepstool in front of the server rack. Eli was slow to respond, and, when she looked back up at him, Sabrina swore Eli seemed to be anxiously surveying their surroundings like he expected someone else to be there.

"Hey!" she barked. "You said the drive's near the top, right?"

Eli jumped with a start before turning his attention back to Sabrina. Even though her phone's flashlight was still pointed at the floor, there was just enough of a glow for her to see the worried look in his eyes.

"Huh? Oh, yeah. Yeah, it should be plugged into the second terminal from the top."

"Got it," Sabrina grunted. "We still clear out there, Nolan?" she called over her shoulder as she got onto the stepstool.

"Looks like it," he reported flatly.

"Good. Then we shouldn't have to worry about someone sneaking up on us right now," Sabrina said somewhat pointedly to Eli. Based on the look in his eyes, he didn't seem to be fully convinced, though.

Shrugging it off, Sabrina turned her attention back to the server rack and pointed her flashlight towards the top quarter of it. With all the black boxes, wires, and blipping lights, she wondered if she'd ever be able to spot the drive. Before long, though, the beam from her phone's flashlight swept over a bright red logo and her eyes immediately latched onto it.

Sabrina leaned in the best she could from her perch and peered into the area behind the terminal. Her heart fluttered a little when she spotted the object the familiar red logo was stamped onto. The drive was almost exactly the way Conrad had described it the other day.

"Found it," Sabrina announced eagerly. Her voice was shaking a little, but it was hard for Nolan or even Eli to hear it against the distorted noise resonating from the gym.

"You think you'll be able to swap it out alright?" Nolan chimed back while briefly glancing away from the hallway.

"Well, we're about to find out," Sabrina replied. She bit her lip and braced the hand that was holding her phone against the shelf as she reached in with her other hand. Her mind was racing as her fingers clasped the plastic stick and pulled on it. The drive came loose an instant later.

"Did you get it?" Eli asked uneasily as soon as he saw Sabrina withdraw her hand from the network cabinet.

"Yeah, I got it," she gasped as she backed down the stepstool. Trying to stifle all the excitement surging through her, she quickly directed her phone's flashlight onto the drive once she had both feet back on the floor.

"Now for the tricky part," she grumbled.

Eli shot a bewildered look back at her. "What do you mean?"

Sabrina turned the USB drive over in her hand so the base was pointing back at her. "I need to see if this drive's the kind that you pry open with a penny or a paperclip so we can take it apart and swap it out with the blank drive."

"So, what kind is it?" Nolan asked impatiently from the doorway.

Sabrina was just about to answer when a sudden flash from the overhead lights being turned on stopped her short. An intense twinge of panic shot down her back when she heard another voice behind them.

"I believe you'd need a paperclip, but I don't think you'll get a chance to try it."

Sabrina's next breath trembled out of her lips and she could already see the terrified look on Nolan's face before she got the nerve to look behind her. Superintendent Richter was standing in the administrator's hallway just a few feet away with a campus police officer next to him.

They had been waiting in Principal Espinoza's old office.

A wicked grin squirmed across the superintendent's gaunt face and he jerked his head behind him. "Why don't you come back here and we'll talk about what y'all are doing here, and why you want to take that drive apart?" he suggested.

Nolan let out a panicked yelp and flung the office door open. He only got a step or two into the hallway before he ran face-first into another campus officer that had moved in through the hallway's front doors while their attention was on the superintendent. He barely had time to react before the officer grabbed him by the shoulders, spun him around, and forced him back into the office.

Sabrina's legs gave out and she sank to her knees when she saw the vacant look in Nolan's eyes. The USB drive slipped out of her hands and fell to the floor next to her, but she hardly noticed. Her eyes were watering up by then, anyway.

"Yeah, I wouldn't try to run," Superintendent Richter said coldly as Nolan was led past the reception counter. He jerked a thumb behind him a second later. "Take them into the office so we can get to the bottom of this. I'll be in there shortly. Oh, and be sure to search their pockets for anything else they might have with them."

The officer that had been standing next to Superintendent Richter stepped over and firmly pulled Sabrina to her feet. With one hand tightly grasping her shoulder, he reached into her jacket pocket and pulled out the eraser drive, then grabbed the USB drive she'd dropped off the floor.

"Anything else on your person I should know about?" the officer asked.

Even though Sabrina wanted to say there wasn't, her voice

was stuck in her throat. Ultimately, all she managed was a shake of her head.

It wasn't until the officer gently pulled her hands behind her and snapped on the handcuffs that Sabrina started to sob uncontrollably. She was still sobbing while the officer went through the same procedure with Eli and Nolan, though Nolan ended up getting handcuffed in tandem with another officer due to his cast.

Eventually, the officers put whatever belongings they found in the three's pockets on an empty paper tray and handed it to Superintendent Richter as they were led back to the principal's office. The superintendent waited until he heard the soft click of the door before he tapped the headset in his right ear.

"Okay, you're clear to come in now," he said flatly. A few seconds later Hayashi stepped into the office and Superintendent Richter exhibited Intuitive Degrees' drive to him as soon as he got close enough. He didn't waste a second to take it from him.

"Well, we played it pretty close, but we got 'em,'" Superintendent Richter beamed triumphantly. He was a bit disappointed when the associate from Intuitive Degrees only grunted in response and kept looking over the USB drive to be sure it hadn't been damaged.

Turning his attention back to the paper tray the officer had handed him, Superintendent Richter picked up the eraser drive and pulled the obvious cap off the top of it. He smirked at its crude but effective design.

"Really, I guess it's not too bad for something an eighth-grader thought up. Look at this."

Hayashi took a moment to stop examining the real drive and grudgingly looked at the eraser Superintendent Richter was showing him. He still didn't seem to be very impressed.

"Yeah, it's nifty, alright," he droned. In a lower voice, he added, "I'm glad that kid warned us about all this when he did, though."

"I'm not going to argue with that!" Superintendent Richter seconded. "It's still crazy to think that Espinoza told us one of those two boys could be the prankster a few days ago *and* that you didn't even want to pursue that lead."

"From what Espinoza told us, the kid that saw Reznik in

the locker room wasn't even sure it was him," Hayashi grumbled. "Besides, I'm pretty sure he was just saying that to try and get himself off the hook."

"A desperate plea from a desperate man," Superintendent Richter reflected in amusement. Hayashi took a second to glare back at him.

"And he probably wouldn't have been so desperate if he hadn't caught onto the holes in your test omissions story and actually decided to report it."

Superintendent Richter let out a dismissive grunt but didn't say anything back. He nudged his head at the drive Hayashi was holding a second later. "So, everything look okay, there?"

Hayashi nodded before he disappeared behind the network cabinet's open door and got to work at plugging the drive back in. It seemed to take longer than Superintendent Richter expected.

"Yeah, everything's fine," Hayashi said eventually as he stepped away from the network cabinet and shut the door. He pulled out his cell phone a second later, tapped into the school's audio network for a test, and exhibited the screen back to Superintendent Richter. Based on the vacant look in the superintendent's eyes, he could already tell Richter had no idea what he was looking at.

"The signal's back up," Hayashi explained, causing Superintendent Richter's eyebrows to pop up in satisfaction.

"Oh, okay. Great. I don't think I have to tell you that I don't need a repeat of last week." The pleased look on his face faded as soon as Hayashi glared back at him.

"Yes, well, I don't think I have to tell *you* that the firm I represent wouldn't want you screwing everything up again either. Otherwise, you'll be the one making desperate pleas."

"Yeah, yeah. I know," Superintendent Richter replied meekly. He was already diverting his eyes to the floor when Hayashi spoke up again.

"Just stick to what we agreed on earlier," he commanded. "No arrests, no witch hunts, and no more lie-chasing. Those kids were just influenced by what they'd been seeing on the news and came up with their own crazy ideas."

Superintendent Richter held up his palms in submission.

"Hey, don't worry. I'll stick to the script. You guys just keep the test scores up."

Hayashi gave him another cold look through the corners of his eyes before tossing the key to the network cabinet back to Superintendent Richter. He wasn't ready for it, though, and the key dropped to the floor after glancing against the edge of his hand.

Richter shot him a frustrated look before he knelt down to retrieve it.

"Anyway, I had better get back to the office and send my report into headquarters," Hayashi said. Superintendent Richter quickly waved at him from the floor.

"Yeah, yeah. Go ahead. I can take it from here."

With a parting nod, Hayashi stepped out of the office and started heading for the front doors. He could hear the cheers and shouts echoing down the darkened hall as the third set of the volleyball match started up behind him.

It wasn't until he'd pushed himself through both sets of doors and stepped outside that he allowed himself to smirk a little. Even though nothing had gone the way he wanted it to after he hacked into Eli Reznik's sick day streaming service a few weeks ago and gave him instructions on how to pull the prank, he still managed to get one of the drives without anyone noticing. And thanks to that girl's idea to use a decoy, it would probably be a while before anyone realized the drive he'd hooked up to the terminal tonight wasn't even transmitting a real signal.

At least, Troy hoped that'd be the case as he made it to his car and stepped in. He still had to get to the airport and find a way to disappear before he could even think about leaking the information on the drive in his pocket.

All the same, after years of sitting in silence and wrestling with his own conscience, Troy knew it was finally time to set things right.

It was time everyone knew what Intuitive Degrees was really up to.

32

The End of an Era

A thin smile crept across Nolan's lips as soon as he stepped out of the snow and into Fryer Tuck's. It felt like it had been eons since he'd been there, and he knew being grounded for the rest of the semester was a big part of that.

Thankfully, he was finally free and the familiar scent of grilled hamburger patties had never smelled better.

Based on the text message he got from Sabrina just an hour after his report card came in the mail today, he figured she must have gotten un-grounded, too. But as sure as he was that Sabrina would be waiting for him when he got to Fryer Tuck's, a quick check of their usual table revealed it was empty.

He almost wondered if the light snow shower was holding her up a little.

After nodding at the guy behind the order counter in acknowledgment, Nolan stepped over to the table lining Crescent Avenue and slid into the booth seat. He pulled his phone out of his coat pocket a second later to be sure Sabrina hadn't texted him while he was walking to Fryer Tuck's. There weren't any new messages, though.

Biting his lip, Nolan impulsively pulled up some of the news apps on his phone to see if anything new had been posted. However, it was mostly just the same stuff he'd seen before leaving for Fryer Tuck's. Superintendent Richter was still on the run and the FBI was gradually dismantling the organization known as Intuitive Degrees, which now appeared to be tied to some big wigs in the Bureau of Education.

As much as Nolan was hoping to see something about Superintendent Richter getting caught, he still couldn't believe how much things had unraveled in the last two months–or how it all started with a familiar problem.

Just a week after their botched heist, several classes started noticing concepts on their tests that neither the teachers nor the students knew anything about. And when the teachers checked the syllabus, the concepts weren't listed there either.

At first, Superintendent Richter tried to blame it on another test fraud scandal at Meade since someone messed with the network cabinet right before the problem started showing up again, but it didn't seem to resonate as much as it did the first time around. Neither did his attempts to get Principal Horne put on leave for being part of the suspected new conspiracy.

The situation only got worse when another item appeared in the news a short time later.

Troy Hayashi, a lead programmer at the local Intuitive Degrees office, leaked data from an undisclosed source onto the internet around mid-November. Once the national news outlets picked up on it, Richter's grip on the situation spiraled out of control.

According to the leak, Intuitive Degrees had been paying struggling school districts lots of money in exchange for subjecting students and teachers to subliminal messages. Or, as the news called it, 'Dangerously experimental learning practices.'

Grafton ISD was just one of about ten districts in the country that Intuitive Degrees had been working with, and, in every case, test grades and classroom efficiency had gone up substantially.

But no matter how many times Superintendent Richter tried to save himself by claiming that was the only reason he signed onto the program, it was all overshadowed by the fact that Hayashi's leaks revealed something else.

Intuitive Degrees was just using the schools as guinea pigs. Their real aim was to eventually expand the scope of the subliminal system and influence the masses to the highest bidder, impacting anything from elections to product marketing.

Before long, the FBI got involved, and, from there, the district really began to fall apart. Teachers fed up with all the corruption were quitting left and right, the FBI took over Central Office to comb for evidence, and Superintendent Richter was forced to resign by the end of November.

He went missing a few days later, just as a warrant for his arrest came down the pipeline. Now, nearly three weeks after his disappearance, Superintendent Richter still hadn't been found and some people were even speculating the higher-ups at Intuitive Degrees had somehow smuggled him out of the country.

Grimmer speculations were floating around, too.

Nolan was still reading over the latest story he'd found just as the front door swung open and Sabrina stepped in. Her eyes quickly fell on him, and he waved to her with a smile as she started to stride over to their usual table.

Sabrina barely even smiled back.

"Well, long time, no see," Nolan greeted as she slid into the booth seat across from him. "How've you been?"

Sabrina looked a little frazzled but managed to force a thin smile. "Well, outside of being grounded for basically forever, pretty good, I guess. How about you?"

"About the same," Nolan said with a shrug and a smile of his own. Sabrina suddenly nudged her head down at his left arm.

"I see you got the cast off."

Nolan reflexively glanced down at his left hand before he could stop himself. "Hmm? Oh, yeah. About a month ago."

"Were you able to make the basketball team?" Sabrina asked, vaguely remembering that Nolan had brought it up the last time they met up to compare report cards.

Nolan shook his head and frowned a little. "No. I missed the tryouts for that by about two weeks. Plus, that was when I was still kicked out of athletics, so it wouldn't have mattered anyway."

"They kicked you out of athletics?" Sabrina gasped.

"Yeah, for what we did in October," Nolan said. "It's all good now, though. After the stuff that Hayashi guy put on the internet, Coach Adams took me back in just like how they let Coach Grayson and Principal Espinoza off the hook a few days ago."

"Yeah, except I'm sure they won't be coming back to work here. Like a lot of other people," Sabrina pointed out glumly. Nolan forced a smile when he saw the sour look in her eyes.

"Well, either way, I'm back in athletics now, so hopefully

I'll have a chance to make the track team again this spring."

"Yeah. Hopefully," Sabrina reflected distantly. Across from her, Nolan lightly tapped his thumb against the dark green tabletop before reaching into his jacket pocket to grab his report card.

"Anyway, you ready to see who'll be buying the drinks this time around?" he asked cheerfully. "Honestly, I think I'm kind of glad we were still grounded when our last report cards came out. I don't know if it was because I was stuck in in-school-suspension for a few weeks or because that subliminal messages thing wasn't giving me a boost anymore, but my last grades were pretty crappy."

"Yeah, mine weren't that great either," Sabrina admitted. "But, hey, at least you've got one last chance to beat me."

Nolan had just retrieved his report card when he glanced back at her. "What, you mean for the semester?"

Sabrina diverted her eyes and shook her head. "No. Pretty much forever, actually."

She could feel Nolan's eyes burning into her brow in the pause that followed before she managed to spit it out.

"My mom decided she's through with Grafton ISD. We're moving out of town next month."

Nolan froze. "Oh, my gosh! Are you serious?"

Sabrina nodded, but still kept her eyes on the dark green tabletop in front of her. "Yeah. I think I'm kind of okay with it, too. I mean, Superintendent Evans and Richter really screwed this district up. I don't know how the next person's going to do any better."

"They might," Nolan suggested with feigned optimism. It wasn't enough to change Sabrina's mood, though, and she just shrugged it off.

"Maybe, but I don't see how and neither does my mom," she said flatly. Nolan could see a tear budding in the corner of her eye when she finally gave him a partial glance. "I'm-I'm sorry."

Nolan just stared back at her for a few seconds, doing his best to take in every feature of her withdrawn face. "Well, I guess you don't have to be," he said at length. "It's not like you caused any of this."

A quivering breath trickled through Sabrina's lips and she

quickly whisked away the tears that were streaming down her cheeks by now. "Yeah, I know. And the truth got out there and all that, but it still kind of sucks, you know?"

"Yeah," Nolan seconded absently.

A long pause fell between them before a crooked smile twisted across Sabrina's lips and she pulled her report card out of her jacket pocket.

"Anyway, why don't we forget about that for now and see if you'll be buying me one more cream soda?"

"So, wait, you're telling me you got better grades than her and you still bought her a drink?" Eli snarled. Even though they hadn't really talked since Eli slipped up and admitted he'd ratted them out a month-and-a-half ago, Nolan still called to break the news to him.

"I don't know," Nolan grumbled. "I guess I just kind of felt like it was the right thing to do, you know? I mean, Superintendent Richter kind of screwed up her life."

"Yeah, and this thing kind of screwed me over, too," Eli shot back as he slouched down to the floor and rested his back against the side of his bed. "I mean, it's not like I'm going to make the honor roll ever again."

"Well, you never know," Nolan suggested unconvincingly. "How'd you do on your report card?"

"Four C's, one D, and two A's," Eli grumbled. Just like he expected, Nolan tried to put a positive spin on it.

"Well, that's still not too bad. You still got two A's, at least."

"Yeah, in shop and PE," Eli sneered. "All we do is play dodgeball in one and build crap in the other. You'd have to be trying to get something worse than that."

"And the C's and the D were in English, and algebra, and stuff?"

"Yep," Eli said.

Nolan went silent long enough for Eli to wonder if the call got dropped. When he finally did speak up again, Eli could hear the hesitation in his friend's voice.

"So, I was kind of thinking. What if you and me started meeting every six weeks to see who has the best report card, like what me and Sabrina have been doing for the last few years?"

A short scoff blasted out of Eli's nose. "Why? So you could beat me every single time?"

"No," Nolan said flatly. "It's just… I don't know, I kind of think the way I was always trying to get better grades than Sabrina was sort of a good thing, you know? I mean, it kind of made me try harder. I just sort of thought maybe it would help you out, too."

"How?" Eli growled. "You're in athletics *and* all the Pre-AP classes and you still get straight A's, like, all the time."

"Not all the time," Nolan said. "Plus, I think the stuff the school was doing before Richter got caught was giving me kind of a boost."

Eli rolled his eyes a little. "Okay, maybe. But, still, there's no way I'd ever beat you, man. You'd wipe the freakin' floor with me every single time."

"I'll let you add ten points to your grades," Nolan bartered. When Eli didn't say anything back, he quickly added, "Look, I'm just trying to help you out, alright? I think you've got what it takes to make the honor roll again. You just need the right push."

Eli glanced at his bedroom door. Even though it was closed, he still stared at it as if he could see straight into Eric's room. As smart as his older brother was, taking down the subliminal messages had hit him pretty hard, too.

All the same, he was still making A's and B's on his report card.

An impulsive twinge raced down Eli's back. "Okay, I guess I'll give that a shot when school starts back up," he grumbled.

"Awesome!" Nolan chimed in.

"But, seriously, you'd better give me those extra ten points," Eli snapped. He could almost hear Nolan smirking through the phone an instant later.

"Hey, man. I got it, alright? Ten points, no problem. Just remember, though, I tend to like Cherry Cokes."

"Yeah? Well, I like root beers, so you might want to

remember that," Eli shot back.

Before long, the two started talking about all the things that had happened in the last two months and what they had planned for the rest of the holiday break. The whole time neither would have guessed that Eli would be reminding Nolan about his preference for root beer in just a year-and-a-half, or that he wouldn't even need the ten-point bonus by then either.

At the moment, all they really cared about was what was right in front of them.

ACKNOWLEDGEMENTS

The author would like to thank his family and friends for their support and encouragement through writing this book and getting it published.

The author would also like to extend a very big thank you to the test readers that provided invaluable feedback on this piece, along with their time spent in reading over my drafts.

To all who were involved, thank you!

9 798218 541002